OF LOVE AND CRIME

THE TAINTED LOVE SAGA BOOK 5

KAYLA LOWE

DEDICATION

For Mom and Dad

"Children need love, especially when they do not deserve it." –
Harold Hubert

ACKNOWLEDGMENTS

Thank you Mom and Dad for continuing to believe in me.

Thank you Samantha for all your love and support through everything.

Thank you Sam for always listening to me vent.

Thank you readers for all the encouragement.

I love you all!

CHAPTER 1

I WATCHED Bruce's throat work as he took a drink of his wine, a lit cigarette still held in his other hand. His hair was slicked straight back from his face in that way he always wore it, the receding hairline not diminishing the look at all. Despite his more advanced age, his hair coloring showed no signs of aging. He was no silver fox. Not a speck of white or gray showed in his blondish-brown locks.

He was wearing his customary jean shorts and no shirt, the muscles in his chest and arms flexing with each movement he made, curtesy of the intense military training from his time in the marines.

It had only been about a week since I'd had to attend the victim awareness class to get the latest domestic violence charge against him dropped. That was the deal I'd had to cut with the DA to get him to agree to drop the charges.

And Bruce was still fuming about it. Every time we drank.

He kept ranting about how shitty the cops had been to him, how ridiculous it all was, how anyone in their right mind would know he'd never hurt me, how he loved me. I knew that didn't I?

He needed constant affirmation, and I was weary of always nodding and telling him that, yes, I knew it.

When he'd asked me what all they'd said in the victim awareness class, I'd shrugged it off and told him they'd said a whole lot of nothing. That it had just been a waste of time.

The speaker had encouraged us all to take the papers she'd given us home with us, but I think most of us had left it all sitting on the table. I know I did.

What did I need all those printouts for? I'd listened to the stupid class, and I maintained in my mind that Bruce wasn't abusive. I wasn't in an abusive relationship.

Bruce just got jealous sometimes, but that was because he was so much older than me. Our relationship was more unconventional than most, so it couldn't be judged the way a normal one could.

That's what I told myself anyway.

We'd gone through hell to be together. My family certainly hadn't made things easy for us. And Bruce had never hit me. Okay, so he'd grabbed me and pushed me down, but that was only when he was drunk, and that was only a couple of times. That's not how he really was.

He loved me. He told me so all the time. He wanted to be with me all the time. If he didn't love me, he wouldn't want to have me with him twenty-four seven, would he?

I took a sip of my own wine and shook all negative thoughts away.

I was laying on the balcony on my pink lounge chair, catching some rays while Bruce had the grill going. He'd marinated some chicken breasts in white wine, and now he was grilling them. The white wine made the chicken super tender, and we liked to cut it up into chunks and put it in a Caesar salad for dinner.

Bruce usually had trouble getting me to eat much after we'd been drinking. I usually wasn't very hungry after drinking, but it seemed I could tolerate a light salad better than some heavier dishes. Plus, he was a typical man and just liked to play with the grill, I think.

"This is going to be so good, babygirl," he called out to me over his shoulder.

"I'm sure it will. Everything you cook is always so yummy," I said back to him before taking another sip of wine.

He turned to me then and grinned. "You're damn right it is."

One thing I'd found out about Bruce was that he liked having his ego stroked. I didn't know if all men were like that, but especially when we were drinking, he seemed to be in a better mood if I agreed with him and complimented him. And I was willing to do whatever it took to keep him in a good mood so we didn't end up fighting.

I hated fighting with him. I hated it more than fighting with my parents.

"F— it's hot out here," he said, wiping his hand over his forehead. "I'm almost finished here, angel. Why don't you go on in and grab your shower?"

He came over to where I was laying and gave me a hand. I took it, and he lifted me up from where I'd been laying out in the sun, my skin still glistening with the oil he'd rubbed all over me. I certainly didn't want to sit on the furniture covered in all that oil, so I stepped through the sliding glass doors into the kitchen, the cool air conditioning of the room hitting my warm body. The warmth of my overheated body made the air inside our apartment feel colder than it was, and goosebumps broke out on my skin as I laid my now-empty wine glass on the kitchen table, went into the bathroom, shimmied out of my bikini, and stepped into a warm shower.

As soon as I stepped out of the shower and dried off, Bruce was handing me a refilled glass of wine.

I thanked him and laid it on the vanity before toweling my hair dry, running a comb through it, and then applying a bit of mousse to my hands before lightly scrunching the curls. I tossed the damp mess over my shoulders, slipped on some stretchy shorts and a crop top, and then picked up my glass of wine and went to join Bruce in the living room where he sat smoking a cigarette and watching a cooking show.

He started commenting to me about something the chef was doing, and I just nodded in agreement with whatever he was saying.

I was already over the cooking show, though, and was glad when something more entertaining came on. We watched a judge show together, laughing at the stupidity of some of the defendants, and by the time it was over, we were both on our way to getting pretty buzzed.

I went over to the computer and pulled up videos of some of our favorite comedians to watch. I knew the ones Bruce liked the best, and I loved laughing with him. We watched some of them for a while before our mood changed, and then we started listening to some of our favorite '80s jams and dancing.

After that, Bruce eventually sat down at his computer, which was really just my old computer that I'd given him when I'd bought me a new one, and I sat in front of the glass coffee table with mine.

He listened to some music from his younger days in the '60s and '70s that I wasn't really fond of, and I put on my headphones and watched music videos of songs he wasn't particularly crazy about. Of course, by the end of the night, I switched to musicals. I always ended up super emotional and watching stuff that made me cry like *The Phantom of the Opera*.

Then, he switched back to music we both liked, pulling me up, urging me to dance with him as he kissed me.

That's the last thing I remember before I woke up the next morning.

And that's how our days went for a while. We'd go to the beach, and when we didn't, I'd work on the computer making as much money as I could while Bruce puttered around outside in his garden. By afternoon, I'd drive us up to the liquor store and we'd get wine. Sometimes I'd drink vodka or something else, but Bruce mostly drank wine or beer. He claimed harder liquor tended to make him meaner, but I didn't comment that he'd been drinking the wine the last time the cops were called on us. I certainly wasn't going to argue with him. I didn't want him drinking anything that would get him drunk faster.

After buying whatever we were going to drink, we'd go back to our apartment and fall into that same drinking schedule. We were back to drinking more than two or three times a week, though not necessarily every day.

I didn't even fight it anymore. I was becoming complacent with our schedule. I liked getting buzzed, laughing, and listening to music. Sometimes we still went on walks, and we frequently walked up to the nearest store to get more wine when we ran out and weren't ready to end our party.

I called my family less and less. Bruce seemed to get an attitude when I talked to them, especially if he'd already started drinking for the day, so I only called them maybe once or twice a week. I tried to at least call my parents and grandma once a week. Addison and I still talked every now and then, and I talked to my brother occasionally.

But my world pretty much became Bruce and keeping him happy. I found myself catering to him and stroking his ego more and more in an attempt to keep him in a good mood so he wouldn't start dwelling on negative things when we were drinking.

While Bruce wasn't going out at night and blowing money on scratch-offs as much as he used to, it still occasionally happened. Sometimes I'd check the bank account and see the ATM withdrawals, and it was always on nights I'd blacked out. Bruce always told me I was with him when it happened, so I couldn't really put up too much of a fuss about it. Just because I didn't remember it didn't mean it hadn't happened. I don't know why it seemed like sometimes I would black out more than others when I wasn't doing anything any different.

Perhaps the main reason I didn't say anything to Bruce about the ATM withdrawals anymore, though, was that I didn't want to rock the boat. I hated arguing with him, and I never wanted him to resent me. I knew if something was bothering Bruce, it would eventually come out when we were drinking, and I didn't want a repeat of the last night he'd blown up at me and gotten arrested.

He'd never hit me, but that didn't make it any less scary when he grabbed me and shook me and told me he hated me with his eyes so cold.

Still, it seemed like no matter what I did or how good our day had gone, Bruce would still get into these moods where he just bitched and moaned about everything—most notably my parents.

I felt like I was walking on eggshells. When he'd start talking about my parents, I always had to just agree with everything he said or find ways to turn the conversation to something else. It was exhausting.

Consequently, I found myself drinking faster and faster. The faster I drank, the floatier I became and the less his ranting would bother me.

I began to crave the numbness and escape alcohol provided me, especially when I fueled it with music.

On top of that, the tipsier I kept myself, the happier Bruce seemed to be with me. He liked me being silly and laughing at every stupid thing he said. Even though we oftentimes did the same stupid, mundane things when we were drinking, we actually had fun doing them.

When it was good, it was good, but each time something bad happened, it seemed to be worse than the time before it.

One night I woke up around midnight, my heart sinking when I found the bed empty next to me. Bruce and I had started drinking earlier than usual that day—before noon actually—and I knew I'd been passed out for a while. The sun hadn't even been down before I must have fallen asleep.

I got up to use the bathroom, and then I padded all throughout the house, already knowing in my gut that Bruce was gone.

I went to check my purse, and while my cards and keys were all there, I noticed that Bruce's wallet was gone.

I logged onto the computer to check the bank account, and sure enough, there were multiple ATM withdrawals of insane amounts of money.

I dropped my forehead down to my hands, my elbows resting on the desk, as the knot formed in my belly.

I hated this feeling of betrayal. I hated waking up to find out Bruce had left me alone and was out doing God knows what. He always told me he was buying scratch-offs, but how could it take him that long to do that? He'd stay gone for hours at a time. He had to be doing something else too.

My head started pounding with stress, or maybe it was from the alcohol I had consumed earlier. I didn't know. All I knew was I was pissed and tired of this shit.

I marched resolutely into the bathroom and

brushed my teeth before washing my face. Then, I grabbed a handful of clothes, still on the hangers, and hauled them down the stairs to the garage where I threw them in the backseat of my car. Back and forth I went loading up my belongings, my heart beating fast in my chest.

I can't do this anymore, I kept thinking over and over again. He doesn't love me. If he did, he wouldn't keep doing this. He wouldn't leave me in the middle of the night and go blow all of our money.

When I finally had everything packed up in the car, Bruce still wasn't back, and for once I was glad. I didn't want to face him right then. It would weaken my resolve.

I set my jaw as I thought of Bruce coming home to find me gone. Let him see what it felt like.

My computer and purse were the last items I grabbed before I got into the car and started the engine. I pulled out of the driveway and started driving down the historic, lamp-lined street. I turned onto the main strip and continued driving, careful not to break the speed limit, though. There weren't many cars out this late at night, and I didn't want to draw undue attention to myself by a cop. I knew I wasn't drunk anymore, but I had been drinking earlier that day, and who knew how long that stuff stayed in your system?

I didn't go very far before my cell phone started ringing. I glanced down at it, already knowing the only person who would be calling me this late at night.

Bruce. His name flashed across the screen. I knew he must have gotten home and found me gone.

I didn't want to talk to him, so I let the phone ring. Plus, I hated talking on the phone while I was driving.

The phone only stopped ringing for a second before it started again. Still, I ignored it.

Again, there was only the slightest pause before it started again.

I subconsciously tightened my hands on the steering wheel as I glanced over at my little pink phone, my heart racing, the ring from the phone stressing me out like nothing else. I saw a motel up on the left side of the road and turned on my blinker to turn into the parking lot.

By the time I parked, my phone beeped, letting me know I had a voicemail. With shaking hands, I picked up the phone, dialed voicemail, and held it up to my ear.

"Sarah, baby," Bruce's voice came over the recording, instantly causing my heart to beat faster, "where are you? I know you're pissed, but call me, angel."

By the time the recording ended, my phone flashed with another one. I pressed the button to listen to it. "Sarah, answer the f— phone. Shit, just talk to me dammit." His voice sounded angry, and that only caused my own anger to rise. How dare he get angry! *I* was the one who had the right to be angry. He'd started all this.

With that thought still on my heels, I grabbed my purse and got out of the car. I went into the lobby that was empty except for the clerk behind the counter working the night shift. Without giving it another thought, I booked a room. I didn't want to keep driving because I didn't have a clue what my plan was at that moment, but I knew one thing. I wasn't going to go back and fight with Bruce all night when he had the audacity to get angry at me for leaving for once when he left all the damn time.

I'd purposefully left my phone in my car when I'd

gone in to book a room, and by the time I got back, there was another voicemail. I probably should have just ignored it too, but I was more curious than a damn cat and couldn't suppress the urge to hear whatever else he'd left.

"Angel," his voice sounded broken this time like he was crying, and it caused something within my chest to twist, "You know I can't live without you. Call me and let me know you're okay, princess. I don't want to fight with you. I promise. I love you, baby. God, I'm such a f— up. I'm going to kill myself..." his voice trailed off the line.

My hands were shaking as I stared down at my phone in horror. He wouldn't really do something like that, right? I couldn't get the sound of his pained voice out of my head, and I didn't know what kind of shape he was in. If he was still drunk enough, would he actually do it? I couldn't live with myself if anyone did something like that because of me.

The phone started ringing again, interrupting my thoughts, and this time I answered it.

"Hello," I said quietly.

"Sarah," Bruce's voice was ragged with relief. "Where are you?" he instantly asked me.

I didn't answer him. Instead, I said, "I could ask you the same thing."

He sighed. "I'm home, baby. Wherever you are, please come back and we can talk about all this."

"I can't keep living like this," I said, my voice small.

"I know, angel. I know, okay?"

When I didn't say anything else, his voice came back over the line sounding half panicked, "Are you leaving me?"

Was I? My entire body was shaking with emotion. I couldn't imagine leaving Bruce, but I wasn't happy waking up time and time again to find him gone. I didn't like him breaking promises to me. I couldn't fathom going home to my parents, and I knew that was the only place I had to go.

"Sarah?" he asked to make sure I was still on the line.

"I'm at a motel," I told him simply.

There was an ominous pause on the other end of the line. "Alone?" he finally asked.

"Oh my gosh, Bruce, yes, of course," I hissed at him. "I don't f— know anybody around here except you." My ire was raised again.

He must have believed me because it was almost like I could see him visibly relax over the phone. "Come home, baby," he said. "Everything will be okay. I need you to come back."

I closed my eyes and fought against the war in my body. My head was telling me that he made promises to me over and over again and broke them, but my heart couldn't forget the brokenness in his voice when he'd said he couldn't live without me. My heart remembered all the good times we'd had and how loving he could be when he wanted to be.

"Sarah, I meant what I said," he said softly. "You can't leave me. I love you, babygirl." His voice broke again.

I sat there as his words hung in the air between us like a veiled threat. I closed my eyes, hating myself for being so weak but also relieved. I didn't want to leave him. Not really. I'd reacted in haste.

"Sarah?" his voice prompted me for an answer again. "Are you coming back to me, angel?"

"Okay," I finally answered.

I heard him exhale on the other end of the line. "I'll be waiting up for you, angel," his voice already sounded lighter.

It didn't matter what Bruce did. He was still my husband. As long as he didn't cheat on me or something, I couldn't leave him. I didn't want to have a failed marriage over money.

We'd get through this. We had to.

I wasted money on a motel room I didn't even enter. I didn't even try to get my money back. I just drove home to Bruce.

Just like he said he would be, he was waiting up for me.

I couldn't stop the tears from falling at the sight of him, and he pulled me into his arms as soon as I opened the car door. I burrowed my head against his chest, and he stroked my hair, murmuring words of comfort to me like he wasn't the one who'd caused my distress.

I knew it was f— up. The person who had caused me pain was giving me solace, and here I was taking it from him. But I didn't have anyone else to turn to. All I had was Bruce. I was states away from my family, and Bruce had become my everything. I was really the only one in his life either. We were together all the time. We were each other's world, and I didn't really mind that, but somehow it made it even more devastating when something bad like this happened between us. Knowing that he was the only one I really had made each hurt that much deeper. I felt like I would die without him. That's how used to being with him I was. I didn't even know why I'd left. I couldn't have really left him. I wouldn't have been able to do it.

Bruce looked over my head into the back of the car and swore, "Damn, you packed all your shit." He pulled back to frown down at me. "Were you really going to leave me?"

"I," I stumbled over my words, not sure what to say before I settled with, "No, I was just mad and reacted in the heat of the moment." I was pretty sure that was as close to the truth as I could get. I still wasn't sure exactly what I'd been planning when I'd left. It didn't matter now, though.

Impossibly, his mouth quirked up into a grin, and he chuckled as he commented, "My fiery little Scots-Irish girl. No wonder my mom loved you."

I took a step back and looked up at him dubiously, a bit surprised he wasn't angrier. Not that I wanted him to be angry. I'd take this over his anger any day.

"Come on," he told me, wrapping an arm around my waist and leading me over to the stairs. "I'll bring all your shit back in tomorrow."

I allowed him to usher me inside, all the adrenaline from my mad burst catching up to me. When we got upstairs, Bruce poured me a glass of wine, and I accepted it wordlessly.

He stood behind me as I took a sip, and I felt his lips drop to my shoulder. He kissed me there before making his way up the side of my neck, sending shivers along my spine.

He plucked the glass of wine from my fingers, set it on

the table, and then turned me to face him. "I love you, Sarah," he said before giving me a bruising kiss.

Maybe I was a fool for forgiving him time and time again.

But I did.

CHAPTER 2

IT WAS foolish of me to think that me leaving Bruce would go unspoken of. While Bruce didn't express any anger the night I came back—on the contrary, he was intent on having passionate, punishing make-up sex—it eventually came up again in the following weeks when we were drinking.

I wasn't really surprised when Bruce started dwelling on it. That was his way. Anything that was bothering him would always come up when we were drinking, no matter how mundane. Of course, this wasn't necessarily something mundane. Bruce had thought I was going to leave him, so of course it bothered him. But still, it pissed me off when he brought it up, trying to make me feel guilty about it when he'd been the one leaving me in the middle of the night for months now, senselessly blowing money on gambling.

I couldn't really say anything about those nights I blacked out and later saw the ATM transactions and he'd told me I'd been with him, but that night I'd woken up and found him gone. If I'd been too drunk to go out with him, he should have just stayed home with me. Hell, I told him that even if I was drunk and he could get me to go with him, he shouldn't be going out spending that kind of money. I just didn't understand it. It frustrated me to no end.

He'd done wrong first, so for him to keep dwelling on my reaction to finding him gone was bullshit.

"Do you want to leave me, angel?" Bruce asked me casually. I wasn't fooled by his nonchalant tone, though. I knew he would get more and more bitter by the second.

I blew out a breath. "Do we really have to go over this again?" I asked crossly, taking another sip of my Pinot Grigio.

"I'm just asking," he continued stubbornly, taking a gulp of his own wine. "Do you want to go back to your parents?"

I sighed in frustration. I was tired of having the same conversation night after night. "No, Bruce. Of course not."

"Because you know they'd lock you up and never let you leave if you ever went back to them. They just want to control you, babygirl," he went on. "You'd be their prisoner. They'd beat you down until you did every little f— thing they wanted. They'd probably marry you off to some little church boy." He sneered as he made that last statement.

He was probably right. My parents probably would do that, but he didn't have to try so hard to beat it into my head. I knew how they were. That still didn't mean it was okay for him to do what he did and for him to expect me not to ever get mad about it.

"That'd be hard to do when I'm already married to you," I pointed out dryly.

He eyed me before he shrugged. "Yet, you packed all your shit up in your car like you were going to leave me."

"I was mad, Bruce!" I flung my arms out in exasperation. "I woke up and you were gone—again. After you've promised me time and time again you'd stop doing that crap. You're always breaking promises to me. I think I'm allowed to get angry about it every now and then."

His eyes flashed fire before I added, "It doesn't mean I'd ever really leave you."

His mood suddenly changed and he came up behind me and wrapped his arms around me, pulling my back flush against his chest. "I won't ever let you leave me," he whispered against my ear before kissing me there.

He said it softly, almost seductively, but it was almost like there was an underlying threat in his words.

"I don't want to," I told him weakly. "I just want you to keep your promises, and I want us to be happy."

"We are happy," he said as he released me. I turned to face him as he added, "So long as your parents and everyone else stays out of it."

I frowned. I hadn't even told them about that night, and Bruce knew that. I'd reassured him many times I hadn't called them, but it looked like I'd have to do it again. "No one is in it." I made air quotes around *it*.

"Good," he said. He looked me straight in the eyes when he added, "Cause I'd hate to have to come up there and get you if you ever left me, but I'd do it, Sarah. I'd fight your daddy and your whole damn family to get you back. I'm an ex f— marine. I worked in recon special ops. You know I could do it. You belong right here with me, angel."

A shiver went up my spine at his words. Again, he

said them halfway like he meant them romantically but halfway as a threat like he was telling me he wouldn't accept it if I ever decided to leave him. I didn't know exactly how that made me feel. I guess it didn't really matter since I didn't ever truly plan on leaving him. When I'd given myself to him sexually, I'd known I'd never want to be with anyone else. I only ever wanted to be with one man. Even before we were married, Bruce had been it for me in my mind.

I hugged him in an attempt to placate him. It must have worked because I felt his arms go around me and heard him say, "You know I'm crazy about you, babygirl."

I knew that was something people said. That they were crazy about the person they loved. It was supposed to be just an expression.

I couldn't help wondering if it was more than that when it came to Bruce and me, though.

Bruce's love was jealous and possessive. That's just the way he was, I told myself. Part of it was probably because he was so much older than me. A part of him was afraid that one day I'd change my mind and leave him for a younger guy. It hurt me that he ever thought that, though. He should know me better than that by now. Besides, I'd never lied to him, though he'd told me plenty of lies.

Bruce justified everything he did, though. He always had an excuse, and I let him off every single time. I wasn't perfect, but most of the time the stuff he got mad at me about were imagined wrongs. Thinking I liked the attention from other guys when we went out. Imagining that something had happened between me and my old boss, Don.

The one time I actually did something—started to

leave him—he acted like he was never going to let me live it down.

For the hundredth time since that night, I found myself wishing I'd never packed up my stuff and left. I didn't like this hanging over us. I knew Bruce had a hard time letting go of stuff.

Although I knew Bruce had started it by breaking his promise, I couldn't help feeling like our current situation was all my fault.

I never should have even threatened to leave him, and I was afraid I was going to hear about it for a long time before he ever got over it.

If he ever did.

I sat in the sunroom sipping wine. It was hot in the sunroom, but it gave me some space from Bruce. He'd been in a foul mood all day, and I needed a breather from hearing him bitch and moan about everything under the sun.

It had been one of those days when everything seemed to go wrong. We'd gotten stuck in traffic when we went to the grocery store. The lines to check out had been long. It was swelteringly hot, and we'd both been sweating by the time we'd lugged all the groceries up the stairs.

Of course, after the day we'd had, Bruce had announced that we "needed" a drink. He could twist anything into a "need a drink" situation. Seeing as how I was high-strung myself from hearing him gripe all day, I wasn't disinclined to agree with him, though.

I'd been drinking in the living room with him, but I'd finally come out here for a few moments when he'd started replaying events from the past again. I was hoping if I stepped out for a few moments, it would get his mind off all that before he started in about my parents. The subject was getting old, and I don't know why he always wanted to drone on about them when we were drinking.

It wasn't five minutes before I heard the sunroom door opening, and I had to fight back a frustrated groan.

Bruce stalked into the sunroom and over to the glass table where I sat sipping my wine, muttering an expletive under his breath, "F— it's hot out here, angel. How can you stand it?"

He frowned down at me, and I just shrugged. "It's not that bad. I just wanted some fresh air."

"Well, come back in the house, baby. I need to talk to you."

It was on the tip of my tongue to tell him that I didn't want to come back in yet, but one look at his face, and I knew that would probably lead to an argument between us, and I didn't want that. I might hate hearing Bruce gripe about shit, but I'd rather him be ranting and pissed off at the rest of the world than at me.

So I dutifully grabbed my glass and walked back into the cold living room. I had to admit that it felt good in there after sitting in the hotbox that was the sunroom in the summertime. It didn't matter that we had all the windows open out there. The sunroom had a greenhouse effect. I'm sure that's why all our plants grew so well out there. We had several philodendrons and spider plants hanging in pots suspended from the ceiling. The philodendrons loved it so much out there they were trailing all the way down to the floor.

Bruce wasted no time in addressing what was on his mind once he got me back into the air conditioning.

"I'm out of smokes, baby, so I need you to drive me up to the store to get some. We'll go ahead and grab a couple more bottles of wine while we're there."

I stilled, the glass of wine halfway to my lips. I set it down on the coffee table without taking a sip and frowned at him. "No way, Bruce. We've been drinking. We can't drive."

Bruce shrugged like it was no big deal. "You've only had two glasses, babygirl. You're fine. You don't feel drunk at all, do you?"

I shook my head. "No, I don't, but that's not the point."

He scoffed. "You know it takes you damn near a whole bottle before you start getting wasted. I've seen you talk to your parents after having more than you've had now."

I swore, taking the Lord's name in vain. I guess Bruce's speech was rubbing off on me more and more. I was swearing more myself than I ever had, but I usually drew the line at taking God's name in vain. I knew it was one of the Ten Commandments and had always taken care not to say those words as curse words. I'd always been taught that was highly disrespectful to God, and I immediately felt a twinge of guilt at saying it, but I ignored it and channeled my irritation toward Bruce. "Why didn't you get more cigarettes when we were out earlier?" I was pissed he was even putting me in this position, and it was ridiculous. We were just out earlier that day.

"I was too f— irritated, and I forgot," he ground out.

"Let's just walk up to the store together," I offered. "It's not that far, and it'll be safer that way. You know I never wanted to even chance driving after drinking."

Bruce scowled and cursed. "It is too damn f— hot to be walking up to the store, baby. I'm ill as shit, and I need a smoke, and I just want to go and get back. I'll f— drive myself if you don't want to go."

I felt a flare of panic rise within me. I knew Bruce had had more to drink than I had. He always drank faster than me unless I chugged to keep up with him, and I also knew if he got caught driving at all—drunk or not—it'd be back to jail for him.

I hesitated, and Bruce started grabbing his wallet. He picked up my car keys and held them out to me.

I looked at them helplessly before his jaw hardened. "Have it your way, then," he muttered as he started walking for the door.

"No! Wait!" I called after him. He stopped and turned back to me expectantly.

I felt a sinking feeling in my chest. I knew if I didn't drive Bruce up to the store, there would be hell to pay no matter what happened. If he got pulled over and went to jail, then it'd be my fault for refusing to take him. If he went on his own and made it back, he'd still give me shit about not driving him.

I took the keys from him, grabbed my purse, and headed down the stairs to the car.

Bruce cranked the air conditioner on high as I backed out of the garage. He was right that I didn't feel impaired at all. I hadn't really drank enough to be drunk yet. Still, I was extra careful on the short drive up to the store. I made sure to come to a complete stop at every stop sign and didn't break the speed limit by even a mile.

I relaxed when I finally killed the engine the parking lot and got out to go into the store with Bruce. We got his usual brand of cigarettes and picked up a couple of magnums of Pinot Grigio. I didn't argue because I certainly didn't want us to run out of wine and then for him to throw a fit for me to drive up here again.

We were out of the store quickly, and then I was driving back to our apartment as Bruce lit up a smoke. His mood instantly improved and he looked over at me and grinned. "Shit, baby, I think you drive better when you've been drinking."

I frowned and said, "I'm never doing this again, Bruce. I mean it. It's too risky."

He waved my concern off. "You're doing fine, angel. We're almost back to the house and nothing's happened."

I allowed myself to relax the tiniest bit. He was right. Our apartment was right up the road. I was at the last stop sign before our driveway. Like I'd been doing, I made sure to come to a complete stop. I looked both ways. There was nothing on the left side. A motorcycle holding a man and woman pulled up on the right, but I knew they'd have to stop. I had the right of way, so I pulled forward to cross the intersection.

But the guy on the motorcycle didn't stop. He ran the stop sign and ran right out in front of me.

My heart jumped into my throat as I slammed on my brakes. Bruce cursed next to me, "That f— ran the stop sign!"

Fortunately, I hadn't been going fast at all. I'd barely started moving the car from a complete stop. The motorcyclist had been going faster than me.

The front of my car collided with the side of his

motorcycle. "Oh my gosh, oh my gosh," I chanted. "Bruce, what do we do?"

"Stay calm, baby," Bruce told me as he got out of the car to go over to the man and woman. The motorcycle was laying on the ground, but they were both standing up.

I felt the bile rising up in my throat and threw open my car door right before I got sick and emptied the contents of my stomach onto the pavement. This was a nightmare. I didn't know what was going to happen, but I couldn't believe I'd been in an accident.

I heard Bruce's voice cutting through the air. "Y'all alright man?"

"Yeah, we're fine," I heard the man telling Bruce. The woman was on the phone, though, and I saw Bruce frowning at her before I heard him saying, "You want our insurance, and then we can just skip the hassle of waiting for the police to show up?"

The guy said something I couldn't make out, and then I heard Bruce's voice sounding slightly pissed. "You know you ran that f— stop sign, man."

The man said something else, and then Bruce shook his head before stalking back over to me.

"Bruce, what's going on? What do we do? Do we have to stay here, or do we leave, or what?" I was panicking. I truly didn't know what to do. I'd never been in an accident before, and I was freaking out.

"The cops are going to show up, Sarah. Just be calm and tell them that f— ran the stop sign. This accident wasn't your fault. You came to a complete stop. That f— idiot over there is the one at fault. Everything's going to be okay."

I nodded, his words calming me. If I wasn't at fault for the accident, then I'd be okay, right? He was right. I wasn't at fault. I'd stopped at the stop sign.

Flashing lights pulled up, breaking me out of my thoughts, and an officer stepped out of the cop car. Another cop car pulled up right behind it, and another officer emerged. Why did cops always have to travel in pairs?

One cop walked over to the motorcyclists. The other walked over to Bruce and me.

The officer who came over to Bruce and me asked us what happened. I let Bruce do all the talking, merely nodding my agreement when the officer glanced at me for confirmation.

The other officer was likewise talking to the couple on the motorcycle, and then the officers met in the middle to discuss together. I glanced over at Bruce, but he was frowning at the two cops talking together.

After just a few minutes, the one who'd initially talked to us came back over and pulled me to the side to speak to me alone. My eyes shot to Bruce, and he looked pissed that the cop was pulling me away on my own.

The police officer asked me to show him my license, so I got it out of my purse and handed it to him.

He spoke into his walkie talkie before turning back to me. "You've never been in any kind of trouble before, have you, Miss MacKenzie? Never been arrested or anything, have you?"

I shook my head, "No, of course not. I've never even gotten a speeding ticket."

He grinned before he glanced over at Bruce and

frowned. "Who is he to you?" he asked as he nodded over to Bruce.

"My husband," I answered simply.

His eyebrows rose up, and I could tell he was curious like almost everyone else who found out I was with Bruce, but he didn't ask the questions I'm sure he wanted to ask, such as what I saw in such an older man, why I was with him, etc. Instead, he jumped straight to the business at hand.

"You were the one who was driving, weren't you, Miss MacKenzie?"

I nodded, "Yes, sir."

"Where were you going?" I frowned. He already knew all this. Bruce had already told him all this.

"We were on our way home. We live right up there," I pointed to the driveway, and the officer's eyes followed in the direction I pointed.

"Have you been drinking tonight?" he asked me, and my heart plummeted. Why was he asking me that? I wasn't acting drunk. At least, I didn't think I was.

I didn't even consider lying to him. I'd just thrown up, so maybe he smelled it on me. Plus, wasn't it considered perjury to lie to the cops?

"I had a couple of glasses of wine earlier," I admitted.

"How long ago was that?" he asked me.

"I don't know," I said slowly. I wasn't sure how much time had passed. "A while?" It came out sounding like a question, and I wanted to kick myself for sounding like an idiot.

The officer nodded and then asked me if I'd be willing to submit to a field sobriety test.

I'd heard the term, but I wasn't too sure what it was. "What exactly is that?" I asked him cautiously.

He told me it was just a few mobility tests that would help him determine if I was under the influence. If I passed, I'd be fine.

I nodded my acceptance. How hard could it be, right? I wasn't drunk, so I should be able to pass, shouldn't I?

He instructed me what to do, telling me to walk in a straight line placing each foot directly in front of the other. I thought I did fine, though I wobbled a bit at the end. It was difficult to keep balance when placing each foot directly in front of the other.

I looked at him hopefully, and he nodded, giving nothing away before he asked me to recite some of the letters of the alphabet backwards.

I frowned. What? My mind was a jumble of nerves, and I struggled to think of the alphabet backward, "Um, Z...Y..." I stopped to mentally sing the alphabet song to myself to figure out which letter came next. How the hell did reciting the alphabet backwards help them determine this?

He stopped me by holding up a hand. He studied me for a moment and then asked me if I would take a breathalyzer test.

I paused, wondering what to do. My eyes flickered over to Bruce. I wanted to ask him what I should do, but the cop moved to block my view of him. It was obvious he wasn't going to let me talk to my husband at all.

I didn't know what would happen if I refused. Could I even refuse? Weren't you supposed to pretty much do everything the cops said? I ultimately decided that was the best course of action. If you cooperated with cops, they were more willing to issue you a warning and be easy on you. Besides, I didn't feel drunk at all, so I should pass the little test, right? I heard myself agree, "Okay."

He led me over to his squad car where he pulled out a device and held it up to my lips. He had me blow into it for a long time, until I was almost out of breath, and I watched him as the number registered on the machine. I wasn't sure what it said, but he asked me to repeat the test, so I did.

He checked the number again before he looked up at me and informed me, "Your numbers have too great a difference between them. One was pretty high and the other was low. It could just be a malfunction in the equipment, but I'm going to have to take you in, and we'll do one at the station with our machine there that has a higher accuracy rating."

I digested that. Take me in? I felt a hard knot forming in my stomach as an awful mixture of fear, disbelief, and dread overtook me. "Are you arresting me?" I asked incredulously.

"Based on the field sobriety test and the breathalyzer, I have to take you in, ma'am." Surprisingly, he sounded halfway sympathetic, like he didn't really want to, but he was just doing his job.

I didn't know what to say, so I just stood there numbly, and he pulled out a pair of handcuffs and came up behind me to place them on my wrists.

I felt like I was in a nightmare as he gently pulled my hands behind me and cuffed me. I'd never been in a pair of real handcuffs before. Sure, my brother and I used to play with toy ones when we were kids, but these were the real deal.

"Is that too tight?" the officer asked me, and I felt tears well up in my eyes that he would even ask. They weren't overly tight, but they weren't loose enough I could get out of them either.

I just shook my head before he went over to the passenger side of his squad door and opened the door. He gently put his hand on my head and led me into his car.

I didn't know much about getting arrested, but I was pretty sure they weren't supposed to put you in the front seat with them. One glance into the backseat where a couple of rough-looking guys sat scowling with their hands cuffed behind their backs and I knew why I'd been placed in front.

"Who's the little hottie?" one of them asked, glancing at me appreciatively as the police officer got into the squad door and shut his.

"Yeah, why didn't you put her back here with us, Johnson? We'd have taken good care of her."

My eyes were wide with shock and fear, and I felt tears welling up again.

The police officer gave them both a stern look and said, "Quiet. Don't speak to her." He turned to me then and said, "Don't worry about them. Just look straight ahead and ignore them."

I didn't nod or do anything. I just did what he said, although I could feel two pairs of eyes on the back of my head as the officer drove us along the highway to the jail.

My mind was going a thousand miles a minute. I didn't have a clue what was going to happen. Was I just going to have to take another test and then they'd let me go? Or, were they actually going to book me into jail?

That thought terrified me. I wasn't one of the psycho-type girls who went to jail. I'd never even gotten sent to the principal's office in school. I'd never been in trouble with the law or authority figures in my entire life. The most rebellious thing I'd ever done was be with Bruce. Sure, he'd gotten me to break the law, but I wasn't really a lawbreaker on my own.

Would Bruce come get me? I'd gotten him out of jail, so I had to believe he would do the same for me, right?

Was I being charged? If so, with what?

I had no idea what to expect or what to do. I'd never felt so scared or doomed in my entire life.

I knew I couldn't break down crying in front of all these men, but I couldn't stop the tears that slipped onto my cheeks as I blinked furiously, trying to blink them away.

The squad car turned off the road onto a long asphalt driveway, and the officer spoke into his walkie talkie before a huge gate opened.

I took a deep breath and tried to focus on keeping my heart from racing out of my chest as he pulled into the back of a huge building before turning off the engine.

CHAPTER 3

THE OFFICER PULLED the two guys out of the back of the squad car first. They mouthed off to him and didn't make his job easy, but he led them over to his white van, opened up the back and put them in there with other male prisoners.

Then, he came back over to the squad car and got me. He didn't take me to the van at first. Instead, he took me into a room on the side of the building where there was another officer sitting behind a machine.

They instructed me to blow into the machine. The first time didn't take because I couldn't blow hard enough or long enough, so I had to do it two more times.

When they finally get the readings they needed, I saw them conversing amongst themselves before the officer who brought me in came over to me and lead me back outside to the van.

He took me to the front middle of the huge van and opened up the door. A handful of other women, all with cuffs behind their backs like me, were sitting in the van. He helped me step up into the van, and my face flushed knowing that I must be flashing him a peek at my butt. I was wearing the short sundress I'd thrown on when Bruce had talked me into driving him to the store, and I knew that bending or stepping up very much would reveal everything underneath it.

I tried not to think about that, though, since there was nothing I could do about it. He directed me to sit along one of the benches that spanned the wall of the van. I was crammed in next to another woman.

I heard the buzz of the air conditioner running in the van and looked up to see the vents in the top of the ceiling, but it was still warm in the back of the van from so many of us being squished up together in there.

Nobody spoke to me, and I didn't speak to anyone, too terrified to say anything. Some of the women looked cross, while others wore a mask of indifference. I wondered what they were all in cuffs for, but I knew better than to ask.

I didn't know why we'd all been put in there, but I guessed I'd find out soon enough. I somehow instinctively knew it was better not to ask questions or make waves. So far, I'd been cooperative, and I knew I needed to keep doing that if I didn't want to get on the wrong side of whoever was in charge there.

My arms began to ache as we sat there for at least an hour. And I guess it was psychological more than anything, but I felt itches all over my body since my hands were pinned behind my back and I couldn't scratch. I tried to think of anything else to keep my mind off the points I imagined were itching.

My curls keep falling in my face, and I'd have to awkwardly try to toss them behind my head, but it was hard to do it in such close quarters, and I didn't want to slap the girl next to me in the face with my hair. I didn't think that would go over so well, so I finally resigned myself to letting it hang there.

Some of the women began to talk amongst themselves, but I stayed quiet and didn't make eye contact with anyone. The ones who talked shared stories about how they'd been picked up, and they didn't sound like strangers to the routines. Of course, each of them maintained she was innocent and had been wrongly accused. I wondered with a start if that's how I would sound telling my story about how I'd been in an accident but that it wasn't my fault, the other guy had run the stop sign and I hadn't been drunk but I'd been taken in just because I had alcohol on my breath from puking my guts out.

Some of the other women mumbled, and one who was getting particularly frustrated with our tight confinement began to bitch loudly, cussing at the cops. All that got us was a pounding on the outside of the door and a "Settle down!"

I don't know how long we sat there. Maybe it was two hours or longer. All I knew was time ticked by slowly, and by the time the doors opened back up and the cops started ushering us out, the sun had gone down.

They took us inside the building, and then we were lined up to be what I guess they call booked in.

Everything happened in a blur. The guys were being booked in ahead of us, and many of them glanced over at us lasciviously, spouting filth at us. The officers warned them not to look at us or speak to us, but some of them continued to do it anyway until things escalated to the point that the officers had to restrain them.

I was standing there shaking with terror at this unhinged, dark world I was suddenly thrust into. I'd been sheltered from stuff like this my entire life. Yeah, I'd seen movies and read books about criminals, but nothing could have prepared me for the reality of it.

One guy was obviously strung out on something and flipped, trying to break free of the cops and screaming. They subdued him, wrestling him to the ground. I stared with wide eyes before a female officer got my attention by repeating herself with irritation, "Step forward, please."

She removed my handcuffs, and I almost sighed at the release from my bondage. Even though the arresting officer hadn't cuffed them too tight, they'd still started to dig into my skin after all the time of sitting with them like that.

I stood where she directed me and faced forward before turning to each side so she could take my mugshot. Tears pricked my eyes at the knowledge that I now had a mugshot. Only criminals had mugshots. I was officially a criminal.

Next, I was prompted to step over to this machine where the officer took each of my fingers and rolled them all along this device that looked like a scanner. I stared at the monitor in amazement as it showed my fingerprints being scanned and captured. After she rolled each of my fingers across the device, she did my palms as well.

Another female officer intercepted me and took me into a room where she mechanically ordered me to strip.

I did as instructed, embarrassment overtaking me at being stark naked in front of a total stranger.

She seemed unaffected by my nudity. Of course, this

was routine for her, but it did nothing to settle my nerves or feeling of shame.

She made me open my mouth so she could look inside, and as if my embarrassment and shame couldn't get any worse, she told me to bend over and cough. I didn't really understand why I had to do that, but I did as instructed.

Only then did she allow me to stand back up and hand me an orange jumpsuit. "This'll be too big on you, but it's all we've got left at the moment, so you'll have to make do," she told me.

I vaguely registered that jail clothes weren't black-and-white stripes like cartoons and TV shows always made them out to be.

I quickly got dressed in the one-piece outfit that was too big for me.

Then, I was led down a long hallway before I was put into a huge cell on the right side. The walls of the area were thick stone on each side except for the front where the door was made of long, thick vertical bars.

Four or five other girls sat spread out on the benches that lined the wall. At least it looked like we wouldn't be cramped together in here like sardines like we had been in the back of the van. Of course, I didn't recognize any of these women, so they weren't the same ones I'd been in the back of the van with.

The door closed behind me with a clang and a sense of finality.

I wasn't sure what this area was. There weren't any beds, so surely this wasn't where we were going to stay indefinitely. There was a toilet and a sink over in the corner of the room, and I shuddered just thinking about going to the bathroom in front of strangers.

One girl stood up and walked over to where there was a phone hanging on the wall. I hadn't even noticed it.

I was still standing at the front of the cell, so I moved to get out of the way as she walked up. I went to the empty corner of the room to sit as far away from everyone else as I could get.

Everyone seemed to be giving each other their space as there were huge gaps between the five or six of us who were in the cell.

She spoke softly into the phone. When she finished her call, she went and sat back down on the bench, her shoulders leaning against the wall and her legs spread wide with her hands hanging loosely in between them.

Silence stretched between all of us, and I wondered what time it was. Of course, there wasn't a clock in the cell. There was nothing of convenience in the spartan place, and why should there be? Jail was a punishment after all.

A few more moments of silence ticked by before one of the women spoke. "You know you can make a phone call, right?"

I looked up and found her looking at me. She was tall and slim with blonde hair that was in a thick French braid. Her eyes held no menace, and her voice was even. She was pretty with thick lashes and full lips.

"First time?" she asked me when I didn't immediately say anything.

I just nodded. "Yeah."

She looked at me with something akin to sympathy

and understanding before she got up and moved to sit closer to me.

She didn't offer her name. She just started talking—or asking questions rather.

"What are you in for?" she asked me.

"DUI, I think," I answered carefully.

She nodded. "Did you blow?"

"What?" I asked her.

"Did you submit to a Breathalyzer test?"

"Oh, yeah. I thought it best to just cooperate."

She shook her head. "You shouldn't have blown. The case is almost always dropped if you refuse to blow because then they don't have any chemical evidence you were over the legal limit."

My brow furrowed. "I didn't know that," I admitted.

She nodded again. "Yeah, most first-timers don't, but it's a sure way to beat the system. Hell, almost every lawyer in the city has been arrested for a DUI, but they know how to get off. Don't blow, and your case has to be thrown out. Now, you won't be able to drive while your case is ongoing, but that's a small price to pay to not get the conviction."

I didn't give her any other details about my incident, and thankfully she didn't ask. Instead, she started talking about how she was picked up for trying to see her kids. Her ex-husband, their father, had custody of them and wouldn't allow her to see them.

I didn't ask her any questions. I just let her talk.

Eventually, she nodded over to the phone again. "You really should call someone and have them be here tomorrow to get you. The judge almost always RORs people on their first charge ever—especially if it's just a misdemeanor."

She said "if it's just a misdemeanor" like a misdemeanor was no big deal. I guess in this criminal world it wasn't. It was child's play here whereas a felony was the real deal.

I stood up and walked over to the phone, trying desperately to remember Bruce's number. We never dialed each other's numbers, though, since they were just programmed into our phones. Hell, we hardly called each other anyway since we were always together.

After wracking my brain, it was obvious I wasn't going to be able to come up with Bruce's number, so I dialed my own. I hadn't had my cell phone or purse or anything on me when I'd been arrested, so it should all be home with Bruce.

My phone rang until it went to voicemail. Damn it. Bruce didn't answer. I didn't know what time it was, but he might be asleep, or he might not have even gotten my purse in from the car, so he might not have heard the phone ringing.

I hated myself for not memorizing his number. I never planned on being in this situation again, but I made a mental note to memorize his number when I got out of here in case I ever needed it.

I put the phone back in the cradle and hung my head. This was the most f— up situation I'd ever been in. I felt tears stinging my eyes again, but I blinked them back. I couldn't break down here in front of all these women. I didn't know much about jail, but I knew you couldn't break down and show that kind of weakness.

I took a deep breath and then picked up the phone

and dialed the only other number I could think of to call, the phone number that had been ingrained in my head since childhood.

Dad answered on the fourth ring, just when I'd been getting ready to give up and put the phone down, thinking that they weren't going to answer either.

"Hello?" his voice was sleepy, cautious, and worried at the same time.

"Dad?" my voice came out on a croak, and I swallowed to clear my throat.

"Sarah? It's one thirty in the morning," Dad said. I did the math, and that let me know it was two thirty here. "Is everything okay? Where are you at? This call came from a Florida county jail," he asked me, the dread in his voice letting me know that he already knew where I was.

"I'm—I'm okay, but I'm in jail."

I heard my mom in the background, "What happened? Why is she in jail?"

I closed my eyes at the worry in their voices. "It's a long story," I began, "but to make it short, a guy on a motorcycle ran a stop sign and ran into me."

"Was anyone hurt?" Dad asks.

"No," I rushed to assure him. "Everyone's fine, but I was arrested because..." I stumbled over my words, dreading revealing the truth to them, "because I'd been drinking earlier in the day."

I heard Mom murmur something, but I couldn't make out what she said. Instead of being met with the expected anger, a disappointed silence just stretched over the line.

"I wasn't drunk, though," I rushed to add. "And I'm sorry I called y'all, but I can't get ahold of Bruce, and I didn't know who else to call," my voice broke at the end.

"You can always call us, Sarah," Dad said heavily. I could tell they had a ton of questions, but an automated voice came over the line telling us we only had one minute left.

"We'll call the jail and see if there's anything we can find out," Dad said, "and we'll see about getting ahold of Bruce too."

"Thank you," I managed.

"And we love you," he said before he added, "and we'll be praying for you. It'll be okay."

His soothing words were almost my undoing.

Just then, the line clicked off, and I replaced the phone before I went back to my corner.

The girl with the braid looked like she might want to talk more, but I wasn't in the mood, so I balled my knees up on the bench and laid down facing the wall.

My mind kept replaying the events of the night. Bruce getting mad at me and wanting me to drive him to the store. Me giving in.

I was angry at him for getting me into this mess. This was all his fault. If he hadn't pushed for me to drive him to the store to get some damn cigarettes, none of this would have happened. If he'd just remembered to pick them up when we were already out...if he hadn't been such a lazy asshole. If, if, if...my mind flooded with all the ifs. If I hadn't driven after I'd been drinking, I wouldn't be here.

I could blame Bruce all I wanted, but this was ultimately on me. I'd given in. I'd driven the car. Yeah, I didn't think it was fair that I was charged when the motorcycle dude ran the stop sign, but I'd still broken the law by getting behind the wheel after I'd been drinking.

My mind thought of that statistic that said most accidents happen within a mile of the home. How ironic that'd been proven true with me. We were only a short block from our apartment when everything had gone to hell.

I was also resentful that I was in here and hadn't been able to get Bruce on the phone. What was he doing? Was he sleeping, unbothered by the fact that I was locked up? When he'd been in jail, I'd sat by the phone. I'd paced and been unable to sleep at the thought of being separated from him. Had Bruce just gone home and continued to drink and party like I wasn't going through the worst thing to ever happen to me?

All those thoughts were making me bitter, and the only shred of hope I had to cling to was what the girl with the braid had told me. Since this was my first time ever being arrested, surely the judge would be lenient on me and let me go without setting a bail. Surely, they wouldn't make me stay in jail. Panic and fear pricked my chest at the thought of staying in here longer than it took to get before the judge.

My thoughts were thankfully interrupted when I heard the bars of the cell clang open again. An officer stood at the door and instructed us all to get up.

Then, she herded us along several more hallways before we got to a huge steel door. She spoke into her walkie talkie, and it buzzed open.

Another officer was standing by a table with supplies heaped on top of it. She gave us each a bundle as we passed by her: a blanket, a flat pillow, toothbrush, a small tube of toothpaste, soap that looked worse than the stuff they provided in hotels.

They walked us into a huge common area that was empty this time of night even though the fluorescent lights lit it up brightly. Cells were buzzed open, and we were separated into them one by one.

When it was finally my turn to be placed in one, I watched as the huge royal blue door slid open, and then I stepped into the darkness within.

The door closed shut behind me, but enough light still peaked in from the window on the door for me to see. There were two bunks on the right wall.

A huge black girl rolled over from where she lay on the bottom bunk and peered up at me. She thumbed up to the bunk above her, "You're up there, sweetheart. Ain't no way my big ass climbing up there."

I tossed my stuff to the top bunk, and then gingerly put my foot on the edge of her bunk to climb up to it.

"Hey, watch the f— bed," she barked at me, and I flinched as I quickly flung myself onto the top bunk.

"Sorry," I mumbled. Seriously, though, how the hell did she expect me to get up here without climbing upon her bed? I was too short to just jump up there.

She mumbled and rolled back over facing the wall. I stuffed the supplies against the wall and spread the blanket out over me, doubting I'd be able to get any sleep. Although I was physically exhausted, my mind was working in overdrive. I was too scared about what my fate in the court system would be. I was regretting having called my parents and getting them involved in all this too. I dreaded the questions that I knew would come, and

I'd have to answer them. They'd have a right to know why their daughter had called them in the middle of the night from jail.

Bruce would be furious with me for calling them, but I didn't care. If he hadn't wanted me to call them, he should have answered the phone.

Now that I was finally encased in darkness, and I heard the snores of the fearsome girl below me, I allowed my tears to fall.

It was freezing cold in the jail, and the thin blanket they'd given me didn't do anything to ward off the chill. My nose felt like a block of ice, and my wrists hurt from where they'd been bound in handcuffs.

Worse than all that, though, was the feeling of doom that settled over me. I felt trapped and helpless. My freedom had been stripped from me, and I was caged up like an animal. I had no idea what to expect about how the DUI charge would turn out. Would I be able to get it dropped? Or would I be convicted? If I was convicted, would I have to do more jail time? I didn't ever want to be in here again.

The tears continued to roll down my face, wetting the flimsy pillow I was laying on as I continued to lament my situation until exhaustion overtook me and sleep finally claimed me.

CHAPTER 4

I AWOKE with a start as bright, piercing light suddenly flooded my vision. Although my eyes were still closed, I could see the sudden brightness through them.

I heard the clang of the door as it opened. The girl below me stood up and stretched before making her way out of the door.

I glanced over at the toilet and cringed. I hated the thought of using it, but I really had to pee, so I hopped off the bed and hurried about my business while there was no one in the cell but me.

Then, I made quick work of washing my hands and face and brushing my teeth. I didn't even bother going to take a shower. I shuddered at the thought of a bunch of other women seeing me naked. Plus, if the girl with the blonde braid had been right, I should be out of here today. I could shower as long as I wanted once I got home.

"Come on! Line up!" I heard a guard saying, so I reluctantly stepped out of the cell into the common area where countless women were grouped together. Many of them chatted amongst each other like they knew each other well. A few newbies like me hung back on our own, and the ones who'd obviously been in there longer were eyeing us, obviously sizing us up.

There was a clock up in the common area, and it showed it was insanely early. Just after four-thirty in the morning, which meant I couldn't have slept for more than an hour.

The group of women began to fall into a line as we were herded out of the area and down hallways until we reached a huge cafeteria.

There were already several groups of women there. I guess they'd been brought in from other parts of the jail. Just how huge was this place? I'd never been inside the little county jail in the town I grew up in, but I could remember from the small size of the outside of the building that it wouldn't have even been able to house half of these female inmates—much less the males.

I wasn't hungry at all, but I noticed that everyone fell into line to get a tray, so I did likewise, not wanting to draw undue attention to myself.

After picking up a tray and grabbing a pack of plastic utensils I had no intention of using, I stood uncertainly, my eyes roving over the tables.

Suddenly, I was back in high school, but my best friend wasn't there, so I didn't know who to sit with— except this was a million times worse. It was like every table was full of mean girls, except these mean girls were the real deal.

In an amazing stroke of luck, the girl with the blonde braid appeared by my side holding a tray of her own.

"Hey, you," she smiled down at me. "Come on, let's go grab a seat."

I was relieved to have been rescued by the only familiar face in there. Well, that's not true. The black girl who'd been my cellmate was sitting at a table with other girls just as big and fearsome looking as she was, but I knew she had no intention of taking me under her wing. She hadn't spoken a word to me after jumping down my throat for daring to use her cot as a steppingstone up to my bunk.

I wordlessly followed blonde-braid girl over to a table where we sat with a few seats between us and another group of girls.

"So, how'd you fare last night?" she asked me, taking a huge bite of toast.

I shrugged, "Okay, I guess."

"I'm glad nobody messed with you. Sometimes these bitches try to give newbies a hard time just because they can, you know?"

I nodded, though I didn't really know, and I said a silent prayer of thanks that I'd been spared from that.

She took another bite from her plate and then looked at my untouched plate before she motioned to it with a handful of toast. "You better eat something."

I shook my head, my stomach turning at the thought, "I'm not hungry."

She glanced up, and I followed her gaze over to where an officer stood surveying the room. "Still, you better eat a little something. If they see someone not eating at all, it can get ugly. They'll think you're trying to starve yourself or something and lock you up in solitary."

I glanced up at the officer she was looking at and saw

her gazed trained right on me. I swallowed and looked down at the tray that held a slice of fried bologna, scrambled eggs, sausage links, and a piece of toast. I took a tiny bite of the toast and forced myself to chew and swallow it. I had absolutely no appetite, and it tasted like sawdust in my mouth. It physically took everything within me to swallow it. I took a sip of the black coffee to wash it down before forcing myself to keep nibbling.

"The food here's actually not that bad," blonde-braid girl commented. "Not like at some jails."

I wondered how many jails she'd been in but didn't ask. She seemed nice enough, but I was reminded just how little I knew about her or anyone here.

I continued to pick at my plate, taking tiny bites and pushing food around just to make it look like I was eating. Blonde-braid girl finished her plate and then eyed mine. "I can help you if you want."

I pushed my plate her way, "Take it, please."

She glanced over at the guard and swapped our plates when she wasn't looking.

Apparently, they didn't want us sharing our food with other inmates in here either.

After our allotted time for breakfast, we were herded back into the block we'd come from. Most of the women stayed out in the common area and chatted noisily, cursing and laughing. I went back into the little cell to get away from anyone, wondering what would happen next.

I wasn't alone long before my cellmate came stomping into the room. Her eyes zeroed in on me, letting me know she'd been looking for me. I felt a prickle of fear go up my spine, knowing that if I'd pissed this woman off enough that she wanted to beat me up, there'd be nothing I could do to stop her. She was more than twice my size and burly like a man with her hair swept back from her face in cornrows. Hell, I'd never been in a fist-fight before in my life. I didn't know the first thing about how to defend myself in a physical altercation. I vaguely thought back to how Dad had tried to teach me the basics of boxing, but I'd wanted no part of it, shrugging it all off, stating that it was classless and unladylike for girls to fight. I'd never anticipated needing those skills.

I was starting to wish I'd let him teach me.

"Yo, you going to first appearance today?"

"Wh-what?" I tried to keep my voice from sounding too wobbly. Show no fear. Maybe she'd lose the scent of blood if she didn't think I was afraid of her.

"You been before a judge yet?" she asked me with exasperation.

I shook my head, "No."

"What you in here for," she jutted her chin out at me.

"DUI," I answered simply.

"This your first time in jail." she said it like a statement, not a question, but I answered her anyway.

"Yes."

"You likely gonna walk then. Dibs on your stuff."

"My what?" I didn't have a clue what she was talking about.

"The soap and other shit they gave you when you checked in here."

"Oh, I glanced over at the pile in the forgotten corner of my bunk and gathered it all up to hand it to her, relieved that that's all she wanted. "Here. It's yours."

She didn't say thank you. Instead, she just took my offering and stashed it with her other stuff before she walked back out into the common area after staking her claim.

I sat there in silence for a while after she left until I heard a police office in the common area calling for quiet. Then, she began to call out surnames. I stood when I heard mine and walked out to stand in the line that was already forming.

I guess we were the newbies who were being taken to what they called first appearance.

The first appearance before a judge.

The moment that would decide whether we'd get bail or be detained.

I was anxious to get it all over with. My stomach was all twisted up in knots. I'm surprised I didn't throw up the few bites of toast I'd had.

I wondered if Bruce would be there in the courtroom. If he'd be waiting in the lobby to get me out like I'd done for him when he'd been arrested.

I wondered if the judge would even let me out. I didn't know anything about how this all worked. But that girl had seemed really sure when she'd told me I'd probably be released on my own recognizance.

I had to hang onto that hope. It's all I had.

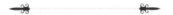

We hadn't been put in vans and taken to the courthouse or anything, and I remembered from when Bruce had been in jail that the first appearances were held in a courtroom right there at the jail. Instead, we were just led down a series of long hallways before we were put into a huge holding area similar to the one we'd been in where we could make a phone call, except this space was quite a bit larger with a longer bench spanning all along the walls.

We had to wait there as we were taken into the courtroom in batches. There were so many of us who had to go before the judge that I guess they couldn't take us all into the courtroom at once, so they took us in groups of about ten. Fortunately, I was among the second group to get to go.

It was humiliating being herded into the courtroom full of people in handcuffs and a jumpsuit. They'd cuffed us all again in the hallway that led to the courtroom.

At least our hands were in front of us this time. It was much better to be cuffed with them sitting in our laps than with our arms stretched behind us. At least this way if our faces itched or something, we could lift both hands to scratch. And I could more easily move my hair out of my face.

I wished for the millionth time since I'd gotten locked up that I had a hair elastic to pull my hair up with.

I quickly scanned the courtroom when we entered, my eyes looking for Bruce, but there was nothing but a sea of unfamiliar faces. Granted, that didn't mean he wasn't there because I hadn't gotten a chance to really look at every face in the courtroom before we were motioned to sit down facing the judge and away from the courtroom of people.

I was a nervous wreck waiting for my name to be called. I was quickly learning that everything to do with the judicial system was waiting. Waiting to get booked into jail, waiting to see the judge, waiting for your name to be called. Waiting, waiting, waiting.

I was so tired of waiting. I just wanted to get all this over with and get out of there and never look back.

When the judge finally called my name, I stood up on shaking legs and approached the podium.

He read my charge off to me as well as my rights. The only question I was asked was whether I understood my rights. "Yes," I said, though I didn't really understand half of what he said.

He then started talking to the DA, who told him my record was clean and considering that, he recommended releasing me on my own recognizance on the conditions that I wasn't to partake of any drugs or alcohol while my case was ongoing. It was something about pretrial release conditions. In other words, they'd let me leave jail, but I wasn't supposed to have any drugs or alcohol. The drugs certainly weren't a problem, and the alcohol wouldn't be either. It's what had gotten me into this mess. I never wanted to drink again.

My heart leaped within me. That meant I'd be able to get out of there. No bail required.

The judge nodded and followed the DA's recommendation, ROR-ing me, telling me to make sure I showed up at my next court date.

I didn't even know when that would be or how I'd find out about it. All I knew was I was getting released, and I couldn't wait.

Some of the weight that'd been on my shoulders ever since I got arrested lifted. Of course, not all of it because I knew I still had to deal with the worry of being convicted and what all that would mean, but first things first.

I just couldn't wait to get out of there.

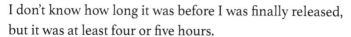

I don't know how long it was before I was finally released, but it was at least four or five hours.

We had to wait until all the other women prisoners went before the judge before we were taken back to our cells.

Then, began more waiting. I sat on the bunk anxiously waiting to be called to leave. I didn't understand why they couldn't just let us go immediately, but I was finding out they had very strict rules and procedures for how they did everything, and those rules and procedures weren't designed for the inmate's convenience, which I never would have cared about until I was one of the ones being held in there.

Finally, my name was called along with the other women who had either been RORed like me or who had posted bail.

We had to turn in our bed linens and pillows, and then we were taken back up front where we had to sign a form to get our belongings.

I quickly changed into my sundress and flip-flops, happy to turn in the jumpsuit and clog-type sandals the jail provided.

At last, I heard the buzzing and clanging of the huge metal door, and I followed the rest of the women out of it to freedom.

I recognized the lobby, only this time instead of me being the one waiting in it for Bruce to come out, I was on the other side of things, coming out from the hellhole that was lockup.

My eyes frantically scanned the area, searching for

Bruce. He had to be here. He just had to. He wouldn't leave me here all alone, would he?

My stomach dropped as I realized he wasn't there.

I walked out into the blazing sun and saw all the other women getting into cars. The ones who weren't were talking on their cell phones they'd retrieved from their personal belongings. I hadn't had a phone or anything on me when I'd been brought in. I had no money, no way to get ahold of anyone.

The jail was on the highway in the middle of nowhere. I knew the closest gas station was at least a couple of miles down the road.

Before I had a chance to ask anyone if I could use their phone to make a call, everyone was gone.

I hugged my arms around myself, feeling like I was going to cry.

I was alone out there and didn't know how I was going to get back to the apartment. I knew I couldn't walk all that way. It was a good twenty-minute drive out here. I'd never make it all that way. At least not in one day.

I squared my shoulders and roughly brushed my hands over my eyes. I could not break down out here. At least I wasn't locked up in that horrid jail anymore. At least I had the freedom to go where I wanted even if I didn't have the means.

I did the only thing I could and began walking up the side of the highway, determined to at least make it to the gas station. Maybe I could borrow a phone from someone there and somehow get ahold of Bruce.

It was the only option I had at that point. Surely, I'd be able to find some good Samaritan who'd let me place a call on their phone. Because I couldn't fathom the alternative of having to keep walking on foot and sleeping in the woods until I finally got back.

I hoped it wouldn't come to that.

I walked in the hot sun until my feet ached and I was a sticky mess. My thin flip-flops weren't ideal for such long hauls. I could feel my shoulders getting burned by the sun. The humidity had turned my hair into a frizzy mess. My mouth was parched. I was dying for a drink of water. I hadn't had hardly anything to drink during my time in jail, and I was thirstier than I ever remembered being.

Cars whizzed past me. The speed limit on this double lane highway was seventy miles an hour, so of course nobody stopped to offer me a ride. I wasn't sure I'd have accepted one anyway. I'd always been warned of the dangers of accepting rides from strangers. You could be getting into a car with a serial killer and not know it.

As hot and tired and thirsty as I was, I'd have almost been willing to chance it, though.

The gas station finally came into sight, and I walked with greater purpose, intent on getting there so I could get a drink of water and get out of this heat for a moment.

All my energy seemed to leave me when I finally made it there. Each step took effort, but I made it inside, the cool air hitting my face in a rush of heaven. I headed straight for the bathroom where I splashed my face and neck with cold water and then cupped my hands and took a sip.

I normally couldn't stand the taste of city water, but I was so thirsty it didn't bother me in the least.

Thankfully, nobody came into the bathroom to see me cupping handfuls of water and drinking it like an animal, but I'm not sure that would have stopped me then anyway. My survival instincts had kicked in, and I just needed to quench my thirst.

I stayed in the bathroom until my body had cooled down to a manageable temperature before I finally made myself walk back out into the store and then outside.

I was aware that this wasn't the safest-looking gas station around. It wasn't one of the more noticeable chain ones, and its close proximity to the jail meant that plenty of unsavory characters stopped there.

But then I'd just gotten out of jail, hadn't I?

I glanced around, looking for someone who didn't look too intimidating to ask if I could place a call on their phone.

The place was full of big, burly men, ones who looked like they could crush me with one fist, and I instinctively shrank back from them.

My gaze finally flicked over to an old stone picnic table set up under some trees over to the right of the building. It looked like it could be an employee's outdoor break area.

There were a couple of old men sitting there smoking and talking, and I decided they were my safest-looking bet. I realized I was judging based on appearances, but what could I do?

I started walking over to them, and they both looked up with interest as it became clear I was approaching them.

"Hi," I tried to say nicely and without letting them see how nervous I was.

I'm not sure how effective I was at hiding my nervousness, though, because one of them eyed me and answered back, "Hey there, sweetheart. You in some kind of trouble?"

A nervous laugh left me, and I tried to play it off like everything was fine. "Oh, I'm fine, but I was wondering if one of you had a phone I could use to call my husband?"

I was praying one of them would say yes and that they wouldn't ask any questions because I certainly didn't want to admit that I'd just gotten out of jail and was stuck out here all alone.

Maybe they sensed my reluctance to give out any information, but one of the men pulled his phone out of his faded jeans pocket and handed it to me. "No problem, honey. Here you go."

"Thank you," I flashed them a genuine smile and accepted the phone with shaking hands.

I dialed my cell phone number since I already knew I couldn't remember Bruce's. *Please pick up, please pick up*, I chanted over and over again in my head as I held it up to my ear and listened to it ring.

"Hello?" Bruce's voice finally came over the line, and I almost sobbed with relief.

"Bruce," I began.

"Angel!" he interrupted me. "I've been so worried about you. I'd have been there to get you, but I couldn't get to you. They came and put a boot on the damn car."

My brow furrowed. "A boot?"

"Yeah, it makes it where you can't drive the car."

I felt my stomach plummet. "I need you to come get me," I told him.

He started asking me questions about what all had

happened, but I interrupted him, "Bruce, just please come get me, and then we can talk about everything later."

"Oh, yeah, of course, babygirl. Where are you at?"

I told him.

"I'm calling a cab right now," he assured me.

I had no idea what it would cost to take a cab all the way out here, but I didn't give a shit. I just wanted to get home.

I wondered why he hadn't taken a cab to the jail this morning so he could be at my first appearance and waiting for me when I got out, but I bit my tongue to keep from asking him. I just needed him to come get me right now, and we could talk about everything else later.

I gave the old man back his phone and thanked him again for letting me use it.

They invited me to have a seat with them, but I hesitated. I didn't want to sit and have to talk to them. I was grateful they'd let me make a call, but I still didn't know anything about them and was in no mood to talk.

"Won't nobody mess with you if you're sitting here with us, sweetheart," one told me in a soothing tone like I was a skittish doe or something.

I sat down on the edge of the concrete bench as far away from them as I could get, and they thankfully went back to talking amongst each other, maybe sensing my reticence to talking.

I relaxed a bit when it began clear they weren't going to try to engage me in unwanted conversation.

I sat there and waited.

I was one step closer to getting out of this nightmare.

CHAPTER 5

WHEN BRUCE FINALLY SHOWED UP, he tore out of the cab and came over to where I sat by the two men, wrapping me in a tight hug.

The cab sat idling, waiting for us, and Bruce thanked the men, "Thank you for watching over my wife for me until I could get here. I really appreciate that."

I saw the shock on their faces at how much older than me Bruce was. While one of them responded to Bruce's thanks with a polite 'no problem,' the other man's jaw hardened in disapproval as he just grunted, looking at Bruce scathingly.

As usual, Bruce seemed wickedly amused by the reactions.

"Come on, angel," Bruce led me over to the cab. "Let's go home."

We got into the back of the cab, and although I didn't want to rehash everything that had happened in jail, I did my best to do so since Bruce was full of questions.

"I can't believe you walked all the way up to that gas

station in that," Bruce eyed my legs. "I'm surprised some-body didn't pick you up and kidnap you."

"I'd never been so hot in my entire life," I told him.

"You're telling me," his mouth quirked up, and I scowled at him. I couldn't believe he was making a joke at a time like this. I felt like I'd been to hell and back.

"I can't believe you," I muttered.

He sobered and reached over to touch my knee. "I'm sorry, baby. I bet you're tired, huh, angel?"

"Yes," I mumbled. "Tired and achy, and I just want a shower." Actually, what I really wanted was a nice, long, hot bath, but we didn't have a bathtub in our apartment, so I knew that wouldn't be happening.

Bruce put his arm around me on the back of the seat, and I leaned into the curve of his arm and rested my head against him. I was still pissed that he hadn't been there to get me when I got out, but I refrained from bring it up to him. Now that I was finally in a car on my way back home, the exhaustion was catching up with me. I didn't want to fight about things we couldn't change. He'd already explained to me that the car had been booted, and maybe he hadn't been able to get a cab that early in the morning. I didn't know. I just wanted to get cleaned up and sleep.

"I'm so sorry you had to go through all that, angel," Bruce said before placing a kiss on the top of my head. "Jail is no place for you, babygirl."

I didn't say anything. I wondered if he was apolo-gizing for pressuring me to drive him up to the store, if he was acknowledging that it was partly his fault. If he was apologizing for his part in it, it was in a roundabout way.

I decided it didn't really matter. I didn't press the issue

because I was too grateful to be out of jail and too exhausted to get into an argument with Bruce.

"I'm tempted to never drink again," I told him. "Besides, I can't have any alcohol anymore. It's one of the conditions of my release."

I peeked up at Bruce and saw him frowning, but he didn't say anything. I knew he liked to drink, but I was not about to risk going back to jail by breaking the terms of my release.

When we finally got back to our apartment, Bruce paid the driver while I stepped out and waited for him to unlock the door. I didn't have any keys or anything on me of course.

When we got inside, Bruce pulled me into another hug. "Everything's going to be okay, angel. I still can't believe that f— pulled out in front of you, and you're the one who ends up going to jail."

His eyes flared with anger at the supposed injustice of it all, but I really didn't want to talk about it all. "I'm going to take a shower," I told him tiredly.

"Okay, angel," he let me go.

I stood under the spray for a long time, letting the heat work the knots out of my muscles. When I finally got out and put on one of my comfiest nighties, a dark blue slip-type one that was loose around my thighs, I padded into the bedroom with my curls still damp and just sat on the bed, dejected.

My mind was racing, wondering what would happen if I was convicted. I would have to get a lawyer. Then, I remembered my parents. Oh gosh, I dreaded talking to them. I shouldn't have called them. Maybe I could have kept all this secret if I hadn't called them. I knew I had to call them before I could go to sleep. They'd be worried about me, and they needed to know I was out of that awful place.

Bruce walked into the bedroom holding a plate with a sandwich on it.

"I'm not hungry," I told him.

"Babygirl, you've got to eat something. I already know you didn't eat that jail food, did you?"

I shook my head. "No, but I don't have an appetite."

He frowned at me before he handed me the plate. "At least try to eat some of it."

I sighed and took a bite. After I swallowed, I looked back up at him and told him, "I need to call my parents. They'll be worried. I called them from jail last night."

"I know," his frown deepened. "I already talked to them today. They called my cell phone. Why did you call them, baby? F—, you know better."

I glared at him. "I couldn't get you on the phone! And theirs was the only other number I could remember. I couldn't remember your number, and I called my phone, but you didn't answer. I was scared and all alone," my voice cracked as I felt the tears flooding to my eyes.

He sighed heavily before sitting down on the bed next to me, "I guess it doesn't matter now, babygirl. They know. I told them what happened, though. How it wasn't your fault and you weren't drunk. You throwing up is probably what did it. That can cause the breathalyzer to read a false positive."

"Let me call them and get it over with. They'll want to hear from me," I told him.

He handed me my phone, and I placed the unfinished sandwich back down on the plate before calling them.

I heard the relief in their voices that I was back home safe and sound. I didn't tell them all the details of my time in jail or that I'd had to walk for miles before Bruce came and picked me up. They didn't need to know all those horrors, and I knew that last bit wouldn't endear Bruce to them any.

As I expected, they sounded deeply disappointed at finding out I'd been drinking. Of course, I didn't tell them how long Bruce and I had been drinking or how much. I made it out like it was something we only did a couple of times and that we didn't get drunk when we did it.

Like Bruce, they tried to tell me not to worry and that everything would be okay one way or another.

I didn't stay on the phone with them long. I told them how tired I was, and they let me go. I went into the bathroom and dried my hair before I went back into the bedroom where Bruce was already laying down propped up on pillows, watching TV, waiting for me.

He held the covers up, and I climbed in bed and curled up next to him, my head on his chest. He stroked my head and arms, and it reminded me of how we used to be back in his little apartment in Tennessee, the one he'd gotten when he came up there just to meet me and be with me.

I couldn't stop the tears that slid from my eyes and dripped down onto his chest.

"Don't cry, baby," he said softly, feeling the wetness on his skin.

"I'm sorry," I sniffed. "I'm just so scared. What if I get convicted and they put me back in jail?"

"You won't have to go back to jail," Bruce said with certainty in his voice. "This is your first one, so you might be lucky enough to get the charges dropped or reduced to reckless driving. Even if you don't, worst case scenario is you'll have to do some probation. That's not that bad, angel."

"I wish we'd never started drinking again," I admitted.

Bruce didn't agree or disagree with me. He just kept petting me, and I laid there and listened to the beating of his heart, my body becoming more relaxed and my eyes slipping closed.

Eventually, the steady thump lulled me to sleep.

As soon as I awoke the next morning, that pit of dread settled back into my stomach. I couldn't stop worrying about my charge.

I slipped out of bed where Bruce was still sleeping and went into the living room. I grabbed my little pink laptop and sat on the chaise lounge with it propped up in my lap.

I searched all the possible consequences of a DUI in the state of Florida. That pit in my stomach only yawned wider the more I read.

There were so many variables and so many extremities of punishments for different types of convictions. Sentences were affected by just how high your blood alcohol content had been, if you were involved in a wreck, which I had been, if anyone was injured, which thankfully no one had been.

My hands were shaking by the time Bruce got up and came out into the living room.

"What you doing, babygirl?" he asked me as he pulled

a cigarette out of the pack that was laying on the coffee table.

I just shook my head.

He came over to peer over my shoulder at my computer screen, and then he scoffed. "You don't need to be looking all that shit up, baby. It's not going to be that bad. Trust me, I know."

"I've got to get a lawyer today," I said. I couldn't take the uncertainty of not knowing what was going to happen, and my anxiety about it all was mounting by the minute. I was relieved to be out of jail, but my emotional state might as well still be in there as wound up as I was.

"Relax, baby," Bruce told me.

But I couldn't no matter how hard I tried. It wasn't something I could control or just turn off. The fear and worry were constantly there at the back of my mind, no matter how hard I tried to push it all away.

Bruce went to make coffee, and as soon as law offices started opening, I started calling. I'd look up several and tried to find the ones closest to us—ones that were within walking distance—since I couldn't drive my car at this point.

Bruce and I walked up to see the first one who called me back. He already had the arrest report and everything pulled by the time we got there. His office was right near historic downtown, not far from where we lived at all.

The lawyer was a young guy with dark hair and a strong jawline. His confidence instantly put me at ease. He seemed to really know what he was talking about when it came to all this stuff.

He asked me a bunch of questions during my initial consultation. After listening to Bruce and I recount everything that had happened, he sat back in his office chair and grinned at us.

"The good news is this is your first charge ever, and that clean arrest record will go a long way. I can't promise I can get the charge totally dismissed or even dropped, but I will try. Our first line of defense will be to say that you weren't the one driving. We could argue that your husband," he nodded at Bruce, "was the one driving driving."

"But he's not supposed to be driving at all," I tell him. "He doesn't have a valid license."

The lawyer shrugs. "Doesn't matter. He's not the one who was charged, and they can't charge him after the fact."

I stared at him. I never would have thought of doing that. It was lying, of course, but if it got me off, I didn't really care.

"What happens if that doesn't work, though?"

"If the people on the motorcycle insist you were the one driving, then I'll do everything I can to make sure you get the best deal possible," he told me frankly.

"Will I have to do anymore jail time?" I asked tentatively.

He shook his head. "I highly doubt that. They almost never sentence people to more jail time after the initial arrest when it's a first-time offense and nobody was injured."

I felt myself relax.

"Told you, angel," Bruce said from where he sat beside me, giving my hand a soft squeeze. Yeah, I know Bruce had tried to assure me of that, but I trusted it more coming from a lawyer who dealt with this stuff every day.

No offense to Bruce, but he hadn't always been right about everything he said. He'd also been the one to push me into the situation that had gotten me into this mess in the first place.

The lawyer seemed unfazed by Bruce being so much older than me. There was probably no telling what kinds of people he dealt with on a daily basis, so nothing probably shocked him at this point. Plus, he was a criminal lawyer, so I guess it was his job to be nonjudgmental and to defend whoever was willing to pay for it.

He told me what his retainer fee would be. Thankfully, he was willing to accept a flat fee rather than charging by the hour like some lawyers did. The fee was high, but it was worth it for peace of mind, all the information he'd given me, and what he said he'd do for me. In addition to overseeing my court case, he'd help me appeal to the DMV to get a restricted license so I could drive for business purposes, which basically meant I was only supposed to drive to work, court, school, or church. Of course, he also implied that it would be okay to drive to get groceries and stuff too but that I should stay off the road as much as possible.

We walked back to our apartment with me in higher spirits than I had been. I hoped it wouldn't take too long to settle my case. I was anxious to get it all over with and know the outcome already.

When we got home, I called my parents and told them the good news about how I'd found a really nice lawyer to help me. Of course, I didn't tell them the details of his strategy, about how he planned to try to question whether I'd really been the one driving the car or not even though we all knew I had been. They didn't need to know all that. All they needed to know was that I had legal representation and that everything would hopefully be okay.

Surprisingly, they weren't as judgmental of me as I'd expected them to be. I think they knew how stressed out I was by all of it anyway and were trying not to make it worse, for which I was grateful.

"Damn, all this stress is enough to make you need a drink, huh, babygirl?" Bruce commented casually as we sat in the living room after I got off the phone with my parents.

I shot him an incredulous look, "I am *not* drinking, Bruce, so don't even go there. I'm not risking getting busted and going back to jail. That's one of the conditions of my release—that I don't drink. It's not worth it to me."

"I know, angel," he said, "I was just kidding."

I didn't think he was, though. I knew Bruce liked to drink, and he liked for me to drink with him. But I would put my foot down this time. There was no way I wanted to take the chance of going back to jail.

Thankfully, he didn't bring it up again—even jokingly. It took about a month for my case to get settled, and I only had to appear in court twice—once to say that I was pleading not guilty so my lawyer could begin crafting my defense and then at the end to accept the plea bargain and my sentence.

As my luck would have it, the couple on the motor-cycle insisted that I had been the one driving the vehicle, so that strategy didn't work. It really pissed me off too because they knew damn well he'd run the stop sign, but they were going to milk the situation for all it was worth and have me deemed at fault just because I'd had alcohol in my system when the accident happened. I think it had more to do with trying to prove they didn't have any fault in the accident because then they could get more money out of my insurance company to repair his shitty bike.

Bruce even made a comment to me that he wouldn't be surprised if the guy had run out in front of me on purpose just so he could claim it against our insurance and essentially get him a new bike. That seemed like a drastic measure to take to scam someone—to purposefully get into an accident—but Bruce told me more people did it than I would believe, and I knew that people did do some crazy stuff sometimes.

Still, it didn't matter what his motives had been. All that mattered was their persistence that I had been the one driving screwed me. While I'd been granted a restricted license and the boot had been removed from my car so that I could drive it while my case was ongoing, I couldn't legally drive it for six months after my case was settled.

True to his word, my lawyer did the best he could to get me the best plea deal, all things considered. I ended up having my licensed suspended for six months, during which time I'd be on probation. I'd have to go to DUI school, and in lieu of doing community service, my lawyer had gotten me the option to buy it out, which meant I'd just have to pay more money in fees if I didn't want to go in and work off the community service hours. I was more than willing to pay more money than to have to do all that.

After my suspension period was up, I'd be able to pay the reinstatement fees and get my license back. I didn't have to go back to jail, though, so that was a definite relief.

And while it would be an inconvenience to not be able to drive anywhere, at least we could take the bus.

I just had to get through the probation period, and I knew that would be difficult with Bruce since I wasn't supposed to drink at all when I was on probation.

CHAPTER 6

FIRST THINGS FIRST, I had to meet with my probation officer. She seemed nice enough as she told me the date I had to report to her every month.

She actually seemed pretty fair too, telling me that if for some reason I couldn't make it by my appointed day to just call her and explain and she would work with me. She also told me to make sure I was prepared to submit a urinalysis every month when I came in, that she could decide to do one randomly. She didn't make me do one that day, though.

As we were walking away from the probation office, Bruce threaded his fingers between mine. "Guess what, angel?"

I glanced over at him to let him know I was listening as we walked up the sidewalk together.

"I was talking to some of the people up there, and apparently you lucked out and got one of the best probation officers. She's not a hard ass and never randomly calls people in for a piss test if they're only on probation for drinking-related offenses."

"Yeah, she seemed nice," I hedged, already knowing where he was going with this.

"So..." he drug out the 'so,' "do you want to stop at the store on the way home?"

Translation: do you want to get some booze?

I shook my head, "Absolutely not. No way. I'm not going to chance it, Bruce."

"You're worrying too much, babygirl," he told me lightly. "I talked to a bunch of people up there who have been on probation with her numerous times and said they never had any random calls or problems out of her. As long as you show up every month and pay your fees, she's cool. Besides, do you know how many people in this city are on probation? The ones they're concerned about randomly piss testing are the ones who are on drugs. They don't want to be wasting money on little misdemeanors like yours."

I shook my head again. "I don't care. Alcohol is what got me into this mess. I don't care if I ever drink again."

Bruce frowned down at me before correcting me firmly, "No, what got you into this mess was that f— prick on a motorcycle. I should have beat his ass when I had the chance. Him and his bitch have really f— things up for us."

I sighed in exasperation, "Just because I don't drink, Bruce, doesn't mean that you can't. Stop and get you something if you want."

He frowned at me again," You need to relax, baby. Why don't I get us both something?"

I shook my head and stated resolutely, "No."

He sighed and looked irritated as we walked into the

store. He picked up a case of beer and paid before we walked the rest of the way home in silence.

I knew he was pissed that I was firm about not drinking with him, but how would I be able to enjoy myself when I would be worried in the back of my mind that I might get called in to give a piss test that would come up dirty?

When we got in the house, I settled in to go to work on my computer. Bruce wasted no time in popping the top on one of his beer.

He was in a foul mood since I had pissed him off by refusing to drink with him, so I was totally unsurprised when he started in on me once he was two beers in.

"Angel, you're being too serious about all this stuff. You can drink, and you'll be fine," he eyed me over his bottle from where he sat in his chair.

I saved my work to make sure I didn't end up losing everything I'd just written before I looked up at him. "And what if I get called in tomorrow randomly? What if I pissed dirty? Would my probation be revoked? Would I be put back in jail to serve the rest of my sentence? Excuse me for not wanting to take that risk," my voice was dripping with sarcasm by the end of my monologue.

Bruce laughed. He actually laughed at me. Not only did it anger me, but it stung too, like he thought I was stupid or something."

"Oh, babygirl, The alcohol wouldn't even show up in your system in the morning if you didn't drink too much. It would have already made its way out of your body. Not only that, but even if you did piss dirty, you are not immediately thrown back in jail. You're usually given a warning. The jail is overcrowded as it is, as you saw when you were in there. They're not gonna throw you back in jail for something small like breaking your probation once. Hell, I know some f— who broke their probation five times or more before finally be sentenced back to jail. I promise you you wouldn't be immediately violated."

"Just like you promised me nothing would happen if I drove you up to the store after I'd been drinking?" The words were out of my mouth before I had a chance to even think about them.

He leapt up from his chair, his hands balled at his sides. "So, you're blaming me for everything now?"

His eyes flashed fire, and despite myself, I felt a shiver of fear run up my spine. I wasn't drunk or even tipsy now, so I lacked any sort of liquid courage.

"That's not what I was saying," I tried to say as reasonably as I could. "I just don't want to drink and think you should respect that. I didn't want to drive that day either, but you pushed and now here we are."

His chest was heaving with rage as he stalked over to me.

I tried not to cower back against the sofa in the face of his anger.

"You've been talking to those f— parents of yours, haven't you? They've put this shit in your head. Always trying to turn you against me. Always trying to tear us apart."

"That's not true," I denied. "They haven't said anything like that. I didn't even tell them why we went up to the store."

Bruce wasn't listening, though. He was stomping around the living room in one of his rages, going on about how they hated him and always would.

I knew I couldn't concentrate enough to work with him going on like this, and besides, he wouldn't let me anyway.

I closed my computer screen and got up to go into the bedroom and try to get away from him, but he grabbed my wrist as I started to walk past him.

"Where do you think you're going?"

"I'm just going into the bedroom," I said meekly.

"Why? So you can try to leave me again?" he spat.

I winced as if he'd slapped me.

"No," I answered softly, thinking it would be better to try not to fight with him than to engage and make him even angrier.

"I'm just tired. I think I'm going to lay down," I lied. I wasn't tired, but I would go lay down if it would keep him off my back.

"What the f— ever," he said before releasing me and taking another swig of his beer.

I could tell he was determined to stay pissed. That was just the kind of mood he was in, but he was letting me go, so I didn't linger. I took my escape and locked myself up in the bedroom. Granted, the door wasn't really locked, but I crawled under the covers and cried. I hated it when Bruce got like this, and it was just that much worse when I wasn't drinking too. At least if I'd been drinking with him, it wouldn't have hurt so bad. The alcohol would have numbed some of the pain.

I heard him eventually playing some of his music from the '60s and '70s that I hated. I tried to just go to sleep, but I couldn't. I was miserable. I really want to go get my computer, but I was afraid if he saw me, he'd start in again, and I really didn't want to fight with him.

So, I just lay there all night until he finally stumbled into bed.

He seemed to have forgotten he was mad at me because I felt him press his chest against my back and pull me close. "Babygirl, you awake?" he asked me.

I kept my eyes closed and my body still. There was no way in hell I wanted to have sex with him right now—not after what he'd done and with him smelling like a smoky brewery.

When I didn't answer, he thankfully grunted and rolled over. It wasn't long until I heard the sounds of his snores and I was finally able to get up and pad back out to the living room.

There was no way I'd be able to get any sleep that night. My nerves were too on edge, so I'd at least make the most of my insomnia and try to make as much money as I could. I'd certainly need it to pay all the court fees I now had.

The next day Bruce got up and acted like nothing had happened the night before. I was quiet and withdrawn all day, though I didn't bring up his behavior the night before. I didn't want to rehash it all or get him going again.

"How long you been up, angel?" He asked me by way of greeting when he got up.

I shrugged, my eyes never leaving my computer screen. "A while."

He pulled a cigarette from his pack and lit up. He didn't say anything else, and I didn't either.

I went back to what I was doing, which was signing up for the court-mandated DUI school.

I signed up to go to DUI school as soon as I could. I wanted to hurry up and get that out of the way. It consisted of going to classes for four hours each a few nights a week or giving up a whole Saturday. I opted for the former rather than the latter.

"So, I'm all signed up for DUI school," I finally broke the silence.

"Okay, babygirl," Bruce answered. "What days you got?"

I told him, and he nodded. My next class was the following night.

"You're smart to just get it out of the way, baby," he told me.

"Yeah, I want to get all this over with as soon as possible."

He came over to look at the computer screen to see where they were held. When he saw the address, he nodded and commented, "I know right where that is, baby. That's perfect. It's not far at all. Right downtown within walking distance."

I was glad for that too because I had dreaded having to go through the hassle of taking a bus. Although my lawyer had gotten me a restricted license, it was only good for while my case was ongoing. Once I was convicted, I had to go through six months of no driving whatsoever, so yeah, it was really convenient the DUI school was close to where we lived. It was much quicker to just walk if it was within walking distance than have to go on the long, drawn-out route the bus would take us just to go a few miles up the road.

Bruce walked me to class every night, and every night when I got out of class he was waiting there to walk me back.

"I'm not going to let my angel walk these city streets alone at night," he commented the first day he walked me up to the building before pressing a chaste kiss on my lips in view for everyone to see before telling me he'd be waiting for me when I got out that night.

Bruce seemed to like kissing me in front of people and letting people know that I was his. I didn't really mind, though I did sometimes wonder if that was the only reason he did it, like he wanted to show me off more than he just truly wanted to kiss me.

Class went from four in the afternoon until nine at night. The instructor seemed nice enough, but she informed us first thing that if anyone came to class drunk or high, they would immediately be asked to leave and wouldn't get credit for the class. Then, they'd have to start all over again and pay the expensive class fee again. She wasn't going to make us all submit to a breathalyzer test every time we entered class, but we'd be asked to take one if she suspected we were under the influence.

It made me feel like I was in a room full of drunks and criminals. But then again, I guess I was. Of course, that thought led to if that's what they are, what does that make me? I was in there with them.

The instructor quickly tried to clear up any of those types of feelings we might be having, though. The first lecture she gave was about how just because we were charged with a DUI didn't mean we were alcoholics. Of course, she then went on to define what a true alcoholic is and stated that actually true alcoholics very rarely got

DUIs because a true alcoholic didn't believe they could go without alcohol, so they would do anything they could to make sure they'd never be put into a situation where they couldn't drink. She went on to tell us a story about her father, who had been a true alcoholic. Many people didn't even know it. That's how good he was at hiding it. According to her, there were different types of alcoholics, some of whom were functioning ones and who just kept a steady stream of alcohol in their systems all day. They functioned while under the influence, as in they went to work and went about their daily lives while secretly drinking all the time but never or rarely to the point of blacking out.

Then, there were social drinkers who pretty much only drank when they were in social settings. Then, there were binge drinkers who might not drink often, but when they did, they drank large amounts and were prone to blacking out.

She went on and on with different scenarios.

The classes consisted of about what I thought they would. We had to watch films about drunk drinking. We had to go around the room and introduce ourselves and tell our stories about how we'd gotten arrested, if this was our first offense, and so on.

It was boring and tedious, but thankfully the time went quickly. We had little ten-minute breaks periodically to accommodate the smokers in the group. I usually just sat at the table and waited for the time to be over since I didn't smoke. A few other people at my table didn't smoke either, and I listened to their conversations as they talked amongst themselves. They tried to draw me into the conversation, and I'd answer and smile politely, though I didn't really want to talk. I didn't want to be a snob, but I wasn't there to make friends. I just wanted to get through it, get my certificate, and move on with my life.

When they were talking, I couldn't help noticing how they all talked about probation, and everyone said the same thing Bruce had said. Several people who were in the class were there for second or third offenses, and they assured those of us who were first-timers that there was nothing to worry about, that we would never be randomly called in for a urine test, that we only needed to worry about being clean the date that we had to report to our probation officer, that that was the only time she might make us take a test.

I finally had to concede to myself that maybe Bruce had been right. Maybe I was worrying too much, and maybe I should let up and drink with him after my last class. I certainly didn't want to deal with his attitude every time he drank and I didn't. Plus, maybe it would take my mind off everything and help me relax.

And honestly after sitting through all those classes, I could use a drink, in the words of Bruce.

So the last night when Bruce came to walk me home, I was ready.

"How was your last night of class, baby?" he asked. "I bet you were glad to get that shit over with."

"Ugh, yes. It was brutal. I could really go for a drink," I told him.

He looked down at me in surprise for a moment before he grinned widely and then laughed. "Spoken like a true Scots-Irish lass," he said.

He took my hand and eagerly started leading me to

the store. "Come on. We'll celebrate your graduation, angel," he joked.

We bought some wine and wasted no time popping the corks once we got back.

Bruce was in a great mood because he had me back as his drinking partner, and I felt myself starting to relax as well as I let the alcohol course through my body.

For the first time since that fateful night when I'd been arrested, I wasn't worrying. I felt bubbly and happy as I watched our silly little shows with Bruce and listened to music.

I wasn't thinking about the overwhelming things I had to do to get my license back or the chance of violating my probation. I just got lost in music and talking with Bruce.

Bruce talked about when we first met, when we used to talk on the internet, things that happened back at the Putnam.

Every time my glass started to get empty, he was right there filling it back up, urging me to drink more.

And I did because the numbness that was overtaking me was far more preferable to all the anxiety and worry that had been my life ever since this DUI nightmare had begun.

I knew that once again I was breaking the law. I was violating the terms of my probation by drinking when I wasn't supposed to touch a drop of alcohol. Hell, part of the terms of my probation was that I wasn't even supposed to be in a bar or a liquor store.

But I thought of how many people in the DUI school broke their probation, and nothing had happened to them.

And really, if I wanted to get technical about it, I'd been breaking the law for a while now. Bruce had given me alcohol when I was technically too young to drink, but that hadn't stopped me from accepting it.

Why get high and mighty about following the law now when it seemed that drinking was going to be a great way for me to escape from all my worries?

And that's what it became: my escape from my troubles.

CHAPTER 7

BRUCE and I started drinking more and more again until we were drinking every other day. We'd drink all day one day, and then the next day we'd lay in bed and recoup from the day before.

We were starting our drinking sessions earlier and earlier too. Instead of waiting until the evening, we were often starting as early as one in the afternoon.

Since I couldn't legally drive us up to the liquor store, we usually just walked up to one of the convenience stores on the corner and got wine. Plus, Bruce said wine would leave my system faster than liquor on the rare chance that I might get called in to do a piss test.

On the days when we didn't drink, I'd call my family. I don't think Mom and Dad had told the rest of the family about my situation, but of course Grandma knew. There was no way for them to get around telling her. We'd always been closer to her, and she made it her business to know our business.

She didn't guilt me over any of it, though. She just had that sad tone to her voice that she always had when she talked to me. It was obvious she wished I would just come back home and that everything would go back to normal, but what she didn't realize is that even if I left Bruce and went back home, nothing would ever be the same again.

I was changed, and there was no going back from that. I couldn't undo getting arrested. I couldn't undo the things I'd done. I couldn't undo giving my virginity to Bruce. I couldn't undo the ridiculous fights Bruce and I still got into when we were drinking and he decided he wanted to dwell on the past.

I couldn't undo any of it, but I could numb it. I could numb it all out if I drank enough. I could get that floaty, I-don't-give-a-shit feeling and eventually I'd black out and wouldn't remember anything. I didn't particularly like blacking out, but at least if I blacked out when Bruce was on one of his rants, I wouldn't remember if he grabbed me or pushed me down—both events that were happening with more and more frequency despite how he'd promised me he'd never hurt me again.

Every month about a week before the day I had to report to my probation officer, we'd stop drinking completely just to make sure I was completely detoxed of any traces of alcohol in my system for in case she made me submit to a urinalysis. Apparently, alcohol could build up in your system if you drank as heavily as we did, and I'd rather be safe than sorry.

She never did make me take a test, though. Still, we went through the week of abstinence as a precaution. I was getting closer to having my six-month probation period over with, and I'd hate to blow it this late in the game.

Summer went by, and as autumn approached, I became more and more depressed. The only thing that seemed to help was drinking, so we began drinking even more. Instead of drinking just every other day, we started drinking nearly every day. The only times we stopped was when I got too sick to carry on and had to take a break to recoup.

I also started drinking even earlier than before, sometimes beginning as early as ten in the morning. I'd usually feel like crap after I woke up, but as soon as I started drinking again, I'd start feeling better.

I was eating even less than before. I found that the alcohol hit me harder if I didn't eat before I drank, and I wanted to feel the numbness sooner rather than later. Food only served to make it so it took the numbness longer to take over my body. Plus, I rarely ever had an appetite anymore. When I woke up in the morning after a night of drinking, the only thing that would make me feel better was more alcohol.

Sometimes Bruce would sleep late if he took one of his Xanax after drinking. When he'd get up around ten or eleven, he'd laugh to see me already drinking.

I wasn't working that much anymore. Instead, I'd watch music videos until Bruce got up. By that time, I usually had a good buzz going, and then when Bruce had one going too, we'd watch our little programs that we watched together. Bruce would always take a nap in the afternoon, during which time I would get back on my computer to watch music videos again, losing myself in the music of whatever I was watching.

When he'd wake back up from his nap, he'd make dinner like usual and drink while doing so. I'd spend more time with him, talking and watching whatever he wanted until we'd eventually turn on music.

And that's when things were going well.

When they weren't, Bruce would rant at me about my parents. He'd tell me how much they controlled me, how they didn't really love me and never had.

He'd call me weak for calling them even when I didn't feel like it. He told me they'd never leave us alone, that they would always have me under their thumb and how that sickened him.

When I'd get tired of hearing him rant, I'd put on my headphones and try to ignore him, but he never let me do that. Bruce was not one to be ignored. He'd yank them off my head, and grab me, hauling me up and shaking me before throwing me down on the couch or bed.

Sometimes I'd fight him. Other times, I'd just lay there numbly and let him have his way. If I was numb enough, I'd be in enough of a haze where I couldn't hardly feel it and didn't care.

Bruce wanted to fight, though. When I didn't fight back, he'd get increasingly violent, grabbing my wrists or arms or pushing me down until he elicited some sort of response from me.

When he got in that kind of temper, I found that the best thing to do would be to cry and agree with him that yes, my parents were horrible. Yes, I could see that they were trying to control me, that they were trying to ruin us, that he was the only one who really loved me.

It's like he wanted my tears because that was the only thing that would sometimes placate him.

Sometimes I would lose it myself and argue with him stubbornly. I'd scream at him that everything that had happened with my DUI was his fault, that *he* was the one who didn't love me, that if he truly loved me, he wouldn't hurt me, that if he truly loved me, he wouldn't call me the vile names that he did, he wouldn't put me in bad situations, and he wouldn't add to my stress by pulling me back and forth between him and my parents.

Bruce never apologized anymore. Not that I really thought any of his apologies before had truly been sincere. I think he'd just been saying what he knew he was supposed to say to mend things over with me so I wouldn't leave him.

Instead, when we fought, he always gaslighted me. He'd deny some of the arguments that I was sure we'd had, telling me that I was drunk and just didn't remember properly. I started to think I was going crazy.

When he did acknowledge our arguments, he was never the one in the wrong. Even when he grabbed me and threw me down, it was *my* fault. He'd tell me he only did that because I did such or such or I said such and such. I made him lose his temper. I knew better than to do or say such and such. It was *my* fault. His actions were *my* fault.

After a while I started to believe it.

If I just did what I was supposed to do, agreed with what he said, acted the way he wanted me to act, everything would be okay.

We'd have fun when we drank if I did that, and he wouldn't try to pull me out of that numb haze I was seeking. He'd let me float happily above it all. We'd laugh instead of fight. We'd make love instead of him violently taking what he wanted.

I could do it, and everything would be okay so long as I stayed somewhat drunk and numb to it all.

But staying drunk so much was taking a toll on my body.

I was losing more weight, making me even skinnier than I'd been before. Bruce didn't seem to have that problem. He still at least ate lunch and dinner, and every time he ate, it was lights out for him. He'd take a nap or go to bed for the entire night.

Sometimes he'd talk me into eating something before bed. More often than not, I would black out before I passed out, but he'd often tell me he'd gotten me to eat before I crashed. I didn't know one way or the other, and I didn't really care either.

The thing that did bother me was how my hands would shake when I suddenly had to stop drinking to get ready to see my probation officer. The first couple of times it happened, I'd freaked out, but Bruce told me that was just my body detoxing from all the alcohol.

It was frustrating when my hands shook like that because I couldn't even hold a pen steady enough to write—not that I handwrote anything much. That was just something I noticed. I guess it was a good thing I didn't wear makeup much anymore because there's no way I could have put on eyeliner or mascara. My hands were too unsteady to do all that.

It was just the most peculiar phenomenon. I never knew that your hands would shake when you were withdrawing off alcohol.

When my hands were all shaky, I usually couldn't sleep either. I'd thought I'd had sleepless nights before, but I realized I'd never had true insomnia until I was purging my body of alcohol to get ready to see my probation officer.

I'd be so tired, and I'd desperately want to sleep but couldn't. Sometimes if I took a couple of Benadryl, I could go to sleep a bit, but even then, I was usually in this half-awake dozy state.

It was awful, and I couldn't really get up and do any work because my hands would be shaking so badly I couldn't hold them still enough to type properly. Plus, I didn't really have the mental capacity to do it anyway.

I'd get through my visit with my probation officer, pay my monthly fees, and keep my hands knotted together the entire time so she wouldn't see them shaking, and then as soon as I got out of the office, Bruce would buy us wine, we'd go back and pop it open, and after a couple of sips, the shakes would stop, and I'd feel better than I had in days.

I wasn't sure if my parents had figured out I was drinking again or not. I always tried to talk to them when I first started and before the numbness set in when I was pretty lucid and knew what was going on.

But the night eventually came when they did find out I was back to drinking again, and it was all my fault.

I was sitting at my computer with my headphones on, minding my own business, watching a stage version of *The Phantom of the Opera*. I was feeling particularly emotional that night, which is why I'd turned to Phantom. If I felt down and felt like wallowing in my misery and crying, Phantom was guaranteed to make me cry. It wasn't just the storyline that made me cry either but also the realization that what I had thought was my own fairy-tale had been somewhat of an illusion too.

I found striking similarities between Christine and myself, but not in the way I'd always wanted. I realized that she too had been tricked into thinking the man she was talking to was someone he wasn't. She'd been naive just as I'd been.

But Bruce didn't have as many similarities to the Phantom as I'd always used to tell myself he did. Whereas everything the Phantom did was out of love for Christine, he would have never hurt her the way Bruce did me. Yeah, Bruce just so happened to be the exact number of years older than me than the Phantom had been, but that was where the similarities ended.

Bruce could be cruel and unrelenting. But then again, I guess the Phantom could be too.

I didn't know if I was still trying to reconcile what I wanted to believe with what I knew to be true. What had become apparently clear was that Bruce wasn't quite as big of a Phantom fan as he'd pretended he was when we used to talk on the internet.

But then this was real life, so what did it matter? I was married to him now, and I had to believe that he loved me. If he didn't, why would he be so jealous and posses-sive of me?

Of course, there was that part of me that whispered to myself that if he loved me, he wouldn't do the things he did to me.

But then I heard another voice telling me that I pushed him to do those things, that it was my fault when he got out of control.

I pushed all my confusing thoughts away, took another sip of wine, and lost myself in the story.

I was crying in no time. Thankfully, Bruce left me be until he reached a certain point in his buzz and wanted to talk.

I wasn't in the mood to talk, though, so I waved him off and kept watching music videos. I'd moved on from musicals to romantic music by some of my favorite singers like Sarah Brightman and Hayley Westenra.

But Bruce was having none of it.

"Babygirl," he frowned down at me as he pulled my headphones from my head, "I'm trying to talk to you." Granted, he didn't rip them from my head, but I was still irritated that he'd slid them off me.

"I don't feel like talking. I'm listening to music," I told him.

He ignored me and began his ranting, "So what did your parents say when you called them earlier? Did they give you a hard time about not calling them yesterday?" Yeah, sometimes Mom would still get in her moods and guilt me about not calling every single day, but I didn't want to talk about all that. I was handling it. It was just a part of life and not something that I wanted to dwell on at the moment.

I sighed in exasperation. "No, and I'm really not in the mood to hear you bitch about my parents today."

I knew better than to say something like that—especially when Bruce was drinking.

I saw the anger instantly rush to his eyes. His jaw hardened as he glared down at me. "F— you then, Sarah," he spat at me. "You'll always f— take up for them no matter what they do. You make me sick. You really have the most dysfunctional relationship in the world with your parents."

Something within me finally snapped. For weeks I'd been being good, agreeing with him, keeping my mouth shut, but I was so tired of rehashing the same stuff over and over again whether I wanted to or not.

I flung my headphones off my head and jumped to my feet. If he wanted a fight, then fine. He would get one.

"No, f— you, Bruce! I'm so sick of your shit! You're always dishing my parents, but you stress me out more than they do."

If his eyes were angry before, that was nothing compared to the cold, hard rage in them now.

He took a step toward me, and I just knew he was going to grab me and throw me onto the couch. I couldn't stand being held down one more time while he rained curses in my face, so I picked up the first thing I could reach—the remote control—and held it up like a weapon.

His eyes flicked to the remote held tightly within my hand, and he laughed. "What are you gonna do, Sarah?"

I didn't say anything. Instead, I just lifted the remote up to my shoulder, ready to throw it at a moment's notice.

He took another step toward me, and I screamed, "No! Don't come near me! I'm not doing this with you today!"

He just laughed again, a cold, heartless laugh that only incensed me in my drunken state.

I flung the remote at him, and it barely whizzed by his head before clattering to the floor.

There was a moment of complete silence as Bruce was totally still, processing what I'd done. When he finally blinked and slowly turned his head back to look at me, fear clawed at my throat at the murderous look in his eyes.

"You're gonna regret that, you little bitch," he said as he began marching purposefully toward me.

I grabbed my phone from where it sat beside my laptop on the coffee table and went running into the bathroom.

I locked both doors to the bathroom and then went to sit in the closet under my clothes that were hanging up.

I huddled up there in the corner and pulled my knees to my chest, crying as I heard Bruce banging on the door leading from the bathroom to the kitchen.

"Open this mother f— door, Sarah!"

I just huddled deeper into myself. I was so tired of fighting with him, and I knew he wouldn't be satisfied until we'd truly had it out.

I don't know how long I sat there. I just know it was long enough for him to come around to the other door leading from the bathroom to the bedroom. I heard his voice closer as he tried it.

I flinched as his pounding got louder and wondered if he would break the door down. Eventually, I heard him stalk away from the door, though I still heard his curses from all the way in the living room.

I pulled out my phone without thinking and did something I probably never should have done.

I dialed my parents' number.

CHAPTER 8

MY DAD ANSWERED on the third ring. "Hello?" he said, sounding sleepy.

Shit, I didn't even pay attention to what time it was and that they might be sleeping, but I hadn't been thinking of any of that when I placed the phone call. I hadn't really been thinking of anything actually. Just that I needed to talk to someone who loved me. Bruce had me so high-strung and stressed out I was shaking.

"Dad?" my voice cracked as I said his name, and he instantly became alert.

"Sarah? Are you okay?" In full Dad mode, he already knew something was wrong.

I started crying, and then I heard a shuffle as Mom took the phone. Her voice sounded surprisingly gentle as she asked me, "What's wrong, baby?"

I started to cry harder at her unexpected tenderness. It was just all too much.

"Bruce is angry, and I'm just so tired of fighting with him," I admitted.

There was a long pause on the other end of the line as

my parents digested what I'd just said. I'd never said one bad thing about Bruce the entire time I'd been with him. I knew better than to ever let on that we ever had an argument. Most couples did have silly arguments that they could fume to their parents about, but not me. I could never say one bad thing about Bruce to my parents because they already hated him so much they'd never forget anything bad I ever told them.

And I was breaking my rule now by talking to them about him.

"Are you okay, Sarah? He hasn't hurt you, has he?"

I hesitated. Something held me back from answering in the affirmative and telling them that he grabbed me and pushed me down and held me down and bruised me.

Instead, I said, "He's always angry about y'all. He gets mad at me for talking to you and says you're trying to control me, but he's the one who's trying to control me. And I'm just so tired of fighting about it."

Mom scoffs, "How the hell can we control you? You're hundreds of miles away from us, and we're lucky to see you two or three times a year." I could tell Mom wasn't angry at me but rather the situation.

Dad's voice came back over the line. "Have you been drinking, Sarah?"

I didn't even bother lying to them. I'm sure they could tell I was drunk anyway. "Yeah, we have," I answered.

"He's been drinking too?" Dad asks.

I gave a hollow laugh. If he only knew what a bizarre question that was. Bruce loved to drink. There's no way he wouldn't drink, and he was the whole reason why I drank now. "Yeah," I just answered.

"Has he gotten violent with you?" Mom chimed in. "Do you want us to call the police? Where are you now?"

I felt panic start to rise within me. No way. There's no way they could call the police. If the police came here, they'd run my name, see I was on probation, and then arrest me for drinking when I wasn't supposed to be.

"No! No, I'm fine," I assure them. "It's nothing like that." *Though it was.* "You can't call the police. I'm on probation, and I'm not supposed to be drinking. They could arrest me." I couldn't keep the fear of going back to jail out of my voice.

I heard my dad sigh, recognizing the truth in my words, and one thing I knew my parents didn't want was me back in jail.

"Sarah, why did you drink when you know you're on probation?" Mom asked me.

"I don't know," I lied. But I do. Because Bruce was giving me hell about not drinking with him. Because I found out that it's the only way I could cope with all my anxiety and worry and depression.

I couldn't tell them that, though, and I was starting to wish I hadn't called them. This was a mistake I knew I'd regret in the morning when the effects of the alcohol wore off.

I sighed. "I'm so sorry I called and woke y'all up. I didn't mean to worry you. Everything's fine. I'll be fine. I think I just had too much to drink and got sad and started missing y'all."

Mom's voice softened. "Why don't you try to lay down and sleep it off? And you know you can tell us anything and call us any time you need to."

I sniffed, overcome again with how nice she was

being. There'd been tension between Mom and me for so long now—even when we were being cordial to each other—that I'd almost forgotten how nice it was to have her be like the mom I'd known when I was growing up, before I'd met Bruce and disappointed both of my parents so deeply with all my life choices.

I heard Bruce trying the door again and quickly bade Mom and Dad goodnight. I had to hurry up and get off the phone with them because if they heard him yelling curses at me like a madman, they might call the police anyway, and I couldn't have that.

It had been a while since I'd had a drink since I'd been huddled in the floor of the closet. Though I was still buzzed, I wasn't buzzing as much as I had been when this whole business had started.

I stood up and squared my shoulders, knowing that I would have to face Bruce eventually. I walked over to the door he was beating on and opened it.

He was livid. His eyes flicked down to the phone still held in my hand, and his lip curled. "Who were you talking to?"

"Who are the only people I ever talk to?" I countered back at him bravely.

His eyes darkened. "What? You called your mommy and daddy to tell them how horrible I'm being to you?"

I didn't say anything as I walked through the bedroom and out into the living room where my glass of wine was waiting.

"Oh, that's f— great, Sarah. As if your parents don't f — hate me enough. They had to have known you were drinking. Now they're never going to shut up about that. They'll be on your ass every day about it."

He might be right, but what was done was done. It had been stupid on my part, but I was drunk. Bruce was always getting passes for doing stupid shit and blaming it on alcohol. Now, it was my turn.

I still didn't say anything to him, and that enraged him. Bruce hated being ignored, especially when he wanted to fight.

I took a gulp of my wine, wanting to get back to that numb place where nothing bothered me as much.

I watched him warily over my glass as he pulled his pocketknife from his pocket. He began flicking it back and forth—opened, then closed, opened, then closed.

His eyes flicked up to me, and he smirked, an evil grin that made the hairs on the back of my nape stand up. Then, he suddenly reared back and flung the pocketknife, throwing it so that it embedded into the wall.

I flinched when I heard the thump of the knife hitting the wall. It stuck, the handle sticking out. I didn't know how he always managed to throw it where it would stick in the wall like that.

My mind flashed back to when he'd done that with some kitchen knives when we lived back at the Putnam. I hated it when he did that shit. Somehow it was the most terrifying thing I'd ever seen him do. It was worse than him pushing me or grabbing me or shaking me or holding me down and forcing himself on me.

Maybe it was the half-crazed look he had on his face when he did it. When he started throwing knives, I always knew he'd reached another level that I didn't understand.

I took another huge gulp of my wine and looked away from him.

His laughter boomed out around us. It sounded maniacal, and my hands started shaking.

Then, he came over to me and wrapped his arms around me from behind. I usually melted against him when he did that, but I only stiffened in his hold this time, unsure of where his mind was and what he was playing at. The way he'd taken after me earlier, I'd been sure he was going to hold me down and scream at me, but now his mood had seemed to switch to something else.

He kissed the side of my temple and chuckled. I could feel the rumble of his chest shaking against my back. "What? You don't like it when I throw knives, babygirl?" he asked against my neck.

I didn't answer. He already knew I didn't.

He just laughed again before he finally stepped back, releasing me. He went to get the wine bottle and topped off both our glasses before he went to sit at the computer desk and got on his computer.

He didn't say another word to me, so I sat back down on the couch in front of my own computer, slipped my headphones on, and turned on a music video.

I took another huge gulp of my wine, wanting the alcohol to hurry up and settle my frazzled nerves.

I didn't know what the hell had just happened with Bruce, but I didn't like it at all. Somehow his knife-throwing tantrum and then his nonchalance about all of it was worse than his screaming rages.

Surprisingly, my parents didn't say too much about me drinking when I talked to them the next day. They made a comment about how I didn't need to do it anymore since I was on probation. I just said I understood, but then they left it at that, although the long silences that kept creeping up between us over the phone were strained and awkward. I knew they were disappointed in me—again. It seemed that ever since I met Bruce all I'd been doing was disappointing them.

Bruce, on the other hand, had plenty to say about me calling my parents. In fact, he never shut up about it. He made sure to tell me how disappointed they probably were in me, how I'd never measure up to their expectations, how I was an adult for God's sake and should be able to do what I wanted without condemnation from them, how I never should have called them.

I knew I shouldn't have. I messed up.

Now not only did my parents know that I was still drinking after my horrible fiasco with going to jail, but I also gave Bruce something else to rant about.

And rant he did. Every damn day. He'd start out being nice to me when we first started drinking. We'd actually have fun at the beginning of our buzz, but then almost every night he'd end up talking about my parents and how dumb I'd been to call him.

I started drinking even more heavily—so much so that I apparently started calling them and even my grandma when I was blacked out.

I found out I had called my grandma when I called Mom and Dad one morning.

"Why did you call Momma last night when you were drunk?" my dad asked me, his voice clearly pissed.

"What?" my brow furrowed.

Mom's voice came over the line. "You called your grandmother last night speaking nonsense. She knew something was wrong and called us."

"We were trying to keep her from knowing you were still drinking, Sarah," Dad reprimanded me. "Now she's going to worry herself to death over you all the time like us."

I swallowed. I couldn't believe I'd gotten drunk and called my grandma and didn't remember it. I hoped I didn't say anything mean to her. Surely I didn't, right?

"I'm sorry," I said, meaning it. "I'll apologize to her."

"You need to stop drinking," Mom's voice was stern.

"What's wrong with you?" This from Dad.

"Do you want to go back to jail?" This from Mom.

"I don't understand why you would do something that you know could get you thrown back in jail." That exasperated comment came from Dad.

I didn't say anything. Nothing I could say would make them understand. Plus, I didn't want to get into an argument with them in front of Bruce.

"Now, listen," Dad put on his stern, no-nonsense Dad voice, "we want you to be able to call us if you need to, but I'm not gonna have you calling Momma and getting her all upset. I know she didn't sleep a wink last night worried about you."

"And we've got to go to work every morning, Sarah," Mom chimed in. "You don't need to be calling us all hours of the night when you're drunk."

I gave an incredulous laugh and couldn't stop the smart-aleck comment that left my lips, "Ever since I left home, all I've heard is how I don't call enough—even if I call every day—and now I call too much."

"You know exactly what we mean," Dad snapped. "We want you to call us. Just at a respectable hour. Don't be waking us up in the middle in the night when you're drunk and then have us so worried about you we can't go back to sleep and then have to drag into work the next day dead dog tired."

"While you might get to lay up and sleep off your hangovers, we have jobs to go to," Mom spat at me.

That almost made me laugh again. If they only knew I didn't sleep in to get over a hangover. No, I just started drinking earlier. Hell, I was sipping a glass of wine now to keep my hands from shaking.

"Don't worry. I won't be calling and bothering y'all anymore," I told them. In fact, it'd be a relief. It was stressful having to call and report in to them all the time. It'd be a weight off my shoulders.

I took another sip of my wine. Bruce was right. There was no making them happy.

"Sarah—"Dad began. I heard Mom's voice muffled in the background. I'm sure I didn't want to hear whatever she had to say. I'm sure it was something about what a horrible daughter I was. I never did seem to be able to please her.

"Look, Dad, I gotta go. I'm getting another phone call," I lied and then hurriedly hung up.

Bruce was eyeing me knowingly, and I scowled at him.

"I told you," he said. "I told you, babygirl. They're always going to be on your ass."

"It's fine," I said. "It'll certainly be easier on me not calling them so much."

"You can't f— make them happy," he said while lifting his cigarette to his mouth. Funny how I used to hate the smell of smoke, but I'd become so accustomed to it that it was almost comforting now. It was just normal to me now, I guess.

"I called Grandma last night?" I asked him.

He laughed. "Yeah, you were lit, baby."

I frowned. "I don't remember. I didn't say anything mean to her, did I?"

"No, babygirl. You mostly just cried and told her how much you missed her and talked about a song your granddaddy used to like."

"Why'd you let me call her when I was like that?" I asked him.

"Shit, I couldn't stop you, babygirl. You were determined," he chuckled again like it was cute or something, but I cringed.

"Well, I'm fixing to have to call and smooth things over with her now," I told him.

Bruce didn't seem to have as much of a problem with my grandma as he did my parents. He never said too much about me calling her even though she'd once said she wouldn't touch him with a nine-and-a-half-foot pole like he was the Grinch or something.

"Better go ahead and get it over with," he said.

I called Grandma and spent the next half hour assuring her that I was fine and apologizing for worrying her. Although Grandma never sternly reprimanded me the way Mom and Dad did, her guilt trips were almost worse. She always sounded seconds away from tears, and her gentle concern had me kicking myself for calling her when I was blacked out.

Of course, I didn't tell her that I was blacked out when I called her and didn't remember anything about it. I wasn't sure she'd even know what the term "blacked out" meant. Like the rest of my family, Grandma didn't drink, so I doubt she'd know the lingo.

When I finally got off the phone with Grandma, Bruce came up and hugged me. It was strange. It seemed like every time I got on the outs with my parents, it somehow brought Bruce and me closer. He'd be nicer to me, always taking my side in everything, reinforcing how horrible they were to me.

Bruce didn't rant at all that day. It seemed the news that I wouldn't be calling anyone to make sure I didn't call them drunk and upset them had placated him for the time being.

He had me all to himself again, and I know he preferred it that way.

I was starting to wonder if it wasn't just easier that way myself. When it was just me and Bruce—when I didn't talk to my parents—he seemed happier. We had more fun together, and I didn't have to hear him griping about them as much—for a while anyway.

I finally completed my last month of probation. I paid all my fines off and was completely off the hook. Granted, I still had another six months of no driving allowed, but I didn't have to deal with reporting to a probation officer every month anymore, though, which was a huge relief.

I still hadn't talked to Mom and Dad since the day they'd gotten onto me about calling my grandma drunk.

I had talked to Grandma since then—just not when I was drunk. But I was even sparing in how much I called her. I told her the bare minimum about my life, knowing that she would report everything back to Mom and Dad. In fact, our conversations were stilted and mundane, just enough to let them know that I was alive and okay since I wouldn't put it past them to do something drastic if they completely lost all contact with me.

What Bruce was always telling me about my parents was slowly starting to sink in. Even though we lived hundreds of miles away from them, I still felt trapped in a sense. Other people could disappear and go off the radar for a few weeks if they wanted to, but not me. My parents would always be there breathing down my neck, wanting to hear from me and know everything they could find out. I always had that pressure that I had to check in with someone.

I loved my mom and dad, but the more Bruce and I talked about it when we were drinking, the more what he said began to make sense to me. My parents were just so over the top. They were too much sometimes. It probably bothered Bruce more than it did me because his family was so different. I was starting to believe it when he told me that his family was the one that was normal, and I just thought mine was because that's what I was used to. I'd been conditioned to accept their overbearing, overprotective behavior as normal, so that's what I thought was normal.

Was Bruce right?

With me not calling my parents anymore and only

talking to my grandma once or twice a week at the most, Bruce was back to being super sweet and doting on me. Even though we still drank like fish and I was still somewhat depressed, we were having fun again, talking about everything again, listening to music together again, watching our shows together again, and laughing together again.

Instead of Bruce forcing me to have sex when he was angry, he was being gentler with me again, giving me massages again and having me dress up in his favorite outfits.

It seemed this was the story of my life. When I was on the outs with Mom and Dad, I was on the ins with Bruce and vice versa.

And I finally realized that if I had to pick one way or the other, I'd pick my husband. He's the one I had to live with, and he was right. No matter what I did or how good I was, it would never be enough for Mom and Dad. They'd always be disappointed in me simply because of who I'd chosen to be with and how I chose to live my life.

I was still blacking out when I drank, but it was getting to the point where I didn't care. Bruce was with me, and he took care of me when I blacked out, picking me up and carrying me to bed.

I drank slower sometimes, not wanting to black out. When Bruce and I were having fun together, I didn't want the nights to end. I guess I just didn't eat enough or something because it seemed like no matter what I did, I would almost always black out by the end of the night. I'd always wake up in bed, not knowing how I got there. Bruce always told me he'd picked me up off the floor or couch and carried me.

My withdrawal symptoms were getting worse too. When we were getting low on groceries, we'd stop drinking for a few days—long enough to get sober enough to take the bus out to get some, but even after three days of no drinking, my hands would still tremble, and sometimes I would find it difficult to form coherent thoughts. I felt like total shit.

Bruce didn't seem to have that trouble. He might have a slight hangover the next morning after drinking, but then he'd be fine with no shakes or insomnia or any of the things I suffered from. I didn't know if it's because he was bigger than me or he ate more than I did or what.

Anyway, when I'd finally get sober enough that I could get dressed well enough to ride with him to get groceries, we'd hurriedly stock up on what we needed before grabbing some wine and going back home. As soon as I downed a glass, I'd start feeling better again.

It eventually got to where Bruce wouldn't make me go through all that. He'd go out on his own to get our groceries, and I'd stay home and wait for him to get back.

I think Bruce liked it better that way because he was faster getting the groceries on his own, and he said he didn't have to worry about going to jail for beating up guys for looking at me on the bus. Though he'd made that comment jokingly, I thought it strange he would even say something like that since I'd never had anyone try to talk to me when we were on the bus together. I was always sitting right next to him, and he always had his arm around me or his fingers threaded through mine. Maybe he saw stuff that I didn't, though. I never really looked at anyone and minded my own business when we rode public transportation—unlike Bruce who had no problem talking to strangers.

It was nearing the end of autumn and was too cold to go to the beach. Plus, even though we were just a short drive over the bridge to the beach, we hadn't gone hardly at all since my DUI because taking the bus over there took a ridiculously long time due to the weird, round-about routes the bus took. It was also a hassle to cart all our stuff back and forth. It was just so much easier when we kept everything we always used in the car.

It didn't matter, though, because Bruce and I did our own thing in our apartment.

We were together, and we had fun drinking together, and that's all the mattered.

To us anyway.

CHAPTER 9

THINGS WENT okay for a while until one day Mom and Dad called me. I stared down at my phone ringing like it was a snake about to bite me.

It was about four in the evening, but I actually hadn't been drinking for very long. I'd gotten sick earlier in the day and had spent the whole morning puking my guts out.

Eventually, Bruce brought me a glass of wine and coaxed me into sipping it, swearing to me that it would make me feel better.

When I didn't answer my ringing phone, Bruce glanced over at me. "Who was it?" he asked. I think he already knew the answer.

"Mom and Dad," I swallowed another sip of wine. It had been a few weeks since I'd talked to them, though I knew they kept up with me through Grandma.

"You gonna call them back?" he asked me. "It's been a while since you talked to them."

"You want me to talk to them?" I asked him dubiously.

He shrugged like it was no big deal to him one way or another. "It's just been a while," he said again.

I stared at him. Bruce confused the hell out of me sometimes. When I did talk to Mom and Dad, all he did was bitch about it, and we fought about them all the time. Now that I hadn't been talking to them and things had been better between me and him, he acted like maybe I should talk to them.

Just as I opened my mouth to question him about it all, my phone rang again.

They were calling again.

Bruce eyed me over his wine glass expectantly.

My hand hovered over the phone before I sighed and flipped it open, holding it up to my ear.

"Hello?" I answered simply.

"Sarah?" Dad's voice was tentative. "How are you doing?"

"I'm okay," I answered. I started not to ask how they were doing, but I knew that would be too rude, so I eventually asked halfheartedly, "How are y'all?"

"We're okay," he answered back.

He went on to ask how the weather was.

I had to fight back a laugh. Really? I hadn't talked to them in weeks, and when Dad finally got around to calling me, it was to talk about the weather? Not that I wanted to fight with them, but just damn.

I took another sip of my wine and answered something back about how it was kind of cold right now.

Like always, Dad seemed surprised to hear that it was cold in Florida, which was absurd to me since they'd come down to visit me in the autumn before and had seen for themselves how cold it could get down here.

People had this huge misconception that it never got cold in Florida when it actually did.

Dad asked me something else, but I didn't hear him.

And I don't know what happened, but it's like I zoned out or something. I wanted to ask him what he'd said, but it's like my mouth wouldn't form the words. I just felt so tired. So very tired, like it was taking all my energy to talk, and suddenly I just didn't want to do this anymore.

The silence stretched between us, and I heard Dad calling my name, but I couldn't say anything.

I took another sip of my wine, my hands shaking, and then I didn't remember anything after that.

I didn't remember anything—until much later, that is.

When I finally became conscious of my surroundings again, it was nighttime and Bruce and I were drinking and listening to music.

I wasn't even thinking about my parents. I assumed that the rest of our conversation must have gone okay since Bruce wasn't ranting about them. In fact, he seemed to be in a pretty good mood.

He was playing some of our favorite music and hugging me from behind in that way of his, swaying me in his arms while he crooned the lyrics into my ear.

I was buzzing and floaty and didn't have a care in the world in that moment.

I could smell the aroma of something that Bruce had in the oven. He managed to eat every night, but I still rarely did. I wasn't hungry and knew I wouldn't be eating that night either.

Instead, I just drank more of the wine Bruce brought me and got lost in the haze of the music.

I didn't bring up the subject of my parents or any of the bad things that had happened. I wasn't thinking about any of that at the moment. I was content to exist in the moment with Bruce and let the alcohol course through my veins, pleasantly numbing me to everything —all the stress, all the worry, all the pain.

I must have blacked out again because I woke up the next morning in bed with no recollection of how I got there.

I stood on shaky legs and tottered to the bathroom where I took a quick shower, feeling weak.

My hands were shaking as I washed myself, but the warm water rushing over my skin felt good, so I lingered.

When I finally got out, I wrapped my hair in a towel and threw on a nightie, too exhausted to even get dressed.

It was about ten o'clock in the morning, which was later than I ever slept, but Bruce and I must have stayed up late the night before. Bruce was still asleep, but I popped open the fridge and pulled the cork from the bottle of white wine and filled up a glass.

I held the glass with both hands as I brought it my lips to keep it from shaking. I didn't know why I would get the shakes when drinking. Bruce never did, but he always assured me that it was okay, that some people just did that and that it was probably just due to my tiny size.

All I knew was that if I could get about half a glass in me the shakes would stop, and I'd start feeling halfway normal again.

I walked shakily into the living room, still sipping my wine and starting to feel my head clear somewhat. It was strange how when I first woke up after blacking out, the only thing that would make me feel better was more alcohol. I'd start feeling almost sober when I first started drinking, but then as I kept going, I would eventually take that turn where I'd start getting drunk. It was a vicious cycle, and no matter how much I tried to slow down, when it started nearing nighttime, it always seemed to catch up to me no matter what I did—especially when Bruce was the one pouring my drinks. I guess it was because he seemed to keep our drinks topped off more than I did.

I sat down on the couch and reached for my phone that was laying on the coffee table.

I had a bunch of missed calls from Mom and Dad and several from Grandma too. I frowned. Why was everyone calling me so much?

As I scrolled through the call log, I saw that the first few calls had come from Mom and Dad's home phone, and then the rest were from their cell phones. Grandma had called from both her home phone and cell phone too.

I sighed and sat back against the couch, dropping the phone onto the cushion next to me.

So maybe the rest of my conversation with Mom and Dad yesterday hadn't gone as well as I'd told myself it must have. But if we'd fought, wouldn't Bruce have been ranting last night? He was in a jovial mood and hadn't acted like I'd been fighting with my parents.

I vaguely wondered if it was some sort of family emergency.

I frowned and dialed my brother's phone number.

"Hello?" he sounded surprised to hear from me. I guess it had been a while since I'd called him.

"Hey, Alex. Is everyone okay?" I asked him.

"Um, yeah, why? What's up?" he asked me.

"Nothing," I pulled the wet towel from my head and shook my damp curls out behind my head. "I just got a bazillion missed calls from Mom and Dad and Grandma and wanted to make sure no one died or anything."

My brother laughed. "Well, if someone did, they haven't told me about it."

"Okay, so they're probably just being psycho Mom and Dad and Grandma then."

"Yeah, they do that sometimes," Alex said.

"Okay, well, I won't bother you," I told Alex lightly, ready to get off the phone.

"You're not bothering me," he said.

"Tell Lynn I said hi," I told him.

"Okay. Talk to you later, Sarah," he let me go. I'm glad my brother wasn't one to keep you on the phone when you were trying to get off.

Now that I knew no one was dying, I sipped more of my wine. I'd call everyone later. I knew I wasn't ready to deal with them now. I still had zero energy, but I forced myself to walk into the bathroom where I put some mousse in my hair, scrunched it, and then left it to air dry. I just didn't have the energy to hold the hair dryer up and dry it that morning, though I knew it'd make me feel better if I did. It was kind of chilly, and my damp hair wasn't helping to make me warm—nor was the thin nightie I had on.

I turned on the TV and absently watched a sitcom while sipping my wine until Bruce got up.

He chuckled when he saw me already drinking. Then, he went into the kitchen and made a cup of coffee before he came back into the living room and sat drinking it while he had a smoke.

I didn't see how he did that. Bruce would have a cup of coffee and a cigarette and shortly after he was done, he'd start drinking. I didn't see how he could drink right after having coffee, but to each his own, I guess.

The day went about much like usual. As I started feeling better, I finally went to dry my hair, though I chose to stay in my nightie. It was Bruce's favorite one, and by the appreciative glances he kept throwing my way, I knew he wanted me to keep wearing it. The alcohol had the blood flowing in my veins by now anyway, so I didn't feel as cold as I had when I first got up.

I kept meaning to call Mom and Dad and Grandma, but Bruce and I were busy talking and buzzing together, and I didn't want to chance ruining the good mood between us.

I decided I'd wait to call them all back. They hadn't called me that day, so whatever it was they had to say to me—which I probably didn't want to hear anyway— could wait one more day.

It was afternoon when my phone started ringing. It was Mom and Dad calling me again.

I was finally feeling a bit better and was well on my way to a good buzz where I'd actually enjoy myself some- what. Still, I answered the phone anyway.

"Hello?"

"Sarah? Oh, thank God. Are you okay?" Mom's voice sounded relieved and worried at the same time.

My brow furrowed. "Yeah, of course. Why?"

There was a long pause on the other end of the line before Dad answered, "You never answered us yesterday when we were talking. There was just this long silence on the phone, and then the phone went dead. We've been calling you ever since then and you never picked up. We didn't know what had happened."

"Your grandma's been trying to call you too," Mom added.

"Yeah, Momma had a bad dream about you..." Dad trailed off.

Grandma had a bad dream about me? My head was spinning, and I took another sip of wine. What were they talking about?

"Oh, I dunno," I tried to play it all off as no big deal. "I just got tired, I guess, and then my phone died."

"Well, we're about fifteen minutes from your place," Dad informed me.

"What?!" I about choked on my drink. "You drove all the way down here. Why?"

Oh my gosh! They were almost here, and here I was buzzing and in one of my sexy nighties. Bruce was drinking too. This was not good. Not good at all. In fact, it was a recipe for disaster. Part of why Bruce had wanted to move away from them, I knew, was to put distance between us so we didn't have to worry about stuff like this —about them just popping by and invading our privacy.

Yet even eight hundred miles away, they still managed to do just that.

"When we just lost you on the phone and couldn't get

ahold of either you or Bruce, we didn't know what happened to you," Mom explained. "Do you know how scary that was for us?"

"And then Momma had this premonition or something..." Dad trailed off again.

I had to fight from rolling my eyes. A premonition. I never thought my parents believed in superstitious stuff like that.

I pinched my fingers in the center of my forehead, exasperated beyond belief. I really didn't want to deal with them right now. There was no way Bruce and I were going to be able to hide that we'd been drinking, and I already knew from personal experience how much more uninhibited Bruce was when he drank. I certainly didn't want him to get into it with them.

"Well, thanks for the heads-up," I told them sarcastically. "Let me let you go so I can get some clothes on."

I hung up before they had a chance to say anything else.

I walked onto the balcony where Bruce was sipping his wine and smoking a cigarette.

"You'll never believe this," I said.

"What, angel?" he asked me lazily.

"My parents are almost here."

That got his attention. He straightened, and his brows shot straight up. "What?"

"When the phone went dead yesterday and then neither of us answered their calls, they freaked out," I repeated the gist of the story to him.

"So they just decide to jump in their car and drive all night down here?" he asked me incredulously.

"Looks that way. Oh, and my grandma had some bad dream about me or something, like a premonition."

Bruce swore under his breath.

"Yeah," I added sardonically before saying, "I'm going to get dressed."

Bruce followed me into the house, still swearing and commenting about how crazy my family was. I was really starting to see where he was coming from.

I threw on a pair of yoga pants and a tank top while Bruce slipped a shirt on over his jeans.

I went into the bathroom and surveyed my appearance in the mirror.

I looked tired. My eyes had bags under them, and they were slightly red. My curls hung limply around my gaunt face. I was thin. Thinner than I'd ever been.

I looked like hell, and I knew it.

I brushed my teeth while Bruce gathered all the wine and wine glasses up, stuffing them in the fridge before he came into the bathroom and brushed his teeth too.

They were futile efforts, though. They'd know we'd been drinking. There was no way to hide we'd been drinking all day.

We had to just get through this, though. I'd let them see I was okay, and then surely they'd be content with that, and then they'd drive back home. They needed to go to work in the morning anyway. I knew they'd had to have taken off work today to come down here.

I should have known that was wishful thinking, though.

I heard a knock on the door and glanced at Bruce in dread.

I was surprised when he took the initiative to go answer the door. I'd been prepared to do it.

I heard the sound of my parents voices along with Bruce's drifting up the staircase. I couldn't make out what all was being said, but my parents' faces were grim when they came up the stairs into the kitchen.

"Sarah," Dad said my name ominously.

"Y'all shouldn't have driven all the way down here," I told them. "See? I'm fine."

Mom's sharp eyes swept over me. "You don't look fine. When's the last time you've eaten?"

I didn't say anything, but I didn't have to. Bruce jumped in to answer for me, "I've been trying to feed her, but I can't hardly get her to eat anything lately."

I stared at him. How typical of him to jump in and save his own ass and place all the blame on me...though I guess what he said was actually true. Bruce *did* try to get me to eat. I just wasn't hungry much anymore.

And I didn't really want Mom and Dad to blame him for everything. They all already had enough bad blood between them without them thinking that he didn't feed me or something.

Though by the looks on their faces that's exactly what they thought even if they didn't voice their opinions.

Then they all—my husband included—started talking about me like I wasn't even there. I vaguely heard Mom and Dad say something to Bruce about me not looking good. He said something back, but I couldn't make out what he said. Everything was becoming blurry, and I saw all three of them looking at me worriedly.

That was the last thing I remembered.

That was the last thing I remembered until I came to at the hospital.

The funny thing about alcohol is that it takes so much time for everything you drink to get completely into your bloodstream. Although I wasn't completely drunk when Mom and Dad showed up, everything I had drank before they arrived had still been building up in my system, and I guess I'd blacked out.

One minute I was standing in the kitchen of the apartment I shared with Bruce listening to all three of them talk about what to do with me like I was a child, and the next I was in the waiting room of a hospital.

Mom and Dad were watching me warily with worry on their faces, and I was scowling at them, complaining about how I wanted to go back to my apartment.

"Why am I here? How did I get here?" I asked them, confused and angry as hell. "Where is Bruce?"

They exchanged a worried glance. "Bruce told you to come with us," Dad said. "You're deathly pale, Sarah. We just want to get you checked out and make sure you're okay."

I looked down and saw that I had on a jacket I didn't remember putting on.

I stood up, and everything spun. I felt drunk, and I was pissed that I'd been dragged away from my apartment.

Dad stood up too and put a hand on my shoulder. "Don't try to go anywhere again."

I blinked up at him. Again? What was he talking about?

"Take me home," I told him firmly. "I don't want to be here. You can't make me go to the hospital if I don't want to."

Mom's eyes were red-rimmed like she'd been crying, but I didn't know what she had to be crying about. What the hell was going on?

"Sarah, we're already here, and we've got you checked in. You'll be seen soon. Just wait and be seen, and then we'll take you back."

"I'm fine!" I argued. I hated hospitals, and I didn't want to be there. "I don't need to be here. Just take me back."

"You don't even remember how you got here," Mom said. "I bet you don't remember running out in the street and almost getting run over either, do you? If it hadn't been for that woman..." Mom's voice caught and she trailed off, shaking her head.

"What woman?" They weren't making any sense. Everything was spinning, and I just wanted to go home and be with Bruce. Maybe listen to some music and relax with some wine.

Dad took over, "You came with us to the hospital after Bruce told you to, but when we got here, you got out of the car and took off. I don't know where you thought you were going, but you're lucky you didn't get run over. This old lady walked up to you and spoke to you very calmly and told you that your parents were just trying to help you, and you calmed right down and agreed to come in here with us."

"It won't be long now. I'm sure you're next to go back," Dad spoke to me cautiously like I was a frightened deer or something. "Just please sit back down and relax. You don't look so good, Sarah."

I knew I didn't look good, but it was just because I'd been drinking for days. I wasn't going to die or anything, but there was no telling them that. "I want my phone," I told them. "I want to talk to Bruce."

Mom had my purse in her hands, and she handed it to me, though I don't think they really wanted to let me call him.

I dug my phone from the mess that was my purse and hit Bruce's name from my short contact list.

"Angel?" he answered immediately.

"Why did you send me to the hospital?" I asked him, stung by his betrayal.

"Babygirl, you haven't been eating, and your parents were worried about you. It won't hurt you to go and make them happy. I'm worried about you too. Are you there yet?"

I didn't answer him. Instead I just said, "I want to come home."

"I know, baby, and I want you home, but please just do this to placate them, and I'll be here waiting for you when it's all over with."

I didn't like his answer. If he'd been worried about me, why hadn't he said anything before Mom and Dad came down? Was he just in cahoots with them to try to somehow take the heat off himself and be in their good graces?

I sighed in exasperation. "I hate hospitals. I don't want to be here," I whined to him.

"I know, angel princess. I love you. Call me and let me

know what's going on, okay, baby?" He made it clear he was ready to get off the phone.

"Fine, whatever," I said. I started to hang up, but then my conscience got the better of me and I added, "I love you too," before I snapped my phone shut.

Mom and Dad were both watching me with frowns on their faces, and I just lay back against the sofa, too tired to sit up anymore.

I don't know how long I lay there, but things still felt like they were spinning when I finally stood up on wobbly feet.

"I need to go to the restroom," I told them.

"I'll take you," Mom said as she stood and took my arm to lead me over to the restrooms.

"I'm fine, Mom. I can go by myself," I protested, but when I took the first step and felt my legs shaking so bad I could hardly stand, I was actually glad for her arm to hold onto.

What the hell was happening to me? How long ago had it been since I'd had a drink? I was probably just starting to withdraw and it was worse since I was awake. At this stage, I was probably usually asleep. That was probably the only reason I didn't know what was going on with my body.

Mom took me into the huge handicapped stall and hovered near me while I peed. I felt like a little kid again, but at that point, I didn't really care. I felt cold sweat beading on my forehead, although I was so cold I was almost shivering.

I looked at my reflection in the mirror as I washed my hands and saw why everyone was alarmed. I was paler than usual despite my tan, but they didn't know that I'd be fine if I just went home and slept it off. There was no need for all of this.

We walked back out to the waiting area where Dad was standing by the door to the ER with a nurse who was waiting to take me back. Apparently, they'd come for me while I was in the restroom. Thank god. Not that I wanted to go back, but if it brought me one step closer to getting out of there, I wanted to get it over with.

We were taken back to a room where I was told to lay on the hospital bed while the nurse took my vitals. I don't know what they were, but I saw the frowns on Mom and Dad's faces. The nurse asked what I was in there for, but Mom and Dad answered for me. I didn't really hear what they said. I was tired and just wanted to go home.

The nurse stoically told us the doctor would be with us momentarily.

I didn't know how long it was before the doctor showed up. It might not have been very long like the nurse said, or it might have been an hour or longer. Time was a blur to me as I was coming down from all the alcohol I'd consumed earlier. I felt shitty and just wanted to get out of there.

Just like when the nurse came in, the doctor— an older gentleman—mostly talked to my parents. I heard them saying stuff like "drunk all the time," "so pale," and "memory loss."

The doctor was looking at me and nodding, and then he came over to examine me. He picked up my arms and noted the bruises on them. "Where did you get all these bruises?" he asked me.

"I bump into stuff a lot," I told him.

He glanced over at my parents. "Do you mind if I talk to her alone?"

Mom and Dad left the room.

"Is there something you want to tell me that you'd feel more comfortable telling me without them in the room?" the doctor asked me frankly.

I shook my head.

"Your parents seem to think your husband did this to you," he pressed.

"No," I said as I shook my head emphatically. "My husband doesn't beat me if that's what you're getting at. I really do fall down a lot and stuff when I drink."

"And how often do you drink?" he asked me.

I shrugged. "I don't know. Sometimes."

He looked at me knowingly. "Your blood alcohol content suggests it's more than sometimes. Plus, you're shaking like a leaf."

I didn't say anything. He made me sound like an alcoholic or something. I was an adult and could do what I wanted, and I didn't need this doctor or anyone else judging me. There's no telling what my parents had this entire medical staff believing.

"Look, I only came here because my parents basically forced me to. I'll be fine once I go home and sleep it off," I told him. "I just want to go home."

"Do you take benzodiazepines?" he asked me.

"Benzo-what?" I asked him in confusion.

"Xanax, Valium, stuff like that," he confirmed for me.

"No," I shook my head. "Why are you asking me that?"

"Because you've got them in your system," he told me with a frown.

"Do you take drugs illegally?" he continued.

"What?! No! Of course not! I've never done drugs in my life," I spat back at him angrily.

"Does anyone you know get these medications?" he pressed me.

"My husband," I answered slowly, "he takes Xanax sometimes."

The doctor continued to study me before he said, "Mixing medication like benzodiazepines with alcohol is extremely dangerous. You're lucky your parents brought you here when they did."

"I'm fine," I told him. "I just want to go home."

I couldn't even wrap my head around how I'd gotten Xanax in my system, for that's what it had to be. Had I taken some of Bruce's medication? Surely he hadn't put it in my drink without my knowledge. Why would he do something like that? I couldn't even think of it. I wouldn't allow myself to think of it. There had to be a reasonable explanation for it.

"Your numbers aren't where I'd like to see them," the doctor told me in response to my declaration that I wanted to go home. I didn't know what numbers he was talking about, and I didn't really care. I knew my body. I knew I'd be fine if I just went home and slept. "I'd like to keep you for a few days—"

I interrupted him with a firm, almost panicked, "No! I don't want to stay here. You can't make me stay here against my will."

He lifted my left hand and motioned to the cuts on the inside of my wrist. "Do you want to explain those? How did you get those? Have you ever tried to commit suicide?"

I glanced down at the scars. I had no recollection of how they'd gotten there, but I knew I'd never tried to kill myself. "No," I said, "I'm not suicidal."

The doctor studied me. "Well, I can't in good conscience discharge you right now," he told me frankly. "Your BAC is still too high, and you're severely dehydrated, so why don't we do some fluids and get you to eat something for me?"

"I'm not hungry," I answered automatically.

"I'm not asking you to eat much. Just enough to get some nutrition in you. Plus, if you want to leave here tonight, I've got to see some improvement in your numbers. Getting some fluids in you and eating something will make that happen faster."

"Fine," I grumbled.

"I'm going to go out and talk to your parents," he said.

A moment later, the nurse came back into the room and put an IV in my hand. I didn't even feel the prick of the needle. I just lay there shaking.

She started pumping fluids into me and then came back with a tray of hospital food: a sandwich, soup, jello, and juice.

"There's no way I can eat all this," I told her.

"Try to eat as much of the sandwich as you can," she told me kindly. "It has the most nutrition in it."

I picked up the sandwich and forced myself to take a bite. It was pimento and cheese, and it seemed to take forever for me to chew it. Swallowing it was a chore too. I honestly couldn't remember the last time I'd eaten, and it seemed to be taking everything out of me to eat now. I ate slowly and could only get through half the sandwich.

Mom and Dad were back in the room and were trying

to coax me to eat more, but I simply couldn't. They didn't get it. I felt nauseatingly full and even more tired than I'd been before.

I lay there for I don't know how long as they pumped at least two bags of fluids into me before the doctor finally came back.

My head wasn't spinning as much as it had been, but I still felt like death and just wanted to leave.

He finally agreed to discharge me on the condition that I'd agreed to go with Mom and Dad and be monitored by them throughout the night.

I'd have said anything to get out there, but as soon as we were out of the doors, I expected them to take me back to my apartment to Bruce.

I should have known that'd be a no-go.

CHAPTER 10

MOM AND DAD insisted on taking me to a hotel with them. When I balked, they told me it was either that or they'd take me back to the hospital.

I was pissed at having my freedom ripped from me and couldn't help thinking that this just proved that Bruce was right, that they were trying to control me.

I was tired and didn't feel like arguing with them, though, so I let them call Bruce and explain to him what was going on. I simply didn't have the energy to do it.

When they were done talking to him, Dad passed his phone to me, saying Bruce wanted to talk to me.

"I'm glad you're okay, angel," Bruce's voice came over the line.

"I want to come home," I told him.

I saw Mom and Dad exchange a glance.

"I know, baby, but stay with your mommy and daddy tonight. It'll make them feel better. You can come home tomorrow."

I felt betrayed, like they'd all ganged up on me together.

"Fine," I didn't argue with him.

"I love you, baby," he told me.

"Love you too," I answered mechanically before hanging up.

Mom and Dad already had a condo lined up to stay in. They must have booked one either on their way down here or when we were in the hospital.

I barely took notice of the elegant furnishings as Mom walked me to our room. I tried to stand on my own as much as I could, but Mom gripped my arm, and I found myself sagging against her. My damn legs were so shaky, and I hated it. I just wanted to sleep and have all this shaky stuff pass, though I knew from experience it would take at least three days—if not longer—before my body would stop shaking.

I dreaded it. I dreaded the withdrawing.

When we got to the room, Dad laid down on one of the double beds while Mom led me into the bathroom and helped me take a bath.

I hadn't had a bath in so long. The warm water felt heavenly and made me even more tired. Mom washed my hair and back for me like I was a child again, only speaking to give me gentle commands to tilt my head back.

She held onto my arms to steady me as I stood, and all the anger I'd felt toward her and Dad earlier vanished. Instead, I now felt shame.

They'd driven all the way down here overnight and then sat in the hospital with me for a good part of the night. Yeah, I hadn't asked them to do it, hadn't wanted them to do it, but I knew they had to be exhausted.

"Thanks, Mom," I told her, tears choking my voice.

She just pulled me into a warm hug and then towel dried my hair before she pulled the hair dryer off the wall and dried it. I didn't even care that I didn't have all my hair products and that it was going to be a poufy mess. I just wanted to get warm and dry.

When Mom finally had my mane completely dry, she helped me dress into a huge T-shirt to sleep in and then guided me into the bedroom and tucked me into the other double bed before climbing in next to me.

"You're not gonna sleep with Dad?" I asked her as I curled onto my side.

"Not tonight. I'm going to sleep with you. You let me know if you need anything."

I simply nodded before I closed my eyes and succumbed to exhaustion.

One of the worst things about withdrawing off alcohol was the insomnia. I was so tired, but my sleep wasn't good at all. I dozed a lot and had very strange, vivid dreams that I kept jerking awake from. I half wished I had a drink because I knew when I got like that the only thing that would actually help me sleep was more alcohol.

I heard Mom and Dad talking several times throughout the night when they thought I was asleep.

They were talking worriedly in hushed tones about how I would jerk and spasm in my sleep, about how I would thrash about.

I heard them talking about how the doctor had told them he was surprised I was still alive in the condition I was in. I thought he must have been exaggerating. Yeah, I felt like crap, but I'd be fine. I'd been through this before when I had to stop drinking to get ready to see my probation officer. Okay, maybe this bout was worse than any other I'd had, but still. I'd be fine.

My night was spent in restless sleep, and when morning came, I was ready to go home to Bruce.

Mom and Dad had other plans, though.

They begged me to come home with them.

"Sarah, you're still shaking like crazy," Mom noted with a frown.

"And what about the Xanax in your system? The doctor said that's probably why you're so bad off. You've got medication and alcohol mixed together in your system. Are you a drugatic too now?" Dad added.

"I don't know how that got in my system," I was quick to defend myself.

Mom and Dad shared a glance before Mom proposed, "Maybe Bruce slipped it into your drink."

I immediately rejected the idea. "What? No! Bruce wouldn't do that," I automatically defended him. No matter that I'd wondered it myself, he was still my husband, and I couldn't have them thinking that of him. I still couldn't believe Bruce would do something like that or why.

"I'll call him now and ask him about it," I said.

Dad scoffed. "Yeah, like he's going to 'fess up about it if he did it."

"Will you please take me back to my apartment?" I asked them in exasperation. "You've got to drive all the way back to Tennessee, so you'll be ready for work come Monday." It was the weekend. They'd taken me to the hospital on Friday, so it was Saturday, and I knew they had the long drive ahead of them back home.

"Why don't you just come home with us for a while?" Dad asked.

"I'm not leaving Bruce," my voice held a note of panic. It was just like Bruce had said. They'd never stop trying to break us up. They saw an opportunity, and they were going to pounce on it.

"Just until you get to feeling better," Mom clarified.

"No," I said more firmly. "You can't make me go with you if I don't want to. I already went to the hospital against my will."

Mom and Dad both looked frustrated, and then Dad pulled out his phone.

He didn't waste any time when he got on the phone with who I quickly figured out was Bruce. "Look, we really want her to come home with us so she can recuperate and build up her strength. Will you talk to her and tell her to come with us?"

There was silence as Dad listened to whatever Bruce said, and then he handed the phone over to me, his lips tight.

"Sarah?" Bruce said when I answered the phone.

"Yeah," I said snippily.

"Your parents want me to tell you to go with them, but I don't want you to do anything you don't want to do."

"I want to come home," I told him.

"Okay," his voice sounded relieved. "Well, I don't want them getting any madder at me than I'm sure they already are. Hell, I'm sure they already think I don't take good care of you now, so we're going to act like I told you to go with them, but you insisted on coming home.

Besides, that's not so far from the truth is it, baby? You want to come home to me, don't you?"

"Yes," I said, relieved that at least Bruce was on my side.

"Okay, give the phone back to your daddy, baby."

I passed the phone back to Dad.

Dad's jaw was tight as he listened to whatever Bruce was telling him. When he hung up the phone, he didn't look happy. He just shook his head at Mom and then blew out a breath.

"You're dead set on going back, aren't you?" he asked me.

I nodded.

I knew Mom and Dad weren't happy. Hell, I'm sure they were pissed, but if anyone had a right to be pissed in all this it was me. I hadn't asked them to go all psycho and drive down here. They'd practically forced me to go to the hospital against my will. They were trying to bully my husband into giving them their way. Enough was enough. I was a grown-ass woman. My life and my decisions were my own.

"Well, let's take her back then," Mom said, her voice betraying her frustration.

The ride back to the apartment was quiet and tense. I was stressed with every second that passed, afraid that at the last moment, Mom and Dad would decide to do something crazy and keep driving, effectively kidnapping me and taking me home with them whether I wanted to go or not.

It wouldn't be the first time they'd essentially kidnapped me and held me against my will since I'd been an adult.

Only when we pulled into the driveway did I feel myself beginning to relax.

"We wish you'd just go back with us, Sarah," Dad tried one last time. "It could be like a vacation or something. We'd take you to the airport so you could come back down here once you're healthier."

"Thanks, but no," I told him again.

"Just leave her alone, Rob," Mom told him. She knew my mind was made up.

Bruce came out to get me. He wrapped an arm around my waist and held me against him while Mom and Dad talked to him.

"She doesn't need to be drinking like that and mixing it with Xanax. That doctor said she had Xanax in her system," my dad told him.

"Yeah, she took one of mine the night before to help her sleep," Bruce said.

I did? I didn't remember that. I never took Bruce's medicine, but maybe I had done it when I was blacked out?

"And she needs to eat more," Mom said.

"I've been telling her that," Bruce nodded. "Don't worry. I'll make sure she gets better. I've told her she doesn't need to drink so much and needs to eat more, but she can be stubborn."

Ha! I was half pissed at Bruce for putting all the blame on me, especially when it was so far from the truth, but then I realized why he did it. Mom and Dad would only be that much worse if they thought Bruce was to blame for everything. I'd rather it be this way than him fighting with them.

And again, they were all talking about me like I wasn't there.

I knew by the looks on their faces that Mom and Dad didn't want to leave me with Bruce. Nevertheless, they finally hugged me goodbye and said a few last words to Bruce before they got into their car and disappeared down the driveway.

"F—," Bruce swore as soon as their car was out of sight. "Let's go inside, angel." I let him usher me up the stairs, grateful to be back and far away from the hospital.

Bruce and I decided not to drink anymore for a while. I had already begun the detox process, so we just let it take its course. I still didn't understand why it all seemed to affect me so much harder than Bruce when he drank the same stuff as I did—and drank more of it.

"Why did I have Xanax in my system, Bruce?" I asked him while we were lying in bed together watching TV. "I've never asked to take your medicine."

"I give you one when sometimes when you can't sleep, baby. You don't remember it because you're blacked out."

I was silent, processing his answer. "The doctor says that's really dangerous."

Bruce scoffed. "I take a Xanax after drinking all the time, baby, and I drink on my Prozac, which they tell you not to do either. Hell, everyone does. They just have to print all that on prescriptions to save themselves from any liability in the rare cases where people mix alcohol with the medications and overdose."

Still," I told him, "don't do that anymore. Don't give me any medicine after I've drank so much."

My head was laying on his chest, and his arm was stroking up and down my back soothingly.

"I just didn't want you to have to lay awake all night with insomnia, baby."

We were silent for a moment before I asked my next question. "Why didn't you come to the hospital with me?"

I felt rather than saw his frown as his hand stilled on my back. "I wanted to, but your parents thought it'd be best if I didn't. And I wasn't really in any condition to argue with them. If they'd have called the cops on me, Sarah, you know they'd have taken me to jail simply because I'd been drinking. That's why I was so cooperative with your parents. I'm lucky as hell they didn't do that. If I'd have been locked up, it would have been that much easier for them to force you to go back to Tennessee with them. I don't think your dad liked it, but I told him I wasn't going to force you to do anything you didn't want to to do."

"I thought you conspired against me with them," I admitted.

He lifted my chin to make my look at him. "Never," he said vehemently. "I was pissed that they came down here and butted into something that was none of their business, trying to take you away from me. Do you believe me now when I tell you how they are? I f— know how they are, Sarah. I get that they love you, but they're over the top. And my hands were tied, so I had to try to do the best I could with the situation. I know your dad was pissed that I didn't pressure you more to go home with them, but how could we trust that they'd really take you to the airport and send you back home to me?"

I nodded. Those were the exact same thoughts I'd been having.

"They're gonna be on your ass even more now," he added. "They'll probably call you all the f— time to try to make sure you're not drinking." He frowned.

"We just need to take it slower," I told him. "Maybe we have been drinking a bit too much anyway."

"You need to listen to me and eat more, baby," he reprimanded me.

"I can eat more if we don't drink as much," I conceded.

Just like Bruce said, Mom and Dad called me every day to make sure I was okay and not drinking again. I assured them I was fine.

I still wasn't sleeping very well, but after about four days, I finally wasn't shaking anymore, and I was able to sleep after taking a Benadryl. On the fifth day, I felt pretty good. I'd been throwing back the water, and my appetite was slowly returning. My hair no longer looked limp. My curls were bouncy looking again, and my eyes didn't look as tired.

I had my first cup of coffee in forever, and I even logged into my writing account and did a bit of work.

Of course, Grandma knew what had happened, so in addition to talking to Mom and Dad every day, I was also having to report in to her frequently. I knew they meant well, but I was beginning to feel controlled and smothered—even from hundreds of miles away.

And Bruce and I were getting bored. It was getting even colder, so we couldn't go to the beach or lay out. We started going for walks again, and Bruce kept me busy in the bedroom, but we were both getting restless.

It wasn't long before we slowly started drinking again.

I always made sure to call my family before we started, and I think we kept it a secret for a while—especially since we didn't drink every day.

But eventually, every couple days turned into every other day, and that turned into every day.

And then I f— up and called my parents and grandma a couple of times when I was drunk, so the cat was out of the bag again.

I started fighting with Mom and Dad on the phone again. Bruce and I had more of our ridiculous arguments that were deep-seated in his jealousy. He ranted about my parents until I got pissed and called Mom and Dad at all hours of the night and took it all out on them.

I never attacked my grandma, though. When I called her, I usually cried to her about how awful Mom and Dad were and how they were stressing me out so much, causing chaos in my marriage. Grandma always listened, but of course, she took up for them too, asserting that they all just wanted the best for me. I couldn't get any of them to understand that the best thing for me was for them to just back off.

So, I stopped answering their phone calls.

Instead of that providing us some sort of relief, Bruce was high-strung, looking over his shoulder all the time. He told me I needed to talk to them, or they might just pop up at the house again.

I couldn't bring myself to do it, so Bruce and I fought about that. I couldn't win. He was pissed when I talked to them and pissed when I didn't.

Instead of showing up at our door again, they sent the cops to do a welfare check.

I'd never in my life heard of a welfare check. The cops simply said they'd received a phone call from my distraught parents saying that no one had had contact with me in a week and they wanted to make sure I was okay.

It was insane. After we assured the cops that I was fine and that I would call them, I called them.

Boy, did I call them. I was pissed, and I didn't even try to hide it. I told them how crazy they were for sending the cops to check on me, how they were smothering me, how I just wanted them to leave me alone and let me live my life. Just because they didn't drink didn't mean they could harass me to death to try to get me not to. They might not like me getting drunk, but I was an adult and could do what I wanted—whether they approved of it or not.

Bruce never argued with them on the phone, but he backed me up one hundred percent and always told me he was proud of me for standing up to them.

And then everything became a blur. I was living on a rollercoaster of emotions. I'd be elated one minute, depressed the next, angry the next, confused the next. Day and night began to blur together, and I was spiraling out of control. Bruce was always there, sometimes loving me with adoring eyes, sometimes ranting at me with dark eyes filled with hate.

And then it all finally came to a head.

CHAPTER 11

MOM AND DAD showed up at our apartment again.

Only this time they hadn't been entirely uninvited.

I'd been deathly sick and couldn't stop throwing up. I would drink, throw up, and then try to drink again, and throw up again.

Bruce seemed genuinely worried about me, so he actually poured out every bit of alcohol we had in the house. I was on day one of detoxing when my parents showed up at our door.

Apparently, Bruce had confided in my parents, worried about how sick I was.

Of course, I'm sure he didn't tell them how he'd been the one bringing me the drinks and promising me it would make me feel better if I kept drinking even after I threw up.

I couldn't blame it all on him, though. I was my own person, and I was the one who kept drinking. It's just that I dreaded detoxing again. I hated throwing up and knew that I'd have to go through all the shaking and insomnia and nausea when I stopped drinking. It was easier to just keep feeding my body with the alcohol that would let me feel pleasantly numb and out of it.

I was livid when Mom and Dad showed up but even more so when they told me Bruce was the one who'd called them.

"What?" I asked him in confusion.

"You've been so sick, baby, and you wouldn't listen to me. I can't get you to eat anything, and I was afraid for you," he told me right in front of my parents.

My head was spinning with confusion. Bruce had been the one encouraging me to drink more, and he didn't want my parents there any more than I did, yet he'd called them? None of it made any sense.

"Bruce thinks it would be a good idea for you to come stay with us for a while, Sarah. We're almost out of school for Christmas break, and we can help you get better," Mom said coaxingly.

"Yeah, and once you get to feeling better, we'll all have a good time. I know your grandma and brother would like to see you—not to mention Addison," Dad added.

What? It was almost Christmas already?

"You want me to leave?" I looked at Bruce in confusion.

"You're so sick, angel. I think it might do you good to get away for a while," he told me.

None of it made any sense. Bruce's biggest fear was that I'd leave him and go back home to my parents, and he'd called them to take me away? Did he not want me anymore?

I walked away from all of them into the bedroom. Bruce followed me, shutting the door behind us.

"What's going on, Bruce?" I asked him, my voice shaky.

He expelled a long breath. "Look, your parents kept ringing your phone off the hook, and they called mine too. They're worried about you, so I finally called them back and told them to come down and take you home with them for a while. Spend some time with them, and then you can come back to me."

My brow furrowed in confusion. "So, you don't want me here?"

He sighed in frustration, "You know it's not that at all, baby. But it's Christmas anyway. You might as well spend it with your family. Hell, I'm not going anywhere. I'll be right here waiting for you to get back, and we'll talk every day."

"You're not afraid they won't let me come back?" I asked him dubiously. That had always been one of the reasons he never wanted me to go up to visit my family.

"They promised me they'll let you come back whenever you want, angel. And besides, I'll come up there and get you myself if I have to." He cracked a wry grin. "You know I will. Nothing would keep me from my angel princess."

"Don't you want to come with us?" I asked him.

"No," he shook his head firmly. "Let your parents have this time alone with you. I know they want it, and then they won't be able to act like I'm controlling or something by not letting you go."

I think Bruce also just didn't want to go. I knew when we visited my family in the past, he always couldn't wait to leave.

"You're not going to go out and blow a bunch of

money on scratch offs while I'm gone, are you?" I asked him worriedly. He hadn't been doing that as much lately, but I still found the large withdrawals on the bank account sometimes when I checked it.

"That's the furtherest thing from my mind, baby. In fact, I'll give you all the cards. You just pull out a bit of money to tide me over for the couple of weeks you're gone. That way you won't even have to worry about me being tempted to do that."

I blinked. Bruce was being so...accommodating. This was completely unlike him.

I physically felt like crap, and honestly, I was getting tired of drinking all the time. Maybe it would be nice to take a break and get away, and I wouldn't have to worry about Bruce if he honored what he said.

And my parents had already driven all the way down here, so it wasn't like I really had a choice unless I wanted to royally piss them off.

"Okay," I agreed.

Mom helped me pack up what I'd need for a few days in Tennessee. It was colder up there than it was down here, so she pulled my long-sleeved stuff from the closet along with my coat and a couple of jackets.

After putting everything in my suitcase, I was exhausted. I had zero energy and had to sit down to keep my legs from shaking.

I saw Mom and Dad exchange worried glances, and they went out to put my things in their SUV, giving me a few last moments with Bruce.

He hugged me and kissed me and told me everything would be okay and that this was for the best for now. While I felt a bit of anxiety at the thought of being away from him for so long—he and I had hardly been separated at all since we'd gotten together—I also felt a bit of relief that I'd be able to relax.

As much as I loved Bruce, he could be exhausting to be around. I always had to watch out for his moods and cater to his whims. Mom and Dad were comfortable and easy. They didn't blow up over stupid little things like Bruce did.

It had been so long since I felt normal without alcohol. If I could just get through this withdrawal period, it would be so great to not drink anymore. I was tempted to say I'd never touch another drop of alcohol again.

Of course, that would require cooperation from Bruce, and he just loved drinking too much, so that would probably never happen.

But he'd stopped drinking for me before. When I'd given him an ultimatum to choose the booze or me, he'd chosen me. Could I do that again?

I hoped Bruce wouldn't do a bunch of drinking by himself while I was gone and then call me with his insecurities. I knew from personal experience that when he drank when he wasn't with me, he'd start brooding on the possibility of me leaving him, and then he'd stress me out by calling me and yelling at me or sounding broken and devastated.

"Goodbye, angel. I'll see you soon." He gave me one last hug and kiss. "Just get through this, and you'll be back in my arms again in no time."

I hugged him back, and he walked me down the stairs out to Mom and Dad's vehicle. He helped me get into the backseat and then told me, "I love you, angel," right in front of my mom and dad.

I was a bit embarrassed, not used to having Mom and Dad around while he told me he loved me, but I wasn't ashamed or anything. It was good of them to see this side of him so they could know that he really did love me and try to take care of me.

"I love you too," I told him before he closed the car door and we drove away.

I mostly lay there in the backseat with my head leaning against the seat that Mom and Dad had reclined for me. Mom and Dad played the '80s channel on SiriusXM, and it was honestly difficult to listen to some of the music since it reminded me of Bruce so much and how we'd lay out tanning together or dance together while drinking.

I still felt like crap. I wanted to sleep, but all I could do was doze. None of us talked much. I think Mom and Dad could sense how bad I felt and knew I wasn't really up to it. Plus, I'm sure they were tired from all the driving they'd done to come down and get me.

We ended up stopping at an O'Charley's right outside of Atlanta to get something for dinner. Mom and Dad had grabbed some lunch stuff from a gas station earlier when they were gassing up, but I hadn't eaten anything then, the thought of food making my stomach turn.

I wasn't really hungry now either, but I knew I needed to try to eat, and Mom and Dad weren't going to settle for me not eating again.

My legs were still shaky as we walked into the restaurant. I didn't really want to go in. I knew I looked like crap. My arms were covered in bruises from where I'd fallen down or bumped into stuff when I was drunk, so I put a jacket on. Thankfully, it was chilly anyway, so it's not like I was out of place wearing one.

I let Mom and Dad order me a bowl of potato soup. I tried to force as much of it down as I could, but I still didn't manage to eat even half of the bowl before sweat was beading on my brow, and I felt impossibly full.

Mom and Dad prompted me to drink all of my water at least, so I did it just to appease them. I knew I needed to hydrate as much as possible.

I was completely exhausted by the time the meal was over with and was grateful to get back out to the SUV. I was extremely self-conscious and felt like the waitress and everyone could tell that something was wrong with me. Was it obvious that I was walking on shaky legs like a foal that had just been born and was just learning how to walk? I felt like it was. It had been everything I could do to try to keep my hand steady enough to raise the soup spoon to my mouth to eat my soup.

Mom and Dad only drove for about another hour before they got us a room for the night. They found a condo compatible with their points in the area. We were about halfway from their home in Tennessee, so they'd drive the rest of the way in the morning. I knew they couldn't go all night again after driving all night on the way down to get me.

Just like the last time I'd been in a room with them, Dad went to lay down and Mom helped me take a bath, washing my hair for me, her tender ministrations bringing me to the point of tears.

I couldn't stop them from falling this time and sat there crying silently.

"Why, Sarah?" Mom asked me gently. "Why do you do this to yourself? I hate seeing you this way, baby."

I didn't know what to tell her. I couldn't tell her everything. I didn't want them to think badly of Bruce. I'd never tell her about how he sometimes grabbed me and pushed me down and scared the living daylights out of me. How he was most terrifying when he threw knives. It was messed up because despite everything I still loved him, and I knew that he loved me too. I had to believe that or everything I'd been through to be with him would have all been for nothing.

So I told her what little I could, "I don't know. I guess because everything has been such a mess since the accident, and I just get so depressed and worried about everything, and drinking makes me forget and feel better for a while. But then the only way I can keep feeling better is to drink some more, and I hate this. I hate withdrawing and shaking and the insomnia and feeling like crap."

"But you're killing yourself, Sarah." Her voice wasn't too admonishing. "Do you shake like this often? I've never seen someone react to just alcohol this way."

I just shrugged. "It'll start going away in a few days." I wished I could just sleep it off, and although I was tired, I knew I wouldn't be able to sleep good. I'd doze and have weird, vivid dreams—sometimes nightmares.

"I don't ever want to see you like this again. You've got to stop doing this, Sarah. Drinking's not good for you, and it's not going to solve anything. Isn't it what got you into this mess in the first place?"

I knew she was right, so I didn't say anything. Instead, I let her help me get dressed into one of Bruce's big T-shirts I'd brought with me to sleep in. I certainly couldn't have brought any of the stuff I normally slept in to wear around my mom and dad. My silky negligees and nighties were too revealing to wear around my parents, even if they did hang off of me these days thanks to how skinny I'd gotten.

Like last time, Dad slept in one bed, and Mom slept in the other one with me.

I'd packed some of my Sleepytime tea to bring with me, and Mom brewed me a cup. Sometimes, it would help me drift off to sleep when I was detoxing and nothing else would work. I'd tried Benadryl, but even if I took three or four, they didn't seem to work when I was coming off of alcohol. Nothing really did, and while the valerian in the Sleepytime tea didn't knock me out or anything, sometimes it would allow me to drift off for a couple of hours at a time.

Apparently, my shaking had gotten worse because when Mom brought me the cup, my hands were shaking so bad that I couldn't even lift the cup to my lips to drink the tea—even holding it with two hands.

I still didn't understand why my body did this, and it frustrated and scared me.

Mom watched me, frowning worriedly, before she went to the kitchen and came back with a spoon. She began spooning the tea into my mouth for me. It was too hot for her to hold the cup up and let me drink it straight from the cup, so spooning it to me was the equivalent of the little sips I should have been able to take from the cup on my own, I guess.

"Thanks, Mom," I said softly. "I'm so sorry," I whispered, shame coming over me and tears pricking my eyes again.

"It's okay," she told me gently. "Everything's going to be okay."

I wanted to believe her.

It felt so weird to be "home," in the place I grew up in, especially without Bruce. The silence of the rural area that I had once found so comforting felt odd. I had gotten used to hearing motorcycles, the zooming of traffic, and police and ambulance sirens at all hours of the day and night that it felt strange to not hear all that background noise from outside.

I was still pretty weak and shaky when we finally got to Mom and Dad's house, and Mom and Dad were worried about how much I was apparently jerking in my sleep, so they had me sleep downstairs the first couple of nights where they could keep an eye on me in case I had a seizure or something. I almost scoffed at the notion. I'd never had a seizure before in my life, but I wasn't really in any position to argue, and going up the stairs took too much energy in my weakened state, so I didn't protest.

I slowly started to get better. Each day I was able to sleep a bit more at night, and I was slowly starting to eat more without getting too nauseous. I was getting my strength back too, and after about five days I was feeling back to my old self and drinking coffee in the morning again. My hair was no longer limp and lifeless. The curls were bouncy and shiny again, and I was no longer shaking like a leaf.

Grandma was ecstatic to see me, and I spent a couple of nights at her house to spend time with her. While it was nice to be back around everyone, it still felt a bit odd to be back by myself without Bruce. What's more is that I felt lost being away from Bruce. I was so used to being with him all the time that I thought about him constantly.

He called me several times a day, though, to check up on me and see how everything was going. He always told me how much he loved me and missed me and couldn't wait for me to get back to him. Sometimes I could tell he'd been drinking, especially when he got in more depressed moods and questioned whether I wasn't happier back with my family.

I hated it when he did that because then I had to spend time convincing him that he's who I really wanted to be with. And it was true. Despite everything, I didn't feel like the same girl I'd been when I'd left my family to be with him. Of course, I wasn't the same girl. I'd been to jail and had experiences my family couldn't even fathom. I was no longer that innocent, carefree girl. I was completely wrapped up in Bruce, and I missed him.

It stressed me out when Bruce questioned my devotion to him, and while it was nice to spend time with my family again, it felt strange too, and I found myself just longing for when I could go back.

When I finally approached Mom and Dad about needing to go back to be with my husband, they shared a glance. Somehow, I instinctively knew something was up.

"You know, your mom and I have been asking around, and there are lots of houses up here for rent. Why don't you and Bruce consider moving up here so you'd be closer to us?" Dad was sitting comfortably on the couch as he threw his idea out.

My mind instantly balked at the idea, something inside me telling me it wasn't a good idea.

"That way we'd get to see you more than once a year, and you could actually save a lot more money here. Rents aren't near as expensive as they are down there in Florida where you live," Mom pointed out.

She did have a point. We'd certainly have more money left over if we didn't have to pay the exorbitant rent prices we paid in Florida.

"How much are rents here?" I asked as if I was considering their proposal.

Dad quoted me a figure. It was half of what we were paying in Florida, and it was for an entire house—much bigger than what we had in Florida.

"I don't know," I hedged. "We need transportation to get around here, and you know I can't drive again yet until I get my license reinstated." The truth about how Bruce couldn't ever legally drive again had come out long ago when I'd first lost my license and had to explain to Mom and Dad why Bruce couldn't just drive us everywhere.

"We can take you wherever you need to go," Dad offered. "We'll take you guys out to get groceries with us. That's not a problem."

"Yeah," I said slowly, letting him know I was listening, though I wasn't sure this was really something Bruce and I should consider.

"We just think you'd do better up here," Dad continued. "I don't ever want to have to drive down to Florida and pick you up in the condition you were in again. You're lucky you're still alive, Sarah," Dad said.

I looked down, feeling bad about what I'd put them

through. I was certainly feeling better and was tempted to say I'd never drink again.

"If you're up here, y'all could spend more time with us, so maybe you wouldn't get so depressed and drink. It's not good for you to be so isolated down there," Mom said.

"I'm not trying to tell you what to do. I'm not trying to control you either," Dad said, "but you don't need to be drinking like that, Sarah. It's not good for your health. Maybe if you move up here, you can both have a fresh start away from all that."

I was quiet as I considered what he said. A fresh start. Away from all the drinking. I could be closer to my family.

It did sound promising. I had to admit it.

But would Bruce be willing to do that? Would he be willing to stop drinking again for me? Would he want to move up here?

He couldn't wait to get away before, but Mom and Dad had been trying to split us up back then. They acted like they accepted Bruce now, so maybe things would be different. Maybe I could have both my family and my husband. Is that what it would take to make me happy?

"I'll have to talk to Bruce about all of it," I finally told them. I wasn't going to make any kind of decision without him. This is something he and I would have to decide together.

Surprisingly, Mom and Dad seemed to understand that, and they should because I know neither of them would make such a huge decision as moving without the other one.

While part of me didn't want to leave Florida, another

part of me actually agreed with Mom and Dad that it would be better for me and Bruce to move back up here.

I'd have to wait and see what Bruce thought, though.

Bruce was silent for so long after I told him Mom and Dad's proposal that I started to worry that he'd hung up on me.

"Bruce?" I said tentatively to make sure he was still there.

"Yeah, angel, I'm here," he said impassively.

"Well, what do you think? I honestly don't know, and of course, I only want to do what you want to do..." I trailed off.

"I think we should do it," he finally said.

"What?" I had to make sure I'd heard him correctly. He surprised the hell out of me by agreeing to it so readily. I'd been expecting him to at least express some concerns over moving back close to my family.

"It might be good for us to have a new start," he said.

"Really?" I asked. "You know we won't be able to drink up here, right? We can't have my family seeing us drunk."

"I know, angel," he said. "That's why I think it might be a good idea. We won't drink. And if your family becomes a problem, we can always move again."

Now it was my turn to be silent. I was dumbfounded by how accommodating Bruce was being. "You'd be willing to stop drinking for me?"

"I did it before, didn't I?" he asked, his voice softer and deeper. "I'd do anything for you, baby. Having you happy and healthy is the most important thing to me."

My heart soared within me. He did love me. I knew he did, and this just confirmed it.

"If you think it would do you good to move back to Tennessee and be around your family, then we'll do that," he went on. "Besides, with rents that cheap, we'll be able to have more money left over every month."

"Yes," I confirmed, "and we can get more bang for our buck too with a bigger place with more privacy."

"I definitely want more privacy, baby, so we can play our music without having to worry about assholes calling the cops for it being too loud."

"How are you feeling, babygirl? Are you eating more?" he asked me. He asked me that almost every day.

"I feel so much better since I stopped drinking, and, yes, Mom and Dad and Grandma are feeding me every chance they get." I laughed.

"That's good, baby. I can't wait to feed you again too. You know I can cook good, too," I could hear the smile in his voice.

"Yes, you can," I agreed with him, sensing he needed his ego stroked. Plus, it was true. Bruce was a good cook.

"I love you," I told him, suddenly feeling happier than I had been in a while.

"I love you too, angel. I guess I'll let you go start making plans with your parents."

We got off the phone, and I went to tell Mom and Dad the good news.

CHAPTER 12

MOM AND DAD WERE ECSTATIC, as was Grandma. My brother commented on how he was glad I was going to be living closer again, and Addison was glad too. We were looking forward to hanging out more again.

Addison and I went out to eat at a Chinese restaurant and catch up. It was nice having my buddy all to myself again, and I could tell she felt the same way. I used to hate Chinese food, but I knew Addison loved it, so when she'd asked to come to a Chinese restaurant, I'd told her I'd give it a try. My tastes must have changed since when I was younger because I found that I liked several of the items on the buffet.

"See!" The look on Addison's face was triumphant as she shoveled some more chow mien in her mouth. "I told you Chinese food is good!"

"It's okay," I relented. "Maybe not good enough to make me want to dig a hole to China, though," I teased her, and she grinned. When we'd been little kids, Addison had always wanted to dig a tunnel to China. I think she'd seen that on a cartoon once or something, and the idea had stuck in her head when we were small.

We talked about her new job and how things were going in her world. I realized with a pang that Addison and I had never gotten to live in an apartment together as roommates like we'd always planned to. Yeah, we'd been dorm mates at college, but then I'd met Bruce and moved out to be with him, and all our plans had gone down the drain. Not that I regretted being with Bruce or anything, but rather, I felt sad at all the "what ifs" and the way things could have been with other important members of my life, like my BFF who was sitting across from me.

Eventually, the conversation had to move to me and why I was moving back up to Tennessee. It was difficult to tell Addison about my no-driving situation. We'd always been the good girls in school, and I was afraid she'd judge me for getting a DUI, but she was actually pretty understanding about it all when I told her how it all happened. Of course, I didn't tell her the part about how Bruce had pressured me into driving him to the store to get him some cigarettes and how really it could all be blamed on that incident. Otherwise, I never would have driven after drinking, but I did tell her about how the dude on the motorcycle had run the stop sign and how I probably wouldn't have been charged with the accident at all had I not been drinking before getting behind the wheel.

She didn't judge me, and I was grateful for that. I also didn't tell her about how much I'd been drinking since my accident. Mom and Dad agreed with me that there was no need for everyone to know all of that, especially since I wouldn't be doing it anymore now that we were moving up here. I was just going to put all that in the past.

Once all the awkward stuff about my DUI was out of the way, Addison and I were chatting about anything and everything like we'd always done. I laughed harder than I'd laughed in a long time, and she did too—until our sides were hurting and tears were streaming down our faces. Addison and I had always had that kind of friendship where we could laugh like that together. It was the best kind of therapy, and I didn't really realize how much I'd missed it until that moment.

Addison must have felt the same way because she said, "I'm so glad you're coming back, buddy. I've missed you."

"Yeah, me too," I told her, my cheeks hurting from smiling so much.

Maybe things were finally starting to look up.

Mom and Dad helped me find a place for Bruce and me to rent. Of course, they'd wanted us as close as possible to them, but Bruce and I had talked about it, and we both agreed that we needed a bit of distance between us, so we were firm about searching for places in the county over from where Mom and Dad lived. Plus, being able to have high-speed internet was a necessity for us, so that knocked out some of the extremely rural places Dad found at first.

Eventually, we finally settled on a place in the small town Bruce had rented an apartment in when he'd first come up to Tennessee to be with me.

The place we found wasn't an apartment complex. The landlord owned three small houses on the same patch of land, though, but there was plenty of space between them. We wouldn't be right on top of the other renters like we had been in our place in Florida, so we'd have more privacy. It was about twenty-five minutes away from where Mom and Dad lived, so it wasn't too far away, but it's not like they were right next door to us either. I wanted to be able to see them, but I also didn't want them in our business all the time.

It was certainly bigger than the apartment we had in Florida. It was two bedrooms, and to my delight, it had a bathtub. I'd sorely missed my baths. We'd also be able to have our own washer and dryer, which was important to us. We didn't want to deal with having to go to a laundromat.

I sent Bruce pictures of everything, and once I got his go-ahead, I wrote the check for the deposit on the place. We'd be set to move in the first of the new year.

Now all that was left to do was get some furniture and have Bruce sell the furniture we had in Florida. While I'd miss some of the pretty stuff I'd picked out in Florida, we knew that it wouldn't be feasible to pay to have it all moved up to Tennessee, so Bruce was going to sell it and get what he could out of it. Then, he'd pack up the smaller things we could fit in our car and Mom and Dad's vehicle, and Mom and Dad and I would drive down to get him and my car when it was time for us to move in.

Time went by quickly as Mom and Dad and even Grandma helped me find furniture for our new place. Mom and Dad gave me my old bedroom set to use for our bedroom, and one of my grandma's friends was selling her basically new living room set because she decided she wanted something different, so I got a great deal on all that. I didn't mind used furniture for an apartment. It didn't make sense to invest in expensive, brand-new stuff for a place we were just renting. When we eventually bought our own place, we could buy some really nice new stuff.

Dad and Alex moved everything into the house for me, and I had everything all set up when Mom and Dad and I finally drove back down to Florida to get the rest of our stuff and pick up Bruce.

Mom drove my car back, and I rode in my car with her while Dad and Bruce rode in Mom and Dad's SUV together. Any anxiety I'd had about Dad and Bruce being alone together was quickly dispelled when we stopped for lunch. They seemed to be getting along well. They mostly talked about sports and fishing and whatnot.

When we finally got to Mom and Dad's house, Bruce and I took Mom and Dad up on the offer to just leave our car at Mom and Dad's place. They had a carport they would park the car under to keep it safe from the elements until I got my license back. They could also start it up and drive it for us every so often, so it didn't just sit there.

Mom and Dad helped us carry all the stuff we'd brought up from Florida into our house, and then they took us out to pick up a few groceries.

And then Bruce and I were finally alone for the first time in a month.

And we were in our new place in Tennessee.

"Did you miss me?" he asked me.

"You know I did," I pouted at him. "It's been so weird sleeping alone." And it had. I'd gotten so used to having him next to me.

"Yeah, for once I didn't have a little cover hog stealing all the covers off me," he grinned at me teasingly.

I feigned mock outrage. "Well, if *that's* the way you feel, I guess you can sleep on the couch tonight."

He laughed as he grabbed my waist and pulled me to him. "Not gonna happen. We're going to sleep together in that little princess bed of yours you used to sleep in when you weren't even legal."

My cheeks pinkened at his insinuation, and I felt a tad bit uncomfortable. Bruce seemed to really get off on our age difference, and it make me wonder sometimes if he'd still want me if we were closer together in age.

He lowered his head to kiss me, and I pushed all those thoughts away. It didn't matter. We were what we were. There was no reason for me to speculate and complicate things any more than they already were.

If I'd learned one thing being with Bruce, it's that I had to savor the good moments when they came. I loved it when he was warm and affectionate like this, and I was still just naive enough to believe that this might really be a new beginning for us—that it just might last.

The first couple days after we brought Bruce up were spent getting us set up with things we needed. Mom and

Dad drove us to the nearest VA hospital to get Bruce registered there so he could get his meds mailed to him every month. They also swung me by the health department so I could get my birth control and all that switched back up to Tennessee instead of in Florida.

We weren't in our new place for two days before Addison and my brother and his wife stopped by one night to see us. They called ahead of time, of course, to make sure it was okay for them to come.

Addison surprised me with a house-warming gift—a floor lamp that we promptly set up in the living room. Bruce and I both thanked her, and then we all sat on the couches and chatted for hours. Well, Addison, my brother, and I did most of the talking, reminiscing about all the silly things we'd done together growing up. Lynn and Bruce mostly smiled and chuckled and listened to us.

It was so great to catch up with my brother and best friend, and it was kind of sweet yet shocking to see how close they'd become in my absence. Even Addison had admitted to me that night at the Chinese restaurant that she and my brother had started hanging out more when I was gone. It was their way of dealing with me not being there, and I was glad they'd had each other. Still, it was kind of weird to see them have their own inside jokes when it had always been me and Addy who had all the inside jokes. I felt a twinge of jealousy, and I realized it was over both of them. I was supposed to be the glue that held the three of us together, and it was a bit disconcerting to see that they'd managed without me.

I shook my head. That kind of thinking was selfish and childish, though. There was no reason to be jealous of them. Alex was still *my* brother, and Addison was still *my* bestie. I wouldn't have wanted them to be depressed with me gone, so I was happy they'd been able to be there for each other.

I think it was more the reminder of all the things I'd missed out on that truly bothered me. Every time Addison and Alex laughed about stupid things that had happened when they were hanging out, it stabbed at my core that I hadn't been there for the fun times.

I looked up at Bruce from where I was sitting nestled into his side in the chair we sat in. The huge recliner that had come with our living room set was oversized and big enough to fit both of us in it. It was a massage chair, and Bruce loved to sit in it with the vibrations going, though we didn't have them on right now.

If I'd been there for every moment with Addison and Alex, I would have missed out on my life with Bruce, and I wouldn't have wanted that, would I? I tried to imagine what my life would have been like without Bruce, but I quickly became uncomfortable and shut those thoughts down. I wouldn't want him picturing his life without me, so I shouldn't do that to him.

He must have felt my gaze on him because he looked down at me, gave me a soft smile, and then kissed my forehead.

I felt content. This was how he'd been ever since we'd gotten here to our new place. He'd been calmer and sweeter, and I dared to hope that this move really was a good thing.

When it started getting later, Addison and Alex and Lynn finally got up to leave. Addy and Alex both had to go to work the next day, and although Lynn was a stay-at-home mommy, they had to go by and pick my nephew up from my grandma who'd been babysitting him that night so they could come over and visit us.

I turned around to face Bruce after closing the door. I figured he'd be ready for bed now. It was nearing ten o'clock, which wasn't terribly late, but we'd been going to be earlier than usual lately. Well, I'd been falling asleep early while Bruce lay beside me in the bed watching TV until he nodded off to sleep too.

"You want to go for a walk, angel?" Bruce asked me.

I laughed incredulously, sure he must be joking. "But it's freezing out there!" It was January, which tended to be one of the coldest months of the year in Tennessee.

He shrugged. "I thought some fresh air might do us good. Plus, there's this little liquor store up on the strip I thought we could walk to. Get us a little nightcap." His gaze didn't quite meet my eyes as he suggested that last bit, and I felt my heart plummet to my stomach.

"Bruce," I began slowly, shaking my head. "You know we can't drink up here. We can't be getting crazy drunk and having my family see us like that. That's *why* we moved up here, remember? So, we wouldn't drink anymore?"

He sat on the couch and started pulling on his boots. "We won't be getting crazy drunk, angel. We'll only have a little bit. I'll have a few beers and instead of you buying a whole bottle of vodka, you can just get a pint."

He stood when he finished putting on his shoes and came over to grip my hips. "Come on angel," he reassured me, "Everything will be okay. I promise. No one will find out. I want to have a drink with my girl and listen to music and laugh and relax. You know the way we do, angel."

"What if you turn mean like you do sometimes?" I asked him, unwilling to let go of the peace and tranquility we'd found in not drinking since he'd been here.

"I'm not in a bad mood, baby, so I won't. I'll be as gentle and loving as a newborn kitten," he joked.

I didn't laugh. I had a bad feeling about opening up this can of worms. I was afraid that once we opened this door, we wouldn't be able to close it again.

But Bruce was already bringing me my boots and coat and a scarf. It's obvious he was going to dress me if I didn't dress myself, so I took the garments he offered and donned them.

"Bruce, you promise this is just going to be like an every now and then thing, right? We can't go back to drinking every night or even every week." I began to chew on my lip thoughtfully. "Maybe we can just do it once every now and then. Can you agree to that?"

"Sure, angel," he said as he grabbed his pack and the keys and began ushering me out the door. "We won't do it all the time, but by god, we're adults and we should be able to have a drink every now and then if we want. I'll watch you. You'll be okay, and I promise not to get belligerent. We won't fight. Your mommy and daddy will never find out, and hell, we can't live our lives trying to please everyone else."

He turned to me when we get to the bottom of the porch and took my gloved hand in his. "Everything will be okay, Sarah. Stop worrying."

Bruce walked us about a mile and a half to the main strip where a liquor store was nestled right in between a bank and a new gas station that hadn't been there when I'd left Tennessee nearly four years ago. I'd never noticed it there before, but the building was old and had probably been there all my life. Funny how Bruce had noticed it right off the bat, though.

It was late when we got there. The store closed at eleven, and we were the only customers in there that late at night. Bruce got him a six-pack, and he selected me a small pint of pink lemonade vodka. I'd never had that before, but it beat just drinking straight vodka with no flavor since that was one of the only flavored vodkas the store owner had in stock that wasn't a huge bottle.

We were freezing by the time we got back to the house. I quickly changed into a warm pair of flannel pajamas. When I came out of the bedroom, Bruce had already poured me a drink in a shot glass and was holding it out to me with a grin.

"To our new beginning, babygirl." He lifted his already open beer bottle in salut.

I stared at the liquid for a moment, already smelling the strong odor of it before I ever lifted it to my lips. I could feel my bitter taste buds clenching up in anticipation of the tart, alcoholic bite I knew was to come from the pink liquid.

I threw my head back and took my first half-shot, my mouth puckering at the taste. But I felt the liquid burn of it all the way down my throat to where it settled in my belly like a ball of fire.

"Is it good, angel?" Bruce asked me.

I shrugged. "It's not bad. It really does taste kind of like pink lemonade," I told him.

He took another pull of his beer and then walked over to where I had the computer set up on the bar-style countertop.

He already had it hooked into our floor tower speaker, and he turned on a playlist of our favorite '80s songs.

I downed the other half of my shot and didn't resist when he pulled me into his arms to dance.

The music was loud, and I started to turn it down, but then I realized that we didn't have any neighbors right on top of us, so it was okay. We only had two neighbors on the hill we lived on, and there was a nice little span between the house above us and the one below us. I doubted they'd be able to hear our music, and I felt a rush of relief crash over me. It was so nice to be able to play music without being all tense and worrying about if the cops were going to show up and tell us to keep it down.

"Feels good, doesn't it, angel? We can play our f— music and not have to worry about some asshole calling the cops on us, huh?"

I nodded my head at him and grinned. The vodka was already hitting me. I hadn't drunk since Mom and Dad had brought me up from Florida, and that had been nearly a month ago, so it was hitting me harder. My limbs already felt light and floaty, and I was giddy, all my worries floating away.

Bruce and I enjoyed the night, drinking our respective drinks until we ran out. For once, I didn't black out— perhaps because I didn't drink as much. Bruce made us a peanut butter and jelly sandwich, and I ate it without protest before we went to bed.

I was asleep as soon as my head hit the pillow while Bruce laid there watching some fishing show.

Maybe drinking every once in a while wouldn't be so bad—so long as we didn't drink much and did it really late like this so we wouldn't have to worry about my family calling and finding out.

I should have known it wouldn't stop there, though. We went a total of three days after drinking that first night before Bruce started in again, trying to renegotiate the terms of our drinking.

"Shit, angel, there's nothing to do up here. It's cold as f —. We can't go to the beach. Can't go fishing. You don't have your license back yet. There's not f— all to do here. I'm going nuts just watching TV all damn day while you work on the computer," he complained.

"At least let us have a bit of fun once a week," he grumbled from where he scowled in the recliner.

"We said we weren't going to do this, though," I argued. "You knew when you agreed to move up here we couldn't drink like we used to. If we start drinking more often—and during the day no less—my parents *will* find out," I reminded him.

"So the f— what?" he finally spat. "We're f— adults, Sarah. We can't let your parents rule our damn lives. You're legally allowed to drink now, so there's not a f— thing they can do about it. The cops aren't going to take you to jail for drinking. You're off probation. You're just waiting for the rest of your license suspension time to be up before you can get your license back. That doesn't mean you can't drink."

I shook my head at him. "Bruce, you called them and had them come get me when I was supposedly near death's door to hear y'all tell it. If they find out we're drinking again, they're gonna freak. They will not let this go." It's like he'd forgotten how tenacious my parents could be when it came to something they strongly believed in. "We need to stay on good terms with them, not only because I want to, but because we need them to take us places to get groceries and stuff." I sighed, feeling the beginnings of a tension headache coming on. "I just want peace, Bruce. Drinking causes nothing but chaos for us."

His jaw hardened, and then he took another drag of his cigarette. "No, it doesn't," he finally said. "It's your parents. They're the ones that cause the problems. They stress you out and make you feel bad for living your life. If you want to have a damn drink, you should be able to do it without looking over you shoulder."

I sighed heavily.

"I knew it was a bad idea to agree to come up here," he muttered.

"Oh no," I shook my head and glared at him, crossing my arms. "No, you don't."

He cut his eyes up at me and puffed on his cigarette again.

"You are *not* about to blame all this on me. I told you I wanted to do what *you* wanted to do. If you didn't want to move up here, all you had to do was say so, and we'd have stayed in Florida. You're the one who said what a great idea you thought it was. I did not beg you to move up here, so don't act like this is all on me."

Bruce didn't say anything while he snuffed out his cigarette. Finally, he stood up and leveled a look at me. "I don't mind living up here, Sarah. It gets you closer to your family, and I thought that would make things better between you and them, but I'll be damned if I'm going to be afraid to do something because of them. I don't mind you being around them so long as they act right and don't try to control you or us. If I want to have a f— drink in my own home, I'll damn well do it, though."

I stared at him helplessly. I could tell his mind was made up. No amount of begging or pleading would change it. Yeah, he might give it up for a while, but he'd resent me, and it would fester between us until he didn't love me anymore.

"So, are you coming with me up to the store or what?" he asked me.

I shook my head sadly. "No, you go ahead. I can't chance people I know seeing me going into the liquor store this time of day and it getting back to my parents."

His lips thinned, but he nodded before pulling on his shoes.

I felt tears pricking my eyes as that little ball of tension settled in the pit of my stomach. I just had a bad feeling about all of this. It was too risky. If we started this again, so near my parents, something bad was going to happen. I just knew it.

Bruce headed for the door, but then he stopped when he got there and turned back. He strode back over to me and dropped a kiss on my forehead. "I'll be back soon, angel," he told me before he turned and finally strode out the door, the soft bang of it reverberating throughout my entire body like the ominous note in an opera bound for tragedy.

CHAPTER 13

I TRIED NOT DRINKING with Bruce, but that went over about as well as it had in the past. Not only did he get on my nerves more when he became intoxicated and I remained sober, but it seemed to eat at him if I didn't join in drinking with him.

He needed me to be his partner in crime, he joked. He couldn't relax and have fun drinking unless I was in the same, tipsy jovial mood.

So, to keep the peace between my husband and myself, I gave in.

Like I always did.

And really it wasn't so hard once I stopped resisting.

That day he'd walked up to the liquor store, he'd brought me back some peach schnapps. He knew all the flavors I liked, and he tempted me with music and laughing.

And when I joined in the drinking, I couldn't deny how the tension would leave my shoulders and how suddenly I didn't care anymore about whether or not we got caught.

Just like I used to do in Florida, I would call my mom and dad and grandma before we started drinking, that way I wouldn't talk to them when I was drunk.

And at first, Bruce and I only drank at night. Then, it got to where we started drinking earlier in the evening around dinner time.

I rarely walked up to the liquor store with him, unless it was late at night and I was pretty sure my family would all be in bed. I didn't want to chance any of them being in town and seeing me walk into the store.

Thankfully, we had an unspoken pact with my family that they couldn't just drop by whenever without calling first. Not only was it rude, but Bruce and I needed to maintain some semblance of privacy.

Even though we lived so close and Mom and Dad and Grandma wanted to see me every weekend, I only agreed to see them every couple of weeks. I didn't want to get into a habit of seeing them too often and having them expect it. Bruce always went with us to pick out groceries, but then he'd usually let me go spend time with my family alone. He never indicated it bothered him, but I could tell by the quiet look in his eyes and the set of his jaw that he was becoming more and more bothered by me leaving every other week.

I hadn't even spent any more time with Addison since that night she and my brother had come to visit us, though we had talked on the phone a couple of times. It was hard to work something out when I never knew when Bruce would want to be drinking, and he already had to share me with Mom and Dad and Grandma.

I knew I was right about his feelings when it came out one day while we were drinking.

"Looks like I'm going to have to buy me some booze," he commented dryly from where he sat spread out on the couch drinking and smoking a cigarette, "since you're going to be leaving me again this weekend."

Great, that was the last thing I needed. Bruce getting drunk and calling me while I was with my family, stressing me out. I couldn't take that.

I took another sip of my schnapps and braced myself. "I don't have to go if you don't want me to, Bruce. All you have to do is say so and I won't go."

He eyed me over his drink but didn't say anything.

"However," I added, "one of the reasons we moved up here was so I could see them more, and if too much time passes without me seeing them, they'll likely become suspicious and wonder why I'm not agreeing to see them."

Perhaps that hadn't been the right thing to say because Bruce scowled. "Them, them, them! It's always f — about them! What about what I want, Sarah?"

I literally bit my tongue to keep from popping back that *everything* was about him. I did every little freaking thing he wanted. I moved away from home for him. I moved back home because he said he wanted us to. I drank when he said drink, ate when he said eat. He snapped his fingers, and I jumped lately.

All to keep the peace. All to keep him happy.

I was tired. So tired of always trying to balance keeping everyone happy. My family. My husband. What about me? What about what I wanted? Did I even know anymore? When was the last time I made a decision that didn't somehow hinge on Bruce or my family?

I didn't say any of that, though. Instead, I just got up

and poured myself another shot of schnapps. At least I could dull some of the irritation this way.

"I don't want you to go this weekend," he finally snapped at me.

I didn't even blink. I just raised the glass to my lips and took a drink.

"Okay," I agreed.

My husband might be happy with me staying home, but I'm sure my parents wouldn't be when I'd already agreed to seeing them this weekend.

I was right, of course. My parents didn't even try to hide their disappointment. "Is something wrong?" Dad asked me. "You were all set to come visit us two days ago."

I pinched between my eyes as I held the phone to my ear and explained, "No, Dad. Nothing's wrong. I'm not mad at y'all or anything. I just feel like staying home this weekend."

"We could come see you if you want..." Dad offered.

I glanced at Bruce who was already shaking his head 'no,' his eyes burning fire at me.

"Uh, that's okay, Dad," I was quick to shut that down, though it was awkward because how was I supposed to tell my parents I didn't want them to come over? "Honestly, Bruce and I aren't feeling too well," I lied. "I think we're just going to take it easy this weekend. I think we might have a bug or something, and I wouldn't want to give it you or Mom knowing y'all have to go to work."

Bruce was nodding his head at me in approval from where he sat smoking his cigarette.

"Okay," Dad sounded deflated. "Well, I guess we'll see you some other time then."

"Yeah," I agreed. "I'm sorry," I added automatically, but I saw Bruce's eyes flashing at me and winced. He hated it when I apologized to my parents for anything, but I *was* sorry I'd let them down and gotten their hopes up for nothing.

No sooner had I gotten off the phone with them did Bruce land into me. "You've got to stop telling them you're sorry for every little thing, Sarah. You're encouraging their controlling behavior when you do that. You have nothing to be f— sorry for. You shouldn't even have to make up a reason why you don't want to see them. You should just be able to say you don't want to, and they should back off. End of story."

I wasn't in the mood for one of his tirades, so I did the one thing I knew would shut him up. I walked over to the fridge and pulled him out a beer before popping the top and carrying it over to sit on his lap as I handed it to him.

He wrapped an arm around my waist and held me with one hand while he took a long pull of his beer with the other, temporarily placated, grunting with satisfaction as he swallowed.

"Go fix yourself a drink too, baby," he told me, nodding at the kitchen.

I moved to obey, not even fighting it anymore. Besides, it felt good to slip into the buzzing, carefree feeling alcohol provided me.

Bruce turned on the cooking shows he liked to watch while we were drinking, and we sat talking and commenting on the recipes and talking about this and that and everything under the sun. As usual, the more buzzed Bruce got the more his thoughts began to drift. He talked about funny moments from our past and some of our sexier moments, but then his talk eventually began to take a sour turn—toward my parents of course.

He was back to bad-mouthing them, talking about how they'd just wanted us to come up here so they could keep me under their thumb and how their eventual plan was to get me away from him.

"Bruce, you agreed to come up here," I tried to point out to him. "We didn't have to do it. We could have stayed in Florida."

He grunted. "I know how they are. They never shut up until they get their way. I shouldn't have agreed to do it. I don't know what I was thinking."

I didn't point out that that wasn't quite true—that if they'd had their way, I wouldn't have married him. But I didn't feel like stoking the fire tonight, so I tried to change the subject back to lighter topics.

Just then, we heard a knock on the door. We both stilled and then glanced at each other. Nobody ever knocked on our door unless it was my family. They were the only people we knew in the area.

Bruce swore and grabbed our drinks and headed to put them in the fridge. I didn't even bother telling him it was no use. Our place reeked of smoke and alcohol. Maybe by some stroke of luck they wouldn't notice? Or better yet, maybe it wasn't them?

Fat chance.

When Bruce had everything put away out of sight, he motioned for me to open the door. Fortunately, I had on a pair of pajamas today instead of one my flimsy nighties.

I opened the door, and sure enough, Mom and Dad stood there.

"Hey, what are y'all doing here?" I tried to keep my voice light and cordial as I stood in the doorway and didn't invite them in.

"We were in the area and thought we'd stop by and see if y'all needed any medicine or anything," Dad commented.

Mom's eyes assessed me critically, and I swear she instantly knew what was going on.

"Aw, that was sweet of y'all, but we're fine really," I said. "Just something that's got to run its course," I added.

I felt Bruce come up behind me. "Y'all want to come in?" he asked. I wanted to stomp on his foot but refrained. Couldn't he see that our best hope of getting out of this without them finding out for sure what we'd been doing was getting them to leave as quickly as possible?

"That's okay," Mom answered this time. "We just wanted to check on y'all."

"Guess we need to be getting home," my dad added.

"Okay," Bruce said. "Good of y'all to stop by." I knew he really thought it was anything but.

We waved them off and Bruce watched them pull out of the driveway from the front window before he turned around and practically stomped over to the fridge to retrieve our drinks.

"Mother— son of a bitch!" he cursed. "Is this how it's always going to be? They don't get their way, so they just show up at our f— house. I won't have it, Sarah!" he roared at me.

I flinched at the loud timbre of his voice. He was really pissed.

But then I straightened my shoulders and glared at him. "It's not my fault, Bruce. I can't control what they do."

"No, but they can sure as f— control you," he spat back at me angrily.

"What am I supposed to do?" I asked him in exasperation.

"Put a leash on your f— parents!"

I snorted. "Yeah, easier said than done. You know that."

He grumbled as he slammed our drinks down on the counter. "Drink," he ordered me. "God knows you need it, baby girl, after that."

I eyed him warily for a moment. So, was he not mad at *me* anymore? I swear, Bruce kept me in a whirlwind of emotions sometimes, one minute raging at me, the next talking to me sympathetically like he understood my plight with my overprotective parents.

I tried to ignore the pit of dread in my stomach as we kept drinking. I kept Bruce distracted with kisses and his favorite music videos and reminiscing about great times we'd had on the beach, but eventually he turned his focus back on what was bothering him.

And then the floodgates released.

He got to ranting and raving about my parents and wouldn't stop. And all I could do was throw back my drinks and try to dull the incessant sound of his voice droning on, going over the same crap over and over, every little infraction they'd ever made against him. How they were trying to take me away from him and would never stop. How they hated him and always would. How they all just pretended for my sake.

Bruce was still droning on while I sat at the computer changing the music, trying to find something that would snag his attention and take it off of bitching for a while, when I got a new email notification.

My stomach dropped when I saw the sender was Mom. Somehow, I just instantly knew that email was not one I would look forward to reading.

With a slightly shaking hand, I clicked to open it.

Sarah,

It's pretty obvious what was really going on when we stopped by to see you this afternoon. It was exactly as I feared when you cancelled coming to see us. I've had a bad feeling ever since you said you weren't coming and turns out my instincts were right.

You are drinking again.

How could you do that to us? To yourself? After all the times we've found you near dead, you would put yourself through that risk again and worry us to death?

When you didn't even invite me and your daddy in, I knew it even more. We raised you better than that, and the guilt was written there all over your face.

You tried to hide it, but I just wanted you to know that we know.

I hope you take care of yourself.

We will always love you no matter what.

Mom

. . .

If Bruce truly loved you, he wouldn't have you drinking like that, killing yourself, either.

That last line there at the end is what caused my vision to blur. She'd stuck it in like a P.S. without labeling it as such as if to ensure it's the last thought I read and the one that would stick out in my mind the most. Mom had always known exactly where to strike and went for the jugular.

If Bruce really loved you, he wouldn't have you drinking like that. Had the thought crossed my mind before? Maybe deep down and I just wanted to ignore it?

No, it wasn't true, and I would't even allow myself to think of it. Bruce could be an asshole. That much was true. He could be a controlling bastard sometimes. He was a bit high-strung, but he *did* love me. He was insanely jealous of me, and he wouldn't be that way if he didn't love me, right?

"Oh, great! And now here come the guilt trips," Bruce sneered from over my shoulder. He must have come up behind me and read the email. I merely downed the rest of my shot, clicked on another song, and then got up to go refill my glass.

"Your mother is really something else..." Bruce began ranting about Mom specifically now and how her emails were toxic to me. I poured another shot and immediately downed it—the whole thing—even though I normally never did a whole shot at a time. I just wanted to tone out the sound of his voice, his anger.

It wasn't five minutes until I felt the languid spread of the alcohol racing throughout my limbs, making me feel lighter. I smiled and walked over to Bruce, who was still scowling.

I sat on his lap and wrapped my arms around his neck, snuggling into him, cutting him off mid-rant.

He looked down at me and a grin finally cracked his face. "You feeling good, baby?"

I nodded into his neck, and he chucked, stroking his hand up and down my back. He took another drink of his beer before he tilted my head up to him. "Come here," here muttered before he leaned down and kissed me.

I don't remember anything else about what happened that night. I woke up the next morning dressed in silky lingerie and in bed even though the last I recalled I'd been wearing warm pajamas and sitting on Bruce's lap.

I felt a warning creep up my spine. I'd blacked out. I'd blacked out for the first time since Florida, which meant that I'd drank too much again.

Surprisingly, I didn't have much of a headache, but my throat was parched, so I got up and slipped on my fuzzy slippers and robe before I padded into the kitchen and got myself a glass of water.

Bruce was still asleep, so I sat down at the computer to check my email. No new ones from Mom, thank goodness. However, I did have a new voicemail on my phone. From Dad telling me to call them when I could.

I walked into the spare bedroom that was on the

opposite end of the house from where Bruce was sleeping and called them.

"Hello?" Dad answered.

"Good morning," I greeted him evenly.

"Good morning," he said back stoically.

"How are y'all?" I tried to act normal, though I knew an inquisition was coming.

"We're okay. How are you feeling?"

"I'm okay," I told him truthfully. Yes, I'd blacked out last night, but it wasn't the end of the world. I didn't even have a headache that morning, and I'd be careful not to do it again.

"Look, Sarah, we know you were drinking yesterday. We could smell it all over you when you opened the door."

I didn't say anything, remaining silent to let Dad say his piece.

"We're not trying to tell you what to do or run your life or anything. We just worry about you. Try to understand. We had to come rescue you from death's door twice because of this. Do you really think it's a good idea for you to start drinking again?"

"It was just a one-time thing," I lied. "It's not something we're going to be doing all the time again."

Dad grunted. I don't know if that meant he was accepting my explanation or he didn't believe me. I guess it didn't matter either way because it was what it was.

"Well, you know we go to church every Sunday down where I pastor. Why don't you and Bruce think about joining us? You know we'd love to have you."

I winced. Church. I'd never been a fan of going when I was growing up, maybe because I'd felt forced to go and it hadn't been my choice. And we'd had to go every time the doors were open: Sunday morning, Sunday night, and Wednesday night—not to count seven nights straight during revival weeks. No matter if I'd had homework or was tired or wanted to do something with Addison instead. Supporting Dad being a pastor had meant all of us—Mom, Alex, and me—had to be there when he was.

I wasn't too keen on the thought of going back to church again where people could be judgmental and self-righteous. Good lord, how would the gentle church folk react to seeing me with Bruce? Someone older than my father. I was halfway surprised Dad would even ask us to go. I wouldn't think he'd want us on display that way.

"I'll talk to Bruce about it," I hedged.

"Okay, just let us know so we can come by and pick you up in the morning if you want to go. I think it'd be really good for y'all, Sarah. You know you were raised in church," Dad started, but then Mom pulled the phone from him, obviously sensing that Dad was only going to push me away if he got too preachy and pushy, as he tended to do when it came to me and church.

"Hey, Sarah," Mom said.

"Hey," I answered back coolly.

"You got my email?" she asked.

"Yes," I answered back simply.

"I didn't send it to hurt your feelings or fight with you. We're just worried about you, and I couldn't sleep last night thinking about it." I was so tired of her not being able to sleep being thrown on me. I didn't tell her that, though.

"This new church your dad was called to pastor is

different from the ones you grew up in. I think you might really like it if you give it a chance."

"I'll talk to Bruce," I reiterated to her what I'd said to Dad.

"Okay. Well, in any case, please don't drink anymore, Sarah. It's not good for you. Your body can't handle it."

"Okay," I simply said, not willing to make promises that I wasn't sure I'd be able to keep. And really, it was like Bruce said. It might not be healthy for me, but I was an adult, and my parents really had no right telling me not to drink if I wanted to.

"Okay, I guess we'll let you go. Call us later and let us know."

"I will," I promised, though I really had no intention of going to church with them tomorrow morning or any morning.

Once again, Bruce surprised the hell out of me by saying, "Sure. Why not? Let's throw them this bone if it'll get them off our backs."

"You want to go to church?" I gaped at him.

He shrugged before chuckling. "I won't burst into flames, angel—though I probably should for some of the things I do to you." He grinned devilishly at his last comment.

I ignored it.

"If we don't go, Sarah," he explained, "they'll find some way to blame me and say I wouldn't let you go. Hell, they already think I'm the damn devil himself. I'm not going to give them the satisfaction of making me the bad guy there."

"But what if I don't want to go?" I asked him because I really didn't think I wanted to.

"We all do things we don't want to," he commented sardonically, taking another pull on his cigarette. "Let's give them this this one time, and we don't have to go back again. That way they won't ever be able to say we didn't try."

"Okay," I nodded slowly, seeing the logic in what he said—even if I wasn't overly fond of the idea of having to sit through a sermon.

"I guess I'll call them and tell them we'll go."

CHAPTER 14

TRUE TO HIS WORD, Bruce didn't burst into flames as soon as we set foot through the church doors. I didn't either for that matter.

I still felt out of place, though. I hadn't been to church since I'd left home for college. I was wearing a black skirt that hung to my knees and a turtleneck sweater, so I think I was dressed appropriately. Of course, my boots came nearly up to my knees, so I'm not sure how appropriate they were, but they were the only ones I had, so they had to do.

Bruce was in khakis and a button-down shirt, but his black leather jacket gave him that bad-boy, biker-looking edge that he never could quite seem to shake no matter what he wore.

I didn't know any of these people, but they all seemed to know who I was. Several of them came over and welcomed Bruce and me before the service started. Bruce shook their hands cordially and smiled appropriately, and it felt weird to see my husband acting so civilized in this polite church world.

Most of the time he was more like a crude sailor or caveman, cursing and being impatient. It was strange, yet kind of nice to see him reigned in.

But I knew that's all it was. He was reigned in for the moment.

We sat in the pew my parents sat in, of course, and Bruce and I shared a hymn book and followed along as the congregation sang songs that I knew by heart from all my years growing up in church. Neither of us sang, though. We just politely sat with our heads bowed over the hymnal reading the words.

For my part, it's not that I was being rude or didn't want to join in praising God or anything. It's just that I never had been much for singing at church. I used to silently move my mouth to the words, but I rarely ever sang in church, even growing up.

When the opening hymns were over, a devotion was read, and then everyone got up to go to various rooms for Sunday school. Apparently, there was a room for the young children, one for the teens, one for the young women, one for the older men, and one for those somewhere in between. Bruce and I simply followed Mom and Dad where they were heading to the one for those in between.

I barely paid attention to what they were talking bout in Sunday school, and I know Bruce wasn't focused on it either. He sat next to me holding my hand and squeezing it ever so often, winking at me over his bible when he got my attention.

I'd try to keep a straight face and look down at my bible piously. Bruce was older than my dad, but he was acting like a teenage boy flirting with me during class. I had to admit that it did help ease some of my tension and lighten my mood, though.

Neither of us commented on anything, and before long, it was over with. Bruce excused himself afterward to go outside and smoke, and I noticed it was a while until he came back in. The congregation had already started singing again when he slipped back into the pew next to me, smelling of menthol cigarettes.

It finally came time for the preaching, and I was relieved to see that it wasn't my dad who would be preaching that morning. He'd arranged for someone else to preach, some guy I didn't know, and I was glad. My dad's preaching had always seemed to get to me more. I don't know if it was because he was my dad and I just assumed that everything he said was aimed at me or what, but his preaching had always made me feel more uncomfortable than anyone else's.

Whoever this guy was, his preaching started out the normal way and then eventually led into how only those who had accepted Jesus Christ as their Lord and Savior would enter into the kingdom of heaven. He said all the usual stuff that I was used to hearing about in church.

I felt Bruce's hand slip from mine at one point, and I glanced over at him curiously. He made a smoking motion to me with his hands, and I just nodded at him to let him know I understood before he slipped back out of the aisle to leave the building for another smoke.

I never wanted to be a smoker, but I was halfway jealous that Bruce had an excuse to leave and get some fresh air—especially when the preacher switched gears and started talking about different sins.

He talked about sexual immorality, drugs, and then

alcohol. I shifted in my seat when he started talking about how Jesus would even save alcoholics, drugatics, and adulterers and turn their lives around, and I couldn't help feeling a bit self-conscious and betrayed.

What all had my parents told this congregation about Bruce and me? This was their church family, so they might have requested prayer for us and told them we were alcoholics or something, that we'd lived in sin before we'd gotten married.

I suddenly just wanted the sermon to hurry up and be over so I could get out of there.

When the preacher finally winded down and the piano began playing softly, he issued an altar call, inviting anyone who wanted to repent of their sins to come forward to the altar.

My chest felt tight, and my hands shook. I'd always hated this part of the church service the most. I always felt like people's eyes were on me expectantly, silently pressuring me to go up to the altar and fall to my knees in front of the whole congregation—something I'd never done before. I couldn't imagine doing that, though—walking up there with all those pairs of eyes on me, and then when I got there, what then? What if I talked to Jesus and nothing happened? How could I stand up and face the congregation and tell them I hadn't gotten what-ever it was I was supposed to get when going up there? That would be humiliating.

So, I did what I always used to do during altar invita-tions. I made my mind focus on something else to keep my cheeks from flaming. I didn't want to look to conspic-uous. I couldn't slip out and go to the bathroom because if you started to move from the pew, people would get all excited and think you were making your way to the altar. I'd made that mistake once and nearly given my poor grandma a stroke; she'd gotten so excited.

At last, the song ended, and everyone resumed their seats without anyone having gone up to the altar. I breathed a sigh of relief as the service was closed out and prayer requests were made.

It was only then that I realized Bruce never had come back into the church house.

"Oh yeah, they most definitely told them about us angel if that preacher mentioned alcohol and sexual immorality in his message," Bruce chuckled and shook his head.

We were back home now after having an early dinner with my parents and grandma after church. Though Grandma didn't go to Mom and Dad's church—she went to the same one she'd always went to, which was right up the road from her house and was the one my mom and dad used to go when I was little—we'd all met up afterward to have Sunday dinner together. Even Alex and Lynn had come with my nephew, and that part of the day had been nice—once we'd gotten through the dreaded church service.

"Well, we got through it, but church just isn't my thing," I said.

"Yeah, never was mine either," Bruce agreed.

"Hey, at least you got to sit out on the last half," I grumbled.

He laughed. "I froze my ass off, baby."

"You should have come back inside and suffered with me," I pouted. "You left me all alone in there."

"I'm sorry, angel," he said. "I didn't want to keep interrupting the service slipping in and out, though."

I scoffed. Yeah, I'm sure that's why he really hung around outside. Truth was he'd been just as uncomfortable in there as I had been.

But that made my heart swell with affection. Bruce didn't have to suffer through that. He'd done that for me. Mom was wrong. Bruce did love me, or he wouldn't keep doing all these things I knew he had no interest in doing just to help me keep the peace with my parents. Sure, he could be an asshole sometimes, but no one was perfect.

As if reading my thoughts, Bruce said, "I love you, angel princess."

He might not be perfect, but he was my husband, and he did love me.

"I love you, too," I told him.

We didn't drink for a few days after going to church with my parents. I talked to Mom and Dad every night that week after they got off work, and I think they were somewhat appeased that they were able to tell we weren't drinking. I talked to Grandma just about every morning like usual too.

By the time Thursday hit, though, Bruce insisted on going up to the store. I didn't fight him. There was no point in it. We were going to do what Bruce wanted to do regardless.

Of course, when we started drinking again, Bruce

started ranting about my parents again. His rants were fueled with even more fire now about how we'd gone to church and everyone had been judging us.

"That was just a show," Bruce sneered from where he drank his beer. "There ain't no telling what your mommy and daddy told those people about us. That I brainwashed you and stole you away from home. That I'm some sort of predator who abducted their innocent young daughter from online. They probably all went home talking about how they'd had a good, hard look at the devil himself," he chuckled self-depreciatively.

"I don't care what they thought," I said, and it was true. I didn't. "I don't even know any of them, and even if I did, I've never cared what people thought of me and you."

"I'd like to see one of them try to take you away from me, though," he said like I hadn't even spoken.

"You know I'd never leave you," I went and sat on his lap, trying to reassure him.

He wrapped an arm around my waist and kissed my neck. "I know you won't, angel. I won't let you," he joked. Or at least, I thought he joked. I think he was half serious too.

Just then, my phone started ringing, and I saw *Dad* flashing across the screen from where my phone sat on the coffee table in front of us.

"You gonna answer it?" Bruce asked me.

"No," I shook my head. "I don't want to talk to them when I'm drinking. For in case they can tell or suspect or something."

Bruce nodded. "Probably a good idea."

They called two more times that night, and still, I

didn't answer. Bruce gave me a look and cursed under his breath after the third time. "I bet you're going to have a pissy email from your mom soon."

"I shouldn't," I commented. "I shouldn't have to jump to answer the phone every time it rings."

"No, you shouldn't," he agreed, "but you know how your mommy and daddy are."

I took another drink of my vodka and turned up the music. "I don't want to talk about them anymore," I told him. I was buzzing and feeling good. "Let's have some fun."

"Whatever you say, baby," he commented with a grin.

Turns out Bruce was right, though. I woke up the next morning to a nasty email from Mom. It seemed that any time I didn't answer my phone or she couldn't sleep, she'd take that time to analyze my life and actions and send me an email dissecting everything that I was doing wrong.

In her email, she expressed how she and Dad suspected I didn't answer because Bruce and I were drinking. How she'd hoped that going to church would help get us grounded but how everyone in the church could tell that we were both extremely uncomfortable.

You were both under conviction whether either of you chose to acknowledge it or not, Sarah. It was written all over your face and obvious in the way you were fidgeting, and Bruce couldn't even stand to stay inside the church house. You both know you are living ungodly lives, drinking and sinning and doing God knows what else...

Her email went on with more of the same judgmental tripe.

Bruce became enraged when he read it.

"How dare she speak to you that way, angel?! Like she thinks she's God himself or something. Who the hell is she to judge us?"

Bruce paced back and forth in his fury before he stomped over to the fridge and pulled out the remaining beer he had left over from last night. He popped the top and took a long drink before he grabbed my shot glass and poured me a shot of vodka. "Here, angel. You need this."

It was only ten o'clock in the morning, but Bruce was right. Parents like mine would drive anyone to drink.

"If every little thing doesn't go exactly their way, your mom is on that f— computer guilt-tripping you like a little kid throwing a temper tantrum. I've never seen grown people act that way. They act like f— children! And I'm tired of it, Sarah!"

"What am I supposed to do?" I asked. "I can't change them."

"No, but we sure as hell don't have to put up with it," he growled before he pulled on his boots and coat and grabbed his pack. "I'm going up to the store. Be back soon, princess."

He didn't need to explain. I knew exactly where he was going. He downed the rest of his last beer in one huge chug before walking out the door.

Any extra money we saved in a lower rent went to alcohol and cigarettes, it seemed. But I knew better than to complain, and besides, I was getting dangerously used to that feeling alcohol provided again—that warm, fuzzy, no-cares feeling.

I downed my shot in one quick drink and then went to take a bath. I laid in the water a bit longer than usual after shaving since I knew about how long it would take Bruce to walk up to the store and back. I thought of how when I was growing up, I used to love reading in the bathtub. I didn't think I'd read an entire book—much less in the bathtub—since I'd been with Bruce. He took up so much of my time and attention I never had time to read. Plus, my life was filled with so much drama on its own, what was the point of reading a book full of it?

I wondered if a lot of girls quit reading when they got married or if it was just me. I'd once said I'd always love reading, and I did still love it, from what I remembered. It had just been so long since I'd gotten to do it. Maybe everyone is like that when they get married, though. If you're busy with your spouse, maybe it's normal to put childish fantasies aside.

My mind drifted to my parents, and I grimaced. It seemed like I'd never be able to make them and Bruce both happy at the same time. If one was happy, the others weren't.

By the time I got out of the bathtub and put lotion all over my body, I heard Bruce coming back through the front door. We had a back door, but we never used it. I vaguely wondered why that was, my mind drifting from topic to topic as it was prone to do when I was buzzing.

I had just slipped on some warm pajamas when Bruce came into our bedroom looking for me.

"There you are, baby," he said coming in to give me a hug.

"I took a bath while you were gone," I told him.

"I can see that," he said, fingering my damp curls. "I need to take me one too."

He pressed his cold, unshaven face against mine, and I pulled back from the scratchiness of his stubble. "You're freezing! And scratchy."

He laughed. "Guess I'll shave too."

"It's only fair," I pointed out. "I shave everywhere every day to be nice and smooth for you."

He smiled lasciviously. "Don't I know it, angel?"

"I'll run you a bath," I told him.

"Thank you, baby," he told me before he started to get undressed.

By the time I had him a bath running, he came into the bathroom holding a little glass. I heard the clink of ice cubes as he climbed into the bathtub and sat the glass down on the lip of the tub.

I saw the amber-colored liquid within it and instantly knew it wasn't beer. Besides, who put their beer on ice?

With a sinking feeling, I realized that Bruce was drinking something much harder today, and I remembered how many of the times we'd had our worst fights he'd been drinking hard liquor.

"What are you drinking?" I asked him, my voice small.

He glanced up at me while soaping up. "Just some scotch, baby."

"Are you sure that's a good idea?" I asked tentatively.

He already wasn't in the best mood because of my parents, and I just knew that was going to come to the surface the drunker he got.

He scoffed. "I'll be fine baby. You and I won't fight. I promise. You know I'd never hurt my baby angel." He smiled at me, trying to reassure me.

I didn't say anything else as I flipped my head over and scrunched my hair while blowing it dry with a hair dryer. It was simply too cold to walk around with a wet head—not if I didn't want to get sick anyway.

When I finished, I went into the kitchen and poured myself another drink.

Looks like I was going to need it.

I was right. Bruce was more volatile when he drank hard liquor. He ranted and raved about my parents for hours. No matter how much I tried to distract him with funny videos, music, or cooking shows, he kept going back to it.

"I though the whole point of drinking was so we could forget about our problems and have fun," I finally snapped at him.

"Oh, so you just want to let them get away with it?" Bruce roared, flinging an arm out in frustration.

"What. Do. You. Want. Me. To. Do?" I bit off, my voice getting louder with each syllable. "I can't f— do anything about it!"

Bruce stood to his full height, glaring down at me. "You call them, and you tell them off. Stand up for your f — self, Sarah! You tell your bitch of a mother—and your father—that you hate them, and you never want to see them again!"

I propped my elbows up on the counter and dropped my forehead into my hands in frustration. Bruce was out for blood today, and nothing would silence the monster within him once he was in this kind of alcohol-infused state.

Before I had a chance to say anything, there was a knock at the door.

I looked up, my eyes meeting Bruce's furious ones.

"I swear to God, Sarah, if that's them..." Bruce left his threat hanging, and I prayed it wasn't Mom and Dad on the other side of the door. I don't know what he'd do if it was, but I had a feeling it wouldn't be good.

My anxiety only ramped up when he strode over to fling open the door instead of letting me open it like he usually did if he thought it was my parents.

I noticed Bruce didn't step back to let whoever it was in. I didn't know who was at the door, but it didn't sound like he was talking to my dad.

"Sure thing, man," I heard Bruce say. "Sarah," he glanced over at me as he called to me and motioned me over to him.

I slid off the barstool and padded over to stand next to him, surprised when I saw a police officer standing in the doorway.

"What's going on?" I asked, my heart starting to beat faster in my chest. Thanks to the time I'd been arrested and the multiple times the cops had shown up at our door in Florida, the appearance of police officers naturally made me nervous.

The walkie talkie on the police officer's belt buzzed

with that staticky sound that walkie talkies make. He pressed a button on it to silence it before shifting his weight and eyeing me. "Are you Sarah MacKenzie?" he asked.

"Yes," I answered slowly. "What's this about?"

"Welfare check," he answered without preamble. "Apparently your parents haven't heard from you in more than two days, say they can't get ahold of you via phone or text or email, so they called the police station to send someone to check on you."

"Unbelievable," I breathed.

Bruce rubbed my back soothingly.

"As you can see, I'm fine," I told the officer.

The officer continued to study me. "Y'all been drinking?" he asked.

Bruce's hand stilled on the small of my back, and I heard the stiffness in his voice as he answered for us. "Yeah. We're here in our own home, aren't causing any trouble, aren't breaking any laws. Sarah's of age."

The officer nodded, surveying Bruce critically like he didn't like him or something, before he looked back at me. "You might want to call your folks, ma'am. They're worried about you. Everything looks fine to me here, though, so I'll leave y'all alone now. Have a good rest of your day."

"You too, officer," Bruce answered for us again before closing the door as the officer began to descend the porch.

I watched Bruce's hand fist on the windowsill where he stood watching the cop car until it pulled out of the driveway.

F—. Here we go, I thought. As if Bruce hadn't been

ranting about my parents enough already, it was only going to be amped up by a million.

"Mother f—!" he yelled as he turned from the window to face me once the cops were completely gone. "You've got to deal with this shit," he said, pointing at me sternly.

"What the f— am I supposed to do?!" I screamed back, frustrated beyond belief at both him and my parents. "It's not my fault!"

Bruce ignored me and went over to the counter to pour himself another drink. Likewise, I poured myself another one too and threw it back faster than I usually did drinks.

I zoned out while his ranting and raving increased. Bruce could go on and on and on when he got on something, and I was so tired of it.

"Sarah!" he finally barked at me, grabbing my arm harshly.

"Ow!" I cried out at his harsh grip. "What the hell, Bruce?"

I tried to yank my arm from his grasp, but he only tightened his hold more.

"Let go of me! You're hurting me!"

"Are you listening to a word I'm saying to you?" he glared down at me.

"How could I not? You won't f— shut up about it," I hissed at him, still trying to free my arm.

He finally sneered at me and flung me away from him. I staggered back, falling into the wall.

"What is wrong with you?" I asked, looking up at him in horror.

"Me?! Me?!" he roared before he swept his hand over

the counter, sending our glasses smashing to the floor, glass shattering. "There's not a damn thing wrong with me. It's your f— mom and dad! And you! You won't f— stand up for yourself or for us!"

"What do you want me to do, Bruce?" I was crying, completely overwhelmed at the situation and scared in the face of his anger.

"Call them!" he grabbed my cell phone and flung it at me. "Tell them to leave us the f— alone. If they can't act better than this, they don't deserve to be in your life! F—, Sarah, they called the cops on us! I can't stand seeing you let them steamroll over you like this. And they keep doing it because you keep letting them!"

I took my cell phone in one hand and pressed the button to dial Mom and Dad's home phone while I walked over to the counter and downed some more liquor.

I don't even remember everything I said to them. By the time Dad answered I was angry. Angry at Bruce, angry at them, and my anger was only fueled by the alcohol coursing through my veins.

I yelled at them for calling the cops just because I wouldn't talk to them. I told them how I felt like they were trying to control me. I ranted at them about how they were trying to put a wedge between Bruce and me and break us up. I spat every evil thing at them that Bruce was telling me to say. At some point when I was finally crying so many angry tears I couldn't see straight, Bruce grabbed the phone from me and started in on them himself.

He told them to leave me alone, to stay away from me, that they were killing me, that I'd never leave him so they might as well give it up, that he'd never let them control me. He cussed at them and said even worse things to them than I had.

I don't know what they said back because I wasn't listening to them. By the time Bruce snapped the phone shut and pulled me into a tight hug, I was shaking, fueled by rage like I'd never felt before.

"I'm so proud of you, babygirl," he encouraged me.

I clung to him and let him comfort him.

At least his anger wasn't directed at me anymore.

CHAPTER 15

AFTER THE CATASTROPHIC phone call to my parents, I drank until I blacked out. I remembered Bruce and I playing music loud and dancing and laughing wildly, but when I woke up the next morning, I had no recollection of how I'd gotten to bed.

I winced when I lifted my arm and looked down to find a nasty-looking bruise where Bruce had grabbed me the night before.

My back ached when I stood, and I lifted up my nightie and twisted to look at my back in the bathroom mirror. I saw a huge, bruised area on it. I guess it was from where Bruce had flung me into the wall. Other little marks dotted my arms and legs—ones I had no recollection of getting.

Bruce came into the bathroom while I was inspecting myself.

"Good morning, angel."

He looked at my bruised body and frowned before chuckling, "Damn, you partied hard last night, baby."

I glanced over at him but didn't say anything.

"You were so drunk you couldn't even stand up, baby," he went on. "I'm surprised you don't have more bruises than that on you. You've got to be more careful, babygirl."

"Yeah," I just agreed. I knew Bruce could be too rough with me when he was drinking, but I also knew how clumsy I was, so if he said I did all those myself, then surely, I did. Besides, it didn't really matter anyway, did it? Bruce would never hurt me when he was sober. If he got too rough when we were drinking, it was just because of the alcohol. It wasn't the real him.

I sat down in front of my computer while Bruce began making coffee.

I pulled up my email and, unsurprisingly, had a long email from my mom.

She basically railed at me for calling her when I was drunk last night. She went on to shame me for how I talked to them and how I let my husband talk to them. She talked about how disappointed they were in me and gave me guilt trip after guilt trip. Then, she went on to get preachy and started quoting the Bible to me.

I gave a humorless laugh and shook my head as Bruce brought me a cup of coffee filled with creamer just like I liked.

"Let me guess," Bruce said sarcastically, "an email from your mom?"

I simply turned the laptop to him by way of answer. I sipped my coffee, glancing at Bruce's face every so often, watching his eyes scan over Mom's scathing email. His mouth hardened into a thin line, and his eyes became more furious looking as they continued to sweep over the email.

"This is it," Bruce said as he pushed the laptop angrily

back over to me. "You're done talking to them. I'm not going to just sit by and watch them treat you this way."

"We already established that yesterday," I said dryly. "They didn't take that very well. Hence, this email." I motioned to the laptop screen.

"I don't give a flying f— how they took it!" He slammed his hand down on the countertop, and I jumped, startled by the sudden movement. Coffee splashed over the rim of my cup.

Bruce didn't seem to notice, though. He continued right on with his bitching and moaning.

"Bruce," I held up my hand to silence him, "whatever. I really don't want to talk about it anymore. I already told them to stay out of our lives. Let's just live our lives and not focus on them. I don't want to keep rehashing everything."

His nostrils flared for a moment, but then he took a deep breath and exhaled. He shook his head and picked up his own coffee cup to take a sip. "You're right, babygirl. I just get so angry reading the crap that your mom sends you. I just can't get over them, man."

"Well, I'm not talking to them anymore, so they can't spoil our fun anymore."

Bruce nodded and pulled a cigarette from his pack. I turned back to my laptop and navigated to the website where I worked when I had time. Granted, I hadn't done much work on there lately. I'd been busy drinking and hanging out with Bruce and spending time on the phone trying to keep my whole family placated. That was the good thing about my "job." Technically, I was considered self-employed, so I could just log in whenever I wanted to and pick from the available assignments. It was perfect for the type of lifestyle I lived with Bruce. I wasn't held back by a traditional nine to five, which meant I was available anytime he needed me for drinking or sex or whatever the hell he wanted to do.

And, of course, Bruce usually kept me too busy to find time to do any freelancing work.

I needed something to take my mind off everything today, though. Throwing myself into a bit of work and making some money would do my mind good.

"What are you doing, babygirl?" Bruce asked me from around the cigarette that was hanging out of his mouth. I watched as he lifted the lighter up and cupped his hands around the end of the smoke as he lit it.

"I'm going to try to do a little bit of work this morning. Haven't done any in forever." I didn't mention the part about how I was using work to get my mind off of all the crap with my parents. I certainly didn't want to get Bruce started on that subject again.

"Okay, babygirl," Bruce said. "I'm going to finish my coffee and then walk up to the store."

I knew what that meant. It meant Bruce was going on a cigarette and liquor run.

"What do you want me to get you, babygirl?"

"Why don't you just get us some wine to share?" I suggested. I was hoping that if I could convince Bruce to just drink wine that maybe he wouldn't get as volatile as he got when he drank hard liquor.

"Pinot Grigio?" he asked.

"Sure, whatever. You know I prefer white over red."

"You got it, angel," Bruce replied before he set off toward the bedroom to get dressed and leave.

I began scanning through the available topics and

picked a couple of orders that looked pretty easy to write. I also made sure to pick ones that were relatively short. I didn't like taking longer ones for two reasons: one, I might not have time to finish them before Bruce wanted me to do something with him and two, I didn't like it when I devoted a ton of time to a project and then it ended up getting rejected over some nit-picky stuff from the client. That had happened to me a couple of times before, and it really pissed me off. There was nothing more frustrating than spending a couple of hours on a high-paying piece only to have it rejected because it wasn't what the client was looking for. I had learned my lesson there, so now I always looked for smaller pieces that I could do more quickly. That way, if something didn't get accepted, it's not like I lost a crap ton of work.

I was already in the process of doing the preliminary research for my piece when Bruce emerged from the bedroom and started putting on his coat and shoes. I barely acknowledged him when he said goodbye and told me that he would be back soon. I was already getting deep into that writing mode, setting up the template for the order I was going to create.

I quickly became wrapped up in my work. They were easy, fun, little pieces. One was about how to choose house plants to complement your home. The other was about the history of the Metropolitan Opera House in New York. Easy to research, easy to write. And, most importantly, they took my mind off of my life and the drama between me, my husband, and my parents.

And by the time Bruce walked back through the door and I heard the clinking of wine bottles in his backpack, both of my orders had already been accepted. It was the first time I had made any money in weeks, and I was feeling particularly accomplished. Not like I had made a ton of money, but it felt good to do something productive again.

"I wrote two articles while you were gone," I told Bruce excitedly, "and they've both already been accepted!"

"That's great, baby," Bruce replied as he began pulling the wine bottles from his backpack. "We should celebrate."

"I want to try and do a couple more first," I told him, turning back to my laptop.

I heard Bruce uncapping the wine, and then I heard the gurgling of the alcohol being poured into the wine-glasses. "You don't want to burn yourself out though, baby."

He brought me over a glass of wine and held it out to me. "You've done good. Take a break and relax with me."

I sighed and then gave him a small smile. "I guess you're right."

He clinked his glass to mine in a toast, and then we both took a sip. My eyes flicked over to glance at the clock on the oven. It wasn't even noon yet, but hey, what the hell.

Like Bruce liked to say, we were adults and could do what we wanted. Since I wouldn't have to worry about talking to my family, I could go ahead and drink without worrying about somebody finding out about it.

And I had to admit that there was a kind of freedom in that. I was tired of always worrying about what my family would think or say.

Besides, I'd been doing better with my drinking than I

did in Florida. I wasn't going through intense shaking and all that. Everything would be fine.

Maybe Bruce was right about everything after all.

I was naive to think that simply drinking wine would be enough to keep Bruce's mind off of all the shit with my parents. He still ranted and raved about them and all the wrongs that they had done. It didn't help when Bruce was on my laptop selecting a music video and an email notification popped up in the bottom right-hand corner of my screen.

Of course, he clicked on it, and it was another nasty email from Mom. She said much the same stuff that she had said in her earlier email, but it only served to enrage Bruce even more — as if he needed any more of an excuse to gripe about my parents.

"Bruce!" I finally exploded at him. "I'm sick and tired of hearing you bitch and moan about my parents! God, I'm not talking to them anymore! What more do you want from me?"

Bruce stalked over to me and grabbed my arm, pulling me roughly from where I was sitting on the couch.

"I want you to see that what they're doing is wrong!" he roared at me.

"I do!" I screamed back at him, tears picking my eyes at the painful pressure of his fingers digging into my arm. "But what you're doing is wrong too. Let go of me! You're hurting me!"

Bruce looked down at where he was holding my arm

as if he just now realized that he was doing it. He released me and shook his head angrily. "This is all your parents' fault. They make us fight like this. This is their intention all along. They want to turn us against each other."

I instantly latched onto that explanation and desperately began to appeal to Bruce, "Then, don't let them. Let's not fight. Let's not talk about them. Let's not let them ruin our good time and what we have together. I just want to be with you. I just want us to be happy.

Bruce came over to me and began to pet where he had grabbed my arm. He stroked it soothingly, as if he was trying to rub away his previous harsh touch. "Every single time we fight, baby, it's because of them. I never mean to hurt you. You know I would never hurt you. They make me like this. And when I feel like you brush it all off and accept the way they treat you, that makes me angry too. But you know me. You know I would never purposefully hurt you."

"I know," I said softly. Maybe Bruce was right. Maybe every time we fought it was about my parents. I tried to think back on it, on the time he went to jail in Florida, but the alcohol was swirling through my veins, and I couldn't think clearly.

"It's all them," he went on. "It's always been them. They're the root of all of our problems. If they would just leave you alone, you and I would never fight. Things would be perfect between us."

I stared up at him, absorbing everything he was saying.

"They don't really care about you," he went on. "If they did, they would want you to be happy. They wouldn't try to control you. That's what it's always been about for them. Control. They act like it's me trying to control you, but it's not. It's them. They're trying to brainwash you against me, and they always have, and I can't take it anymore."

He looked at me seriously. "I hate them, Sarah. I hate them for what they've done to you. I hate them for what they're trying to do to us. You should hate them too."

"Bruce," I started, "they're still my pa—"

Bruce cut me off with, "I don't want to hear that shit! Are you listening to a f— word I'm saying to you?"

I shrank back from him and looked down.

"They don't f— love you. I am the only one who loves you. I am the only one you should care about. *Me*," he pointed to himself. "Your husband. You're the only woman I've ever really loved."

His jaw was set furiously, and I couldn't help trembling.

"You know you're the only man I've ever loved too," I told him.

Bruce scoffed. "What about Don?" He sneered at me now and looked at me with disgust. "You let him put his filthy hands on you."

"This again?" I asked in exasperation. "Bruce, he was my *boss*. I never asked for him to touch me, and it never went too far. I still can't believe after all this time and with you being the only man I've ever slept with you would even accuse me of something like that."

"And how do I know that all that time you were up here without me that your mommy and daddy weren't trying to set you up with some good little church boy?"

"Oh my God," I groaned, "my parents might not be

your biggest fan, but we *are* married, and they would never advocate for me committing adultery."

"I'm sure you wore plenty of makeup when you were up here on your own without me. Like you're looking for a man or something." He downed another huge gulp of his wine.

I just shook my head. "I thought we agreed we weren't going to let them win. If we keep fighting and turning on each other, then they're getting exactly what they want."

"Whatever. I don't give a f— anymore, Sarah. Do whatever you want. Talk to your parents if you want. Just don't tell me that you love me because it's obvious that you never did."

I watched helplessly as he walked over to the door and flung on his coat.

"Where are you going?" I asked him.

"Outside for a smoke and to get some damn fresh air," he answered before slamming the door so violently that the walls shook.

My shaky legs finally collapsed out from under me, and I plopped back down onto the couch. I reached out and grabbed my wine glass and quickly downed the last of its contents before I stood to go get myself a much-needed refill.

I didn't know what the hell to do. I couldn't make my parents happy. I couldn't make Bruce happy. It didn't seem like I could make anybody happy. I just wanted to forget. Forget all of it.

So, I tipped my newly filled wineglass back and took a huge gulp

And then another one.

I was miserable. That day began a chain of drinking and fighting with everyone in my life that I wouldn't be able to break for a long time.

My mom wouldn't let up with the emails. I woke up to one every day, and sometimes I got multiple ones throughout the day. When I got them when I was drunk, I gave in and would write her back, fighting with her. Bruce was right there at my shoulder, egging me on. He even got on the computer and wrote some stuff to her himself. He seemed to take great delight in virtually attacking my parents, actually cackling with glee and toasting to some of the supposedly witty things he said.

Bruce and I still fought too. The more he drank, the more he wanted to dwell on all the bad things and talk about them. The more he would blame me for all of it too. The only way to keep him halfway satisfied was for me to bash my parents too. It's like if we were attacking them together, we were on the same team, but if I ever showed any hesitance or—God forbid—defended them, then I became the enemy too.

I began to seek out that haze that only alcohol provided. I wanted to be numb to everything. So, I began drinking more and more. Sometimes, Bruce and I drank wine. Other times, he would buy the hard stuff because the effects were stronger and we didn't have to drink as much of it, which meant it was cheaper than buying wine.

It eventually got to the point where I began skipping my morning coffee and went straight to a shot when I woke up. Bruce just laughed and called me a true Scots-Irish lass.

Sometimes, all the alcohol made me sick. I would throw up, but then I would be able to go right back to drinking. Sometimes, the alcohol fueled my anger, and I would call my parents and tell them how much I hated them.

Sometimes, I would actually stand up to Bruce. We would argue, yelling at each other until he got physical with me, pushing me down, holding me down, throwing me down, grabbing me, pulling me by my hair if I tried to run into the bedroom and shut the door in his face. I can't even tell you everything that we argued about. My parents, Bruce's imaginings that I had wanted to be with other guys, me just getting pissed off at his shitty attitude. I mean, seriously, Bruce was always bitching and moaning about something. And his negativity just really got on my nerves sometimes, especially if I was buzzing and trying to listen to music and have a good time. He could be such a buzz kill and a downer. He seemed to enjoy fighting—if not with me, then with my parents or with one of his family members on the phone.

One morning I realized that it had been forever since I had talked to Addison, so I texted her just to see how everything was going and to say hi.

I didn't hear back from her that day, which wasn't really a big deal since I knew she was probably at work. However, when the next day rolled around and then the next and then the next and she still hadn't responded to my texts, I started to think that something was up.

Was she not talking to me because of my parents? What was going on? Whatever went down between me and Mom and Dad had nothing to do with my relationship with my best friend.

And it was obviously bothering me, so much so that when I started drinking, all my feelings about it would come out. I would cry and confide to Bruce, wondering what I had done wrong that she would ignore me like this.

Of course, Bruce was right there to take my side in the whole matter. He told me that, like my parents, Addison didn't really care anything about me. That if she did, she wouldn't cut me off without even giving me a reason why. He called her nothing but a little bitch and reminded me of how she had taken my parents' side before.

I finally sent Addison a text message telling her that I didn't know what I had done but that I didn't deserve for her to ignore me and I wish she would at least tell me why she wasn't talking to me.

That message came back undeliverable, which meant that she must've blocked me.

"See?" Bruce raised an eyebrow at me after I told him my message wouldn't send. "She's up your parents' ass. A bitch who doesn't care anything about you — just like I said."

I set my phone down and took a sip of wine, acting like it didn't bother me.

But it did.

Just like before when I had first run off with Bruce, nobody from my family was talking to me — no one but Grandma, that is.

It seemed like it didn't matter what I did, Grandma was always willing to talk to me. Not that I called her that often because she always used her sad grandma voice on me and told me that my parents loved me, always advocating for us all to get along. I tried to tell her a couple of times that it was them — not me — but in typical grandma fashion, she tended to take Dad's side.

So, when I called her, I usually just made our conversations brief. I mostly just called her to let her know that I was okay, and I knew she passed the word along to Mom and Dad, but I didn't really care about that. I refused to talk about them or ask how they were doing. At that point, I really and truly started to believe everything that Bruce said to me — that they didn't really care about me and just wanted to control me, and that they wanted to break up our marriage.

Bruce and I drank more and more, and even though I was no longer talking to my parents or even my best friend, we still somehow fought about my family. It seemed like all Bruce wanted to do was rehash all of the bad stuff. It's like he liked staying angry about something all the time. That got on my nerves, and when I had enough alcohol fueling my own anger, I would snap back at him, which usually resulted in him getting physical with me.

I would kick and scream and call him every vile name in the book while he held me down and did whatever he wanted to me.

It eventually got to the point where Bruce stopped apologizing for his actions. We would just wake up the next morning or sometimes in the middle of the night and start drinking like nothing had ever happened. The few times that I did confront Bruce about hitting me or holding me down and forcing me he would always gaslight me and say that I was drunk and I didn't remember correctly and that anything he did I made him do. That it was all my fault. Me and my family.

I drowned my sorrows in alcohol and music.

But I can't say that I was always sad. What kept me turning to alcohol time and time again was the way when I first started drinking, I would get this elated feeling of complete happiness. Nothing seemed to matter. The music hit different. The funny videos we watched made me happier than they normally did. Even our stupid little cooking shows and court shows were more enjoyable when I first started drinking.

But then as the day wore on, after I had been drinking all day long, by the time the evening came, that elated, happy feeling would be fading to be replaced by an emotional whirlwind. Sometimes I wouldn't be able to stop crying. Bruce didn't help because my tears only angered him, and then we would start fighting. It pissed him off to see me crying over my family. He thought I was weak for wanting anything to do with them after what they had done to us.

Other times, I would get so angry that I would call Mom and Dad in the middle of the night and leave mean messages on their answering machine. I can't even remember everything that I said. All I know is it wasn't nice.

I was blacking out every night again. And I didn't care. I didn't care about anything. I didn't care about trying to work and make a little bit of money anymore. I just lived from day to day, taking whatever happiness I could find at the beginning of my binge every day and then spiraling down into blackness every night.

Through it all, I kept telling myself that Bruce was all

I needed. In those tender moments in the mornings when we were just starting drinking, he would hold me and reaffirm to me how much he loved me.

By the time the end of the day rolled around and we were both soused and fighting, we blamed it all on the alcohol and my parents.

Bruce didn't mean to hit me. Bruce didn't mean to hurt me. It was my fault. For having the kind of parents that I did. For not keeping him happy. I made him angry. I made him do it. He didn't want to do it. But sometimes I brought out the worst of him.

Because he loved me so much.

CHAPTER 16

I REFUSED to take Mom and Dad's calls when they called. I still called my grandma every day or two just so no one would be able to say that they hadn't heard from me and have an excuse to send the cops to our house to do a welfare check.

Everything all came to a head one afternoon, though. Bruce and I had been drinking all day, and while I wasn't totally lambasted yet, as in I wasn't blacked out and still knew what was going on, I was definitely buzzing and probably considered drunk.

There was a knock at the door. Bruce was in the bathroom, so I went over and cracked open the door just a peek to see who was there.

It was Mom and Dad.

I scoffed and rolled my eyes, disbelieving that they would just show up like this. Though why I found that hard to believe considering everything that they had done since I'd met Bruce I didn't know.

I started to slam the door in their faces, but Dad stuck

his foot in the way. "We just want to talk to you, Sarah," Dad said.

"I don't want to fight with y'all," I retorted back.

"We don't want to fight with you either," Mom chimed in. "We just wanted to come and make sure you're okay."

"Can we just come in and talk?" Dad asked.

By that time, Bruce had come out of the bathroom, and I felt him looking at me from over the kitchen counter. I glanced over at him, realizing that he had heard some of what had gone down so far, and he nodded at me, silently giving his permission for Mom and Dad to enter our house.

I stepped back to allow them to enter. I saw both of their eyes immediately flick over to the counter where my open vodka bottle was sitting. My shot glass with half a shot was still sitting there too. Bruce had only been drinking beer that day, but all his beer must have been in the fridge because none of his were sitting out.

I crossed my arms and stared at them. This was my house. There was no need for me to hide what I was doing. It wasn't against the law for me to drink in my own home. I was of legal age.

"We knew you were drinking again," Dad said.

"It's not a crime to drink, Dad," I said sarcastically.

"How can you live like this?" Mom asked disbelievingly.

Although my parents had briefly glanced over at Bruce, I noticed that they hadn't said a word to him. Likewise, he just leaned against the wall, watching our exchange silently.

I latched onto that. "What? So, you're just going to

ignore my husband? You waltz into his house and don't even acknowledge him? How rude are you?"

I saw my dad's jaw tense as he glanced over at Bruce and nodded in greeting. Mom didn't say a word.

"No, it's okay, Sarah," Bruce said cordially. "They were just busy talking to you."

I glanced over at Bruce, wondering what his game was. He hated them. Now he was acting like he was okay with them? "No, it's not okay. They were being rude to you," I ground out from in between clenched teeth.

"Babygirl, it's really okay," Bruce said. "I don't think they meant anything by it. Let's not fight with your parents. Since they're here, talk to them."

I stared at him in disbelief. "Why? What do I have to say to them? They've made our lives hell, and then they just want to show up here without even having the decency to call first."

"How have we made your lives hell?" Mom snorted. "We never see you or talk to you, so how can we be doing anything to you?"

"How about by calling the cops on me!" I screamed at her. "Or how about harassing me every single f— day with emails telling me how I'm going to burn in hell for all of my sins, telling me what a bad daughter I am? You call that doing nothing?"

"This," Dad said, picking up my vodka bottle and going to the sink with it, "this is what is making your life hell. Not us. We're trying to help you."

He tipped the bottle up and proceeded to pour it all out down the sink.

That incensed me.

I immediately flew into a rage. "Don't pour my shit

out! What gives you the right? You can't just barge in here and take over and tell me what to do!"

"Sarah, we're trying to help you!" Mom screamed.

"No, you're trying to control me! That's all you've ever done!"

Mom gave a humorless laugh. "Control you? How can we control you when we never see you or talk to you?"

"You know exactly what you do," I hissed at her, the alcohol coursing through my veins only fueling my anger and making me bolder than I would normally ever be in an argument with them.

"What do we do," Dad asked, "other than want to see you happy and healthy?"

"I am happy!" I lied. "And it's none of your business anyway. For God's sake, will you just let me live my life!"

My hands were beginning to shake, and my breathing became shallower. My chest heaved up and down as I brought my trembling hands up to grip either side of my head. I was completely overwhelmed, panicking, like I couldn't contain the flood of emotions running through me. Anger, anxiety, desperation, and helplessness all flooded my system, causing me to short circuit.

"It's too much," I gasped out. "I can't please any of you. I might as well just f— kill myself," I mumbled. I don't know why I said that. I was certain I didn't mean the words. They were just spoken in the heat of the moment. I wasn't suicidal.

But that erroneous, dramatic statement sent my parents over the top. They shared a worried glance before Dad started walking over toward me slowly with his hand held out like I was holding a gun or something. "You don't want to do that, Sarah. Everything's going to be fine. We're going to get you the help you need."

Out of the corner of my eye, I saw Mom on the phone. Her lips were moving, and her eyes kept flicking over to me frantically, but I couldn't make out what she was saying.

Bruce was still leaning against the wall, his hands crossed over his chest, silently watching as it all played out. Why wasn't he stepping in to defend me? Why wasn't he helping me? He was just going to let them come in here and attack me like this?

Everything started to blur as I looked between all of them: Mom, Dad, and my husband. Mom and Dad's lips were moving, but their voices were garbled and incomprehensible to me, kind of like in the movies when the voices slow down and deepen for that special effect.

I shook my head and tried to focus, and the next thing I knew a police officer was there, towering over me.

His lips were moving, and I finally started coming back down to earth enough to make out the tail-end of what he was saying. "Your parents said you threatened to kill yourself."

I shook my head, "No, I didn't mean that. They're overdramatic and overreacting. I'm fine."

The officer looked down at me critically as if he was trying to assess for himself. "I'm not suicidal!" I adamantly added.

In my peripheral, I saw another police officer talking to Bruce, and I calmed somewhat. He would tell them. He would tell them I wasn't suicidal.

"Did you say anything about killing yourself?" The officer asked me.

Damn me and my penchant for honesty because I didn't even think about how I should deny the accusation. "I did," I admitted. "But I would never really do anything like that!" I rushed to add. "My parents, they're just so pushy, and they overwhelmed me, and I couldn't think straight. I didn't know what I was saying."

The officer's brows furrowed in concern. "You didn't know what you were saying?"

Oh, f—. That made it sound like I was crazy. "I'm not crazy, officer. I'm fine. I just need them to go away and leave me alone!"

The officer switched tactics then, asking me if I could show him my ID. I turned to where my purse was sitting on the table and began to dig through it.

While I was engaged in my menial task, I saw the two officers conferring amongst themselves, and then they spoke to my parents. Again, Bruce was on the outside looking in, like a bystander watching all the drama unfold. He was my husband. If the police should be reporting to anyone, it should be him, but I guess since it was Mom and Dad who called them, they didn't see it that way.

I finally succeeded in locating my ID and held it out to the officer as both officers made their way back over to me. He took it and barely glanced it, which let me know they must not have ever really needed it in the first place. It had all been a diversion to keep me calm and occupied while they spoke to everyone in the room about me but me.

"Miss MacKenzie, will you please put your hands behind your back?" the officer delivered the edict stoically.

"What?" I was shocked, confused, and then outraged. "You're arresting me? What for? I haven't done anything! I haven't broken any laws!"

"We're not arresting you," he replied calmly while his backup officer stood beside him in case I tried anything. I almost snorted. Yeah right. Like I would be a match against one officer—much less two. "We're just going to transport you to the hospital for a psychiatric evaluation."

"But I'm not crazy!" I said desperately. God, I did not want to have to go to the hospital. I just wanted everyone to leave, and then I wanted to continue drinking with Bruce. I wanted him to hold me and tell me everything would be okay. I wanted us to still be in Florida. I wanted us to have never moved back up here.

"It's just standard procedure when someone threatens suicide, ma'am," he tells me robotically.

"But I didn't—"I cut myself off with a groan of frustration before I said with clenched teeth. "I am not suicidal."

"If you don't cooperate, we will have to arrest you," he warned.

I looked beyond the officers over to Bruce. His eyes were hard, his lips pressed into a grim line, but he gave me a subtle nod, telling me I had to cooperate.

So, with tears streaming down my face, I put my hands behind my back and felt the grip of strong hands as they placed me in handcuffs.

I was behind handcuffed again. Like I was nothing more than a common criminal. And seeing as how I'd been convicted of a crime in Florida, I guess I was.

Only this time I really didn't do anything.

I glared at Mom and Dad as the police officers led me past them, hate simmering within me. I'd told them I hated them before when I called them in drunken rages, but I'd never really felt it the way I did in that moment.

I never wanted to see them again.

Of course, that wasn't going to happen, though. The officer drove me to the hospital and escorted me into the ER in handcuffs. I didn't notice any curious looks from the staff, so maybe they were used to people being brought into the emergency room in handcuffs.

It was humiliating, though, but I was beyond caring what they thought. They didn't know me, and all I cared about was getting out of there and going home.

One thing I'll say for being escorted into the ER by a police officer is that it was the fastest way to get priority treatment. I was immediately taken to an open room instead of having to sit around in the waiting room for two hours like the poor folks out front who'd driven themselves to the hospital.

It was really rather ridiculous. Here I was getting the royal treatment of getting to skip line and go first, and there wasn't anything wrong with me. What if there was someone out there in that waiting room who really needed treatment and here they were prioritizing me and wasting time on me because of my parents' overprotective, overbearing, overdramatic bullshit?

The nurse immediately drew blood and had me strip down and put on a hospital gown. I felt a ball of dread settle in the pit of my stomach when they asked me to change into a gown like I would be settling in for a good, long stay.

I was still buzzing from all the alcohol I had dunk that day, and I was restless as I lay there in the bed with a blanket over me. I just wanted to go home. I just wanted to be with Bruce. I just wanted to have another drink and forget all of this. My anger simmered again when I thought of my parents and how this was all their fault. So these were the lengths they would go to now? They would have me committed into a hospital against my will. That right there should be against the law.

The door opened and the nurse walked back in. Followed by my parents.

Oh hell no.

"What are they doing here?"

The nurse looked between me and my parents, though she didn't look surprised. I guess she already been apprised of the situation beforehand.

I didn't give a f—. I didn't want to see them. My fists balled at my sides. "I don't want them here," I said vehemently.

"Sarah, we just —" Dad began, but I cut him off.

"I don't want you here," I said more firmly, speaking directly to them.

The nurse nodded toward the door. "You can wait outside. I'll have the doctor speak with you when he comes in."

"About that," I began, "I don't even need to see a doctor. See, this is all one big misunderstanding. I shouldn't even be here. I'm here against my will."

"Why don't we just let the doctor take a look at you and see what he says?" the nurse said kindly, but I was having none of it.

It suddenly struck me that they couldn't hold me here against my will, could they?

No, they couldn't. I was fairly certain of it. So, with new confidence, I stood and started heading for the door.

"Miss?" The nurse questioned me uncertainly. "Please, you need to get back in the bed and wait for the doctor."

I ignored her and opened the door, clutching the back of the gown together to try to keep everyone from seeing my naked ass. I didn't know where my clothes had gone, and frankly I didn't care. I only had one thought on my brain. Getting out of there.

I didn't know which way I was going, but I started hurrying down the hall. I didn't even really know what my game plan was. I was just trying to get out of the building, and then I would take it from there. Maybe I could find some kind stranger to hitch a ride with back to my house. I didn't live very far from the hospital anyway. It would be maybe a five- to ten-minute drive.

I heard the nurse's frantic voice behind me, though I didn't register what she said. My parents must have spotted me as well because I thought I heard their voices saying something like, "She's getting away!"

The voices were shortly followed by strong footsteps, and then the police officer who had brought me in suddenly stepped around me and filled my line of vision.

"Miss MacKenzie, I'm going to have to ask you to go back to your room and cooperate with the hospital staff," his tone was firm, and it was clear he wasn't asking me to do anything. He was telling me.

I glared up at him. What was he still doing here? He had dropped me off. I thought he was gone.

With more bravery than I felt, I lifted my chin and

retorted, "I don't want to be here. You can't keep me here against my will. I haven't broken any laws. In fact, I think *you're* the one breaking the law."

The officer stared down at me stonily. "When you threaten to harm anyone — including yourself — we have reason to arrest you. At your parents urging, we brought you here instead. But if you don't cooperate, I'll have no choice but to take you in."

My heart fluttered within my chest at the threat in his words. I knew that it wasn't an idle threat either. This police officer would arrest me in a heartbeat. My mind ran back to the time I was arrested in Florida, and I gave an involuntary tremble. I never wanted to relive that horrible, humiliating situation again.

I tried not to let my shoulders slump as I turned and walked back toward the room they had placed me in, the officer right on my heels for in case I made any sudden movements to flee.

"I'll be standing right out here," he warned as he stationed himself right beside the outside of my door.

My face heated as I walked back into the hospital room and climbed into the bed. Unbelievable. There was a police officer standing right outside my room like I was a criminal to be guarded.

A sense of frustration and helplessness overtook me as I realized I had no say in any part of my life anymore. I could tell my parents to stay away from me, but they wouldn't. I didn't have a driver's license anymore, so I couldn't just get in a car and take off anywhere I wanted to. And now I was being forced into medical treatment that I didn't want — or need.

I crossed my arms and fumed at my circumstances

while I sat there impatiently waiting for the doctor to come in so we could get this over with. I knew I had to act fine and tell him whatever he needed to hear so that he would agree to let me go. Even when they did just discharge me, I wasn't sure how I would get home, but I was sure it wouldn't be a problem. One thing at a time. I just had to get out of there.

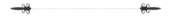

I may have been put into a room fast, but that didn't mean that getting a doctor into the room went any faster than normal. After my blood was drawn, I sat there for what seemed like forever waiting for the physician to enter and give his verdict. I didn't have a phone or watch on, and there was no clock anywhere in the room I was placed in. In fact, the room I was in was suspiciously bare. It was devoid of a computer and all the other hospital equipment that was usually found in ER rooms.

My lips thinned as I realized I'd been placed in a psychiatric room. I was surprised they didn't have padded walls to make sure I didn't bash my brains out against the brick.

I shivered and tucked the blanket closer around me. I noticed that my hands were starting to shake in that way that they did when the alcohol was starting to leave my body.

I desperately needed to get back home and have another drink. Bruce was right. My parents were nothing but trouble. They were trying to control me. Just look where I was.

Finally, the doctor entered the room followed by the

female nurse who had been attending to me ever since I'd arrived. He was a middle-aged man who introduced himself kindly enough, but he quickly turned clinical when he started reading off my chart.

I vaguely recall him saying something about how high my blood alcohol content level was. I noticed his shrewd eyes as they assessed my shaking hands, so I quickly grasped them together in my lap to try to stop the tremors.

I admitted that I'd been drinking but commented that that wasn't a crime and that I was fine.

As the doctor sat on the rolling stool and rolled over to feel my neck and wrists, he continued to question me.

"Have you ever been hospitalized for alcohol abuse before?"

I narrowed my eyes at him. "You've been talking to my parents, haven't you?"

"They said they took you to the hospital in Florida several months ago when you were extremely intoxicated," he stated matter-of-factly.

"I wasn't hospitalized," I pointed out. "They let me go home."

"Have you ever tried to kill yourself before?" he asked me candidly.

"I swear," I muttered under my breath.

"I am not suicidal," I reiterated for what felt like the millionth time that day.

"They said you threatened to kill yourself," he said as he placed his stethoscope against my chest to listen to my heartbeat.

"It was not like that at all. I didn't mean that. My parents can take anything out of context," I told him.

"Look," I told him frankly, "I just want to go home. I shouldn't be here."

The doctor hung his stethoscope back around his neck before sitting back and studying me. His eyes flicked to my arms that were littered with bruises. "Do you mind sitting up for me?" he asked me gently.

I didn't know what for, but I didn't think to ask either. I simply obeyed and lifted my back off of the bed a bit. I was already reclining in a halfway sitting position.

I felt cool air on the exposed skin of my back, which the doctor must've been looking at because the next words out of his mouth were, "Where did you get these bruises all over your arms and back?"

I shrugged. "I fall a lot when I drink."

"Are you married?" he asked.

My brows furrowed, already sensing where he was going with this. "Yes," I answered simply, not giving any more than what was required.

"You mind if I have a look at your legs?" the doctor asked and then began moving the sheet away without even waiting for my answer.

"Like I said," I looked at him evenly, "I fall a lot when I drink."

The doctor appraised me shrewdly, and I ended up breaking eye contact first, looking down at my hands. I didn't like the way his eyes seemed to pierce right through me, like he didn't believe me or something.

Thankfully, he didn't push the issue. Instead, he switched tactics. "And how often do you drink?"

I shrugged, "I don't know. Often enough, I guess."

"Well, your blood alcohol content level suggests that you drink more than just every now and then."

The same words the doctor in Florida had said.

"Is there anything that you want to tell me?" I looked back up at the doctor's kind gaze. When my eyes met his, he went on gently, "You're safe here. You can tell us anything that's going on."

My heart began to thump loudly in my chest. They thought Bruce was abusing me. That's what it sounded like they were implying, at least. Why did everyone always think that? Because of the bruises on me? I bruised easily. I always had.

Besides, even though Bruce was responsible for some of the bruises, he didn't mean it. He would never purposefully hurt me. And it's not like he punched me or anything. And I knew that I was clumsy. When he told me I fell down a lot when I drank, I'm sure it was true. How could I remember what happened when I blacked out? Didn't it make sense that I would be stumbling and falling over drunk when I was blacked out?

"There's nothing going on. I just want to go home," I stressed.

The doctor shook his head. "I'm afraid I can't discharge you just yet. I'd like to see your vitals improve before I release you."

My heart plummeted within me. "But I don't want to be here," I stated.

"Why don't you let us hook you up to some fluids and get you to eat something and then we'll go from there?" the doctor suggested.

I had a strange sense of déjà vu from my time at the hospital back in Florida. Only I knew that this time there was no way in hell I was going to be letting my parents take me anywhere.

I nodded my head to give my consent. The sooner I let them do what they wanted to do the sooner I would be out of there.

"I'm also going to send somewhere in to ask you a few questions."

"What kind of questions?" I asked suspiciously.

"Just answer them as honestly as you can," he prodded. "There are no right or wrong answers.

With that cryptic statement, he left the room, and the nurse began feeding an IV needle into me. Then, she left for a few minutes and returned with a tray of hospital food.

My stomach turned at the thought of eating it, but I forced myself to take a bite of the dry sandwich, knowing they wouldn't discharge me until they felt I'd sufficiently eaten.

And at that moment, my number one goal was to get the hell out of there.

Although I was freezing, sweat broke out on my brow as I forced myself to take the last bite of the sandwich. I tried to shovel down some of the jello too.

No sooner had I pushed the hospital tray of food away from me did the door open and a woman with a clipboard walk-in. She introduced herself kindly enough and then proceeded to ask me a bunch of mental health questions.

Was I depressed? Honestly, I probably was, but there was no way in hell I was going to tell them that. Because they would just read way too much into it and then conclude that I was suicidal.

How was my relationship with my husband? Did I ever fear for my life? Did I have thoughts of harming myself? Did I feel like everyone was out to get me? Was I always looking over my shoulder? Had I ever done drugs? On and on the questions went, and many of them were repetitive, like they were trying to trip me up or something.

I tried to answer as calmly and patiently as I could, though my patience was quickly wearing thin. The food I had forced myself to eat was like a leaden weight in my stomach, and I felt like I could barf at any moment.

I was relieved when the woman finally left, but then I was stuck in another long, torturous wait for the doctor to come back and discharge me.

I should have known that with my luck it wouldn't be that easy.

CHAPTER 17

THE DOCTOR CAME BACK ALRIGHT — but not to discharge me. The asshole said that he wanted to keep me overnight for observation— that it was standard procedure to put anyone who had threatened to kill himself under suicide watch for the night, which basically meant that I had been tricked. The damned doctor knew from the get-go that he wasn't going to release me, but he'd been feeding me his "do this and we'll see's" to get me to comply with his demands.

I balked and protested of course, but one glance at the police officer still standing guard outside my door let me know that it was either this or they'd haul my ass to jail. As much as I hated the thought of having to be in this hospital for a moment longer, it was much better than the alternative.

My parents were waiting outside the room as they began to roll me out on the hospital bed I was still sitting on.

"We'll be right here waiting for you in the morning, honey," Mom said, looking grave and worried.

I bit back my instinctual retort to tell them both to go to hell and instead asked them if they would call Bruce and let him know what was going on.

They glanced at each other before nodding. If anyone was going to be here with me all night, it should be my husband — not them.

Once again feeling like I had had all of my choices and free will taken from me, I was transported up to the fifth floor — a.k.a. the psychiatric ward, like I was a nut job or something.

As it turns out, I wasn't allowed to have any visitors up on that floor. Seeing as how it was nighttime, I guess it didn't matter anyway.

I was still hooked up to an IV and was given fluids all night. A blood pressure cuff was constantly on my arm as well as a pulse oximeter to constantly monitoring my vitals like I was at death's door or something.

I couldn't sleep, and every time I had to go to the bathroom, I had to push the button for a nurse to come help me to the restroom since I was hooked up so much equipment.

I daresay it was the longest night of my life — other than maybe the time I went to jail. I desperately wanted to sleep so that I would just wake up in the morning and it would all be over with, but that wasn't happening. I'd been drinking alcohol for too long, and I was suffering from insomnia. The little bit of dozing that I did was riddled with hallucinogenic dreams. They weren't exactly nightmares, but the nature of them filled me with terror anyway. In them, everything was either freakishly big or I was dreaming that I was awake when I wasn't. Nothing was right, and I kept feeling like I was falling. I woke up alternately in cold sweats or burning up. At one point I even yanked the IV out of my hand during one of them, and the nurse had to come in and reinsert it in the other hand.

Surely, they would have to release me in the morning. They couldn't keep me here forever. I just wanted to go home and be with Bruce and forget about all of this.

And I swore that I was finally done with my parents. They had gone too far this time.

Thankfully, there was a clock in the room I was placed in, so I was able to stare at it every time I woke up from a torturous dose. I willed the hands to move faster.

As the early morning hours finally rolled around, the doctor from the night before finally came in.

"Good morning," he greeted me jovially.

I glared at him, not in the mood for his bullshit, so I cut straight to the chase, "Are you going to let me go home now?"

"Yes," he told me frankly as he came over with his stethoscope to manually check me. I don't know why he was going through all those motions when I was hooked up to every machine on the planet to monitor my vitals, but he was the doctor so whatever. "You get to go home today after you speak with someone from our counseling center."

"Great," I mumbled while rolling my eyes.

I felt a prick of conscience when he ignored my bad manners and continued treating me cordially and professionally.

This wasn't me. This rude, irritated girl, but I was so over my parents' crap.

"It's important that you drink plenty of water in the

coming week," the doctor told me. He rattled off some more instructions about eating healthy and cutting down on the drinking before he finally smiled at me again.

"Thank you," I said softly. It wasn't his fault that I was here — it was my parents'. He was just doing his job.

He smiled at me again and squeezed my arm before he left the room, leaving me to wait for the counselor to come in. My last step to getting back home to my husband.

The counselor was younger than I expected her to be. She was definitely older than me by at least 10 years, but she was younger than my parents. She had big brown eyes that were soft and caring.

If I thought that she was just going to ask me the same typical mental health questions that the lady had last night, I was wrong. Her psychiatric exit interview was nothing like that.

She started off introducing herself and telling me about the counseling center where she worked and how they were always available to talk or whatever. She also reiterated the fact that she was not judging me and didn't assume that I was suicidal or had mental issues just because I was on the fifth floor of the hospital, that this was just standard procedure that they had to go through. I had to admit that her frank, kind manner put me at ease and made me feel better about everything.

Instead of asking me a series of mental health questions, she asked me about the events leading up to why I was there.

At first, I tried to answer as minimally as possible, but at her gentle prompts, I found everything spilling out of me.

"It's my parents," I said. "I'm married to a man much older than me — thirty-four years older than me to be exact. He's older than both of my parents, and they just can't get over that. They're always trying to break us up. They tried to get along with him for a while when I lived in Florida, but I know that was just because they wanted to come see me. Ever since we moved back up here so that I could be closer to them, things have just gotten worse and worse. There's always this strife between them and my husband, and I'm the one stuck in the middle."

I peeked up at her, and she nodded sympathetically, so I continued, "My husband and I drink. But my parents don't believe in drinking at all. They go to church, and they were always strict when I was growing up, and I just feel so overwhelmed sometimes. Like they're trying to control me. I'm here because they just showed up at our house out of the blue and when they came in, my dad took it upon himself to pour out my liquor, and he had no right to do that. I mean, even if I drink too much sometimes, I'm an adult and that's none of their business."

The counselor adjusted her glasses that were perched on the end of her nose before asking me gently, "And your husband? How is your relationship with him?"

"I love him," I admitted, "and he loves me. All of our fights lately are always about my parents. He doesn't like the way they stress me out, and he wants me to stand up for myself, but when I do, this is what happens," I splayed my arms out to gesture toward the hospital room I was sitting in.

She then went on to talk to me about the drinking and about the DUI. Apparently, all that was in my file, which let me know she had spoken to my parents before she spoke to me.

"My husband and I just drink to have fun," I hedged.

"Do you think you have a drinking problem?" She asked me.

I looked at her, trying to detect a hint of judgment but found none.

I shook my head "No, but I'll admit that sometimes I do drink to escape everything."

"And your husband," she began, "he doesn't hit you or abuse you in any way?"

I looked away from her as I answered, "No, he loves me. He would never hurt me."

I knew that if I told her about how he sometimes got physical with me and called me names or yelled at me that she would misconstrue that as abuse. He never did any of that when he was sober. It was only when we were drinking. And to be fair, I lost my temper when I was drinking too and called him names back.

At the end of our conversation, she sat back and pulled her glasses from her nose. "I don't think you're suicidal," she told me, and my heart leapt within me, gratified to see that at least one person believed me.

"I just think that you're very stressed out by this dynamic between your parents and your husband. And if you ever need someone to talk to, you can call me." She slid her card onto the table next to me before going on, "You're a beautiful girl, and you are in control of your life. You're smart, and you can do anything that you want, and if you ever want to talk about your goals or if you need help, you can call us."

She paused before adding her last statement, "And

I'm not saying that this is going on, so please don't take this the wrong way. I'm just required to say this as part of my job. If you ever do find yourself in an abusive situation, we have plenty of resources to help you get out. If you feel like you can't go to your parents, if you feel like you can't go to the cops, if you ever need anything, all you have to do is call us. We will help get you out," she promised.

My throat suddenly felt tight, and my eyes pricked with tears, but I quickly blinked them away, unwilling to show any emotion. I don't know why I was suddenly getting so emotional. This woman was a stranger, yet she wasn't judging me. She just listened to me. She heard me.

I simply nodded before asking tentatively, "Will I be able to go home now?"

She nodded before saying, "I'm just going to have a chat with your parents. They're waiting outside the door. I'm sure the nurse will be in here soon to unhook you from the IV so that you can get dressed."

"Thank you," I told her—and I actually meant it.

While the counselor was gone, the nurse did come in. She unhooked me from all the medical equipment. She also gave me my clothes so that I could put them on. I was thankful to get out of that dreadful hospital gown. The nurse told me to hold tight while she went and drew up my discharge paperwork.

When the counselor came back in the door, she was trailed by my parents.

"The nurse will be in here soon with your discharge

papers. Once you sign them, you're good to go," she told me.

I thanked her again, and then she took her leave, leaving me alone in the room with Mom and Dad. I glanced at them and then looked away. They looked about as comfortable as I felt. Dad's shoulders were stiff as he shifted on his feet. Mom's lips were a thin line as she regarded me.

I wasn't going to be the first one to break the silence, so I waited for them to speak.

Dad stuffed his hands in his pockets before he finally spoke, "Well, I don't know what you said to that woman, but she seems to be under the impression that we are the root of all your problems."

Mom placed a hand on Dad's arm, and I looked away from him again. I certainly wasn't in the mood to argue with them. I just wanted to get out of there. "Did you call Bruce?" I asked.

"Yes," Mom answered.

"Well?" I asked. "Why isn't he here?"

"He didn't want to come," Mom replied back. To her credit, she delivered that statement stoically with no menace or emotion at all.

I looked down, a world of emotions going through me. So, I had to spend the night in the hospital and my husband couldn't even be bothered to come? I don't know why I was surprised, though. He hadn't even been bothered to come pick me up from jail when I was arrested. It hurt more than I cared to admit, the knowledge that if he was ever in the hospital for anything I would have stayed there all night whether I was allowed in the room or not, yet he wouldn't do the same.

"Why are y'all here?" I asked them.

"We've been here all night," Mom answered. "You're our daughter. Do you think we would leave you here all alone?"

Hearing her say that hurt even more. I heard the implication in her words — that they were there for me when Bruce wasn't.

But then I reminded myself that I wouldn't have even been there at all had it not been for them.

Thankfully, the nurse returned then with the papers for me to sign. I quickly signed them and then stood to begin leaving. She stayed me, however, telling me that she would be right back with a wheelchair to wheel me out.

I scoffed, "That's not necessary. I can totally walk on my own."

"It's hospital policy," she informed me, so with a sigh, I sat back down and waited for her to go get a wheelchair.

When she returned with the wheelchair, she glanced at my parents, telling them, "One of you can go down and pull your vehicle around to the front entrance. That's where I'll be taking her."

"I just need to call a cab or something," I told the nurse, not even looking at my parents. I had no plans of getting into a car with them.

I heard Dad huff a frustrated sigh, but Mom is the one who spoke. "We're just going to drive you back to your house, Sarah," Mom said with a hint of irritation in her voice.

"How do I know you're not really going to take me hostage at your house?" I asked bitterly.

"You have my word we're going to take you wherever

you want to go," Dad said, frowning at my distrust in them. But could anyone really blame me?

"I'm only supposed to discharge you if you have a ride home," the nurse chimed in, her eyes flicking between all of us questioningly.

Well, that seemed to settle it. I looked down at the floor, and Dad took that as the acquiescence that it was. He went ahead of us to go get the car and pull it around to the front entrance. Mom walked beside the nurse and me.

I hated being wheeled into the elevator and through the hallways like I was an invalid or something.

I got into the backseat of the car, and Mom got into the front passenger seat. I saw my dad glance at me in the rearview mirror. "I assume you want us to take you back to your place?"

I nodded without speaking.

Mom and Dad shared a glance, but neither of them spoke either.

Thankfully, the ride from the hospital to where I lived with Bruce was relatively short. None of us spoke during that time until we started pulling up the driveway when Dad offered, "You know you can always come home with us anytime you want."

I pressed my lips together to keep myself from saying something smart-alecky when I was so close to being home and simply nodded to let him know that I heard him.

When he finished pulling up the driveway, I hopped out of the car when it had barely stopped, not even taking the time say another word to them.

I marched up the porch steps and entered the

unlocked door, firmly closing and barricading myself inside.

"Angel princess!" Bruce greeted me as I pressed my back against the door and stared at him. He was dressed in a pair of navy-blue jogging pants and a white under-shirt. It was still early, and it didn't appear he had been drinking. However, I saw the smoke curling up from a lit cigarette in the ashtray on the coffee table. "Thank god you're okay!" He said as he came over and tried to wrap me in a hug.

I held up my hands and pushed against his chest when he reached me, unwilling to submit to his embrace.

Instead, I let my anger engulf me as I hissed at him "Where the fuck were you?"

I saw the momentary surprise flit across Bruce's face before he quickly recovered and masked it. I don't think I had ever refused his embrace before, and I'm sure he was realizing the same thing as he stepped back from me with his hands held up in surrender.

"What do you mean where was I? I've been right here waiting to hear something about you. I've been worried sick, babygirl." The lines in his forehead creased as if it pained him to think about it.

I wasn't buying it, though. I snorted and crossed my arms as I looked at him. "You couldn't have been too worried if you couldn't even make it to the hospital to be there with me."

His brow furrowed as he said, "I called the hospital trying to find out whatever I could about you, angel. I couldn't get anyone to tell me anything. Do you know how that made me feel? My wife was in the hospital, and there wasn't a f— thing I could do about it?"

"My parents called you," I accused him. "They said you didn't want to come."

Understanding seemed to dawn on his face, and he shook his head and cursed under his breath before saying, "I can't believe them." When he turned his eyes back up to me, they were smoldering with fury. "They did *not* call me, angel."

"But," I said with confusion, "they made it sound like they called you, like they offered to get you and you just didn't want to come."

"Oh yeah," Bruce's nostrils flared. "I'm sure they f— did." He turned to where his cigarette was burning away in the ashtray and snuffed it out since it was pretty much gone anyway before he yanked another one from the pack laying on the coffee table. "No," he said as he placed the cigarette between his lips and held the lighter up to light it, "they did not call me. Nobody would give me an update on *my* wife. I've been sitting here like a f— chump waiting for any word, worried half to death, and then you come home, and I find out you've been fed all these lies. Do you believe me now? Do you see the lengths that your parents will go to try to tear us apart? That they would lie to you like this..." He trailed off as he took a drag on his cigarette and shook his head.

"Wow," I exhaled a disbelieving breath.

"Yeah," Bruce said, cutting his eyes up to me.

"I never thought my parents would lie to me like that," I frowned.

"I don't know why you're so surprised," Bruce spit out bitterly. "They've made it abundantly clear they'll justify anything they want to do concerning you if they get you away from me. Do you remember how they basically kidnapped you when we first met? Why are you so surprised they would lie to you?"

I just shook my head and continued to lean against the door, taking it all in.

"And now, they've made you out to be a nut job and had you carted off to the hospital. Mark my words, Sarah, if they could have you committed in an insane asylum to get you away from me, they would."

I looked at Bruce with horror, thinking of being locked away in a mental ward. As much as I hated to admit it, what he said rang true. There were no lengths my parents wouldn't go to if they thought they were "protecting me."

"I still can't believe they would do something like that," I was talking about how they'd lied to me and all the other things that they had done too.

Bruce seemed to know what I was talking about because he took another long drag on his cigarette before leveling me with a disappointed look that filled me with shame, "Yet you didn't hesitate to question me — your own husband."

I looked down and licked my lips nervously.

"You were so quick to believe," Bruce went on, "that I didn't even care about checking up on you when you were in that f— hospital. You're so quick to call me an asshole, but you give your parents the benefit of the doubt every damn time. I'm f— sick of it, Sarah."

"I'm sorry," I told him guiltily. "You're right."

He looked up at me from where he sat, and I walked over to sit down beside him on the couch. "I'm done with them. I don't want anything to do with them anymore," I told him. "Last night was the last straw. I just hate it," I looked down. "I wish I could have a relationship with my parents."

Bruce titled my chin up to force me to look at him, "You know you can't, Sarah. They just want to control you. They don't want you with me. They put up a good front for a little while, pretending to get along with me, but they've never liked me, and they never will. You see what they will do now, don't you?"

I nodded, agreeing with him.

He studied me for a moment, as if he was trying to gauge my sincerity, but I was sincere. I really meant it this time. I wasn't going to have anything else to do with my parents.

Apparently, he saw whatever he was looking for because he snuffed out his cigarette and then ran his thumb over my cheek. "Poor babygirl. You had a rough night, didn't you, my angel?"

I swallowed and nodded.

"Let me go run you a bath and fix you a drink and you can tell me all about it."

I smiled at him weakly, and he pressed a chaste kiss to my forehead before he stood and started walking toward the bathroom and kitchen.

It was official. Bruce was all I needed. Him and his love.

I could say that I was done with my parents, but it was obvious they would never be done with me. It didn't matter if I didn't accept her calls. Mom still made sure she got her shots in. I woke up every day to emails from her. I tried to check my emails before Bruce was awake because I didn't want him reading them and them determining the tone of our day.

In one of them, she talked about how the doctor had conveyed to them about all the bruises on me. She came right out and told me how she and Dad believed that Bruce was beating me and how it pained them to think that I would choose to stay with someone like that.

While I hadn't been responding to any of her emails, I couldn't let that one slide by. I typed out a quick response before Bruce woke up.

I denied the accusations, of course, and went on to talk about how Bruce was the only one who loved me. I accused her and Dad of wanting to control me and wanting to break up my marriage. I pointed out how suddenly no one else would have anything to do with me, how Addison suddenly stopped responding to any of my texts or calls.

Granted, I had talked to my grandma once or twice since I had gotten out of the hospital, but the conversations were very short, just long enough to let her know that I was alive and that no, I didn't want anything to do with Mom and Dad after what they had done, calling the cops and having me physically escorted to the hospital like I was a psycho or something.

Mom emailed me back almost immediately, which meant she must've been on the computer checking her email before she went to work that morning. Of course, she refuted everything that I said. She and Dad did not want to control me. In fact, she accused Bruce of controlling me.

As far as Addison was concerned, Mom actually

fessed up and told me that she had told Addison not to talk to me anymore. She claimed that Bruce had called and left some really mean voicemails on Addison's phone when Addison was at work and that they had really upset her and that she didn't understand why he would say the kinds of things he said to her.

I didn't know anything about that. I didn't remember Bruce ever calling her. If he'd done that, it had to have been when I was asleep or blacked out or something. And how could I even know he really did do it? They had lied to me. How could I trust that she was telling the truth now?

Besides, I decided that it didn't matter. If that had indeed happened, Addison should have come to me. She should have talked to me about it instead of just cutting me off and never speaking to me again without even telling me what was going on.

I'm not going to lie. That hurt. Losing my best friend all over again was like cutting into an old wound. She cut me off once before and just stopped talking to me whenever I made the decision to move in with Bruce after my parents had physically tried to keep us apart. History was repeating itself. I got into it with Mom and Dad, and Addison was once again taking their side and not mine.

Mom and Dad had betrayed me. My best friend had betrayed me—again. Bruce was right. He was the only one I could count on. He was the only one who truly loved me.

CHAPTER 18

JUST LIKE THINGS bothered Bruce and came out when he was drinking, I guess I was the same way now. Although I had resolved not to tell him about the emails because I didn't want to get him dwelling on all the stuff with my parents, it ended up coming out when we were drinking. I'd been drinking vodka that day, and Bruce had been drinking scotch.

I shouldn't have said anything, but it was on my mind, and I couldn't stem the flow of words once my inhibitions were down and I got started.

"So, Mom said that the reason why Addison won't talk to me anymore is because you called and left a bunch of mean voicemails on her phone."

Bruce eyed me over the top of his glass, seemingly unfazed by my accusation. "Have you been talking to your parents?" he asked.

If I had been a bit more sober, I might have detected the hint of a threat in his words. As it was, I was oblivious to the storm brewing just underneath the surface.

"She's been sending me emails," I admitted. "I haven't

responded to one until this morning, and that's when she told me that."

Bruce nodded and stood to go refill his scotch. I watched as he popped a couple of ice cubes from the ice tray and then dropped them into his glass with a clink before he poured some scotch from the green glass bottle on top of the cubes.

I grabbed my vodka bottle from the counter and poured myself another shot.

"Well?" I asked him after I downed half a shot. "Did you do it?'

He took a sip of his drink and then slipped the long-sleeved shirt he was wearing off over his head, leaving him bare-chested, wearing nothing but jeans and black socks. I watched the muscles of his arms and back flex with the movement, a testament to all his physical training in the marines that he still retained them even at his age.

He never took his eyes off me as he stripped out of his shirt. "Yes," he finally answered me, looking right into my eyes. "I did it." He stated it unapologetically, almost confrontationally, like he was daring me to be upset about it.

"When?" I asked. "Was I asleep or something?"

"No," he answered back. "You were standing right beside me. You heard every word."

I blinked. I did? I suppose it was possible. I did black out a lot when I drank. I just couldn't believe I could function like normal, walking around and talking and doing things and have no memory of it, but I knew that that was part of blacking out and that it did indeed happen to some people. I'd looked it up on the internet.

Unfortunately, I was just one of those people that it happened to a lot.

"But, once again, your mommy and daddy lied to you," Bruce sneered. "That's not why Addison stopped talking to you. I didn't call her and tell her what a little bitch she was until *after* she stopped talking to you— when you were crying about her not talking to you. I called her to tell her what a piece of shit excuse for a friend she was for dropping you without a word. I was taking up for you because it was ripping my heart out to see you being hurt by your family once again."

"Oh," I said, still trying to wrap my head around everything.

He took a step toward me, saying, "You don't need friends like that anyway."

I didn't immediately say anything. Instead, I downed the other half of my shot.

Bruce took a couple more steps toward me. "That's the second time she's turned her back on you. My buddy, Ron, would never do me that way."

For some reason, that infuriated me. "I get it," I snapped. "Your friend is better than mine."

His eyes darkened as he closed the rest of the distance between us. Without warning, his hand shot out and grabbed my hair at the nape of my neck. He tugged back on it, exposing my throat and forcing me to look up at him.

"You know what's pathetic?" he asked me. "You will defend your family and choose them every single time despite how they treat you."

"I'm not choosing anyone—" I argued with both of my

hands wrapped around his bulging forearm, trying to get him to release me.

"Yes, you are!" he interrupted me, yelling in my face.

"Ow!" I cried. "Bruce, stop! You're hurting me!"

"You're disgusting," he said before he flung me back into the counter.

I felt pain shooting up my back where it collided with the hard countertop.

"You know what? You're f— insane!" I screamed at him, my own temper rising at his harsh treatment of me.

"Insane?!" He repeated, his eyes dark with malice. "Oh, Sarah, you haven't seen anything yet." He lunged at me, and I barely managed to sidestep him just in time. My heart hammering in my chest, I took off toward the spare bedroom that served as the office I very rarely used. I don't know what he was planning on doing, but every instinct within me was telling me to run, so I did.

I instinctively grabbed my phone from where it sat on the counter along the way, a motion that didn't go unnoticed by Bruce.

"What do you think you're doing?" Bruce thundered, charging toward me.

I barely reached the spare bedroom and slammed the door shut behind me, locking it before he was upon it, pounding the door loudly.

Something about knowing I was locked up in that room with my phone made Bruce go berserk. He beat on the door and poured threats through it.

"Sarah, open this f— door! I swear to God if you call the cops, I'm going to kill you, you little bitch! You are not f— sending me to jail!"

I cried and trembled where I sat on the other side of

the room as far away from the doors I could get. Bruce was scaring me. He was still beating down the door and screaming at the top of his lungs, raining threats down. I don't know why he thought I was going to call the cops. I had never called the cops on him. It had always been others who had done that.

As he kept screaming over and over again that he was going to kill me, fear began to prickle up my spine. Surely Bruce wouldn't make good on his threats. This was just the alcohol talking. But then I thought of how he had just slammed me into the counter and how he had been drinking scotch and how he was way meaner when he drank hard liquor than when he just drank beer.

My heart was beating wildly within my chest as Bruce showed no signs of waning. He was still pounding on the door like a madman, screaming and threatening like he was out of his mind.

My hands were shaking as I opened my phone and hit the contact icon for the only people I could think of to call.

My parents.

Dad answered on the first ring.

"Hello?" his voice came over the line, but I couldn't calm myself down long enough to greet him back.

"Sarah?" Dad's voice held a note of panic. "Sarah, are you okay?"

Suddenly, I heard Mom's voice over the line. "Sarah, what's going on?" Mom's voice was urgent.

"It's Bruce," I said in between sobs. "He's—he's—," I couldn't get any more out.

"Sarah, has he hurt you?" Mom asked.

"Yes," I managed to choke out.

I was torn. I didn't want to betray Bruce, but he was genuinely scaring me. And I couldn't think straight. We'd been drinking all day. I didn't know what would happen. Maybe if I just got away from him for a little while, long enough for him to calm down, and then everything would be okay. Everything would go back to the way it was. I shouldn't have brought up anything about my family. This was all my fault.

Dad had the phone now. "Sarah, where you at right now?"

"I'm—I'm locked up in the extra bedroom. He's trying to break down the door," my teeth were chattering with my crying. "He so angry," my voice came out as a pitiful whine.

"We're on our way now," Dad said. "Carol," he spoke to my mom, "call 911 right now."

"No, no!" I tried to protest. "No cops! He said he'd kill me if I called the cops!"

"Sarah!" Mom said urgently over the line, "he might kill you before we get there if we don't."

"Stay on the phone with us until we or the cops get there," Dad said. I heard mom's muffled voice in the background. I knew she was calling the cops, and I didn't know how to stop it. I didn't know if I was doing the right thing or if it was wrong for me to call my parents.

Oh God, if the cops came here, they were going to arrest Bruce. He would be furious. I didn't want him to be arrested. But I also didn't want him to be this angry with me. I didn't want him to hurt me in his alcohol-imbued state.

I screamed when Bruce's foot finally kicked in the door, busting it off its hinges. His eyes were wild with anger as he took in my form huddled up into a ball in the corner of the room with the phone up to my ear.

"Who are you on the phone with?" he roared. "You call the cops on me?" He asked while he stomped over toward me menacingly.

"No! No!" I denied. "It's just my parents. I just thought I would go with them for a while —"

"Rob, he's in the room with her," fear laced my mom's voice as it came over the phone.

I didn't hear anything else that my parents said, though, because I flung my hands up to ward off Bruce's attack as he flew at me in a rage.

"You think you're going to leave me?!" Bruce roared down at me, his face twisted up, making him look demonically menacing. I'd never been more afraid of him than I was in that moment.

His hands came crashing down toward my face, knocking the phone out of my hands. He grabbed the phone and snapped it shut before flinging it toward the wall.

"You are never leaving me! Do you f— hear me! You are mine, and you are never going anywhere! I will kill you before you leave me!"

He hit me repeatedly with open palms, smacking me on my face, my arms, my stomach, anywhere he could reach. Although I felt the pain from the strikes explode across my skin where he hit, it was somewhat numbed by all the alcohol coursing through my body.

I flailed and kicked and fought back the best I could, but he was way too strong. He easily pinned my arms down beside my head.

I landed a kick to his shin, though, and I immediately realized my error when I saw his eyes darken with fury.

"You kick me? Oh, you little bitch!" Bruce let go of one of my hands long enough to rear back and smack me on the face. Pain flared sharply, stars dotted my vision, and I was left gasping for breath. I turned my head, trying to block his blows, but he grabbed my hair and yanked me back.

Bruce had been rough with me before. He had grabbed me. He had pushed me down. He'd left bruises on me. But he had never openly hit me like this. The vile names that he called me in between his hits hurt almost as much as the physical strikes. My heart and soul broke a little bit more with each verbal and physical blow he dealt.

He might not have punched me with fists, but that didn't deter the amount of damage he did.

He didn't stop his assault until there was a series of super loud knocks on the door.

"Open up! Police!" A male officer's voice came through the door.

Bruce glared icy daggers down at me as he cursed. "Well, you've done it now."

He pushed himself up off of me and towered over me were I was still curled up in a protective ball on the floor. "Don't you dare move from that spot," he warned me. "This is all your fault."

I didn't dare disobey. Bruce walked out of the door to the extra bedroom. He tried to close it as best he could, but of course it wouldn't shut properly since he destroyed it in his mad attempt to break into it.

I winced as I sat up with my back against the wall and

pulled my knees up to my chest. I ached everywhere, and I lifted my hand to my face to wipe away moisture that I assumed was tears.

I stared at my hand in shock, though, when I pulled it back and saw it covered in blood. I was bleeding?

I put my hand back up to my face and felt the wetness around my nose. It was my nose. A steady stream of blood was dripping from it onto my clothes, onto the carpet.

I suddenly smelled the coppery tang of it and watched as the droplets turned everything they hit crimson. I held my sleeve up to my nose to try to stem the flood, but every time I pulled it away, it would begin anew, trickling down to the top of my lip.

I couldn't stop the tears from streaming from my eyes. I had moisture running down my cheeks, from my nose. I was a dripping, sniveling mess, and I'd never felt more confused or lost in my entire life. I think I was in shock, in disbelief that Bruce, my husband, the man I loved more than anything in the world would do something like this to me.

I didn't break out of my trance until a police officer stepped into the room. He took in the sight of me trembling in a ball on the floor before he asked me gently, "Ma'am, do you think you can stand up?"

I nodded and stood on shaky legs, leaning against the wall for support.

"Can you tell me what happened here tonight?" he asked me.

I glanced toward the doorway when I heard Bruce speaking loudly to the officer in the other room.

"Everything's fine, man," I heard Bruce's voice drifting

through the doorway. "We've both been drinking. We both had a little bit too much to drink, and we got into a fight about her parents. Her parents are always calling her and harassing us. They're always trying to break us up. We were arguing about that, and she fell. I love her. I would never do anything to hurt her. She's my wife, man."

I listened as Bruce's voice expertly weaved truth with lie.

"How did your nose start bleeding?" The police officer standing in front of me prompted me, pulling my attention back to him.

"I —" I hesitated, reluctant to tell the truth. Something was holding me back from snitching on Bruce. If I told them what happened, they would for sure take him to jail if they didn't take him anyway. I remembered his voice telling me he would kill me. But did I really think he would do that?

But then I thought of the Bruce I fell in love with. I thought of how sweet and caring he was to me when he wasn't drunk like this. I couldn't bring myself to say it. "I fell," I ended up saying.

I knew by the look on the officer's face that he wasn't buying it. "We got a distraught 9-1-1 call from your parents saying they heard your husband saying he was going to kill you. They claim they heard him yelling at you and attacking you. You're safe now," he assured me. "You can tell us the truth. He's not going to be able to do anything else to you."

I trembled and swallowed but didn't say anything else.

"Please don't take him to jail," I begged softly.

"That's already a done deal," the police officer told me

frankly. "He's already in handcuffs. There's no way he's not going to jail when you're standing before me with a bleeding nose and marks all over you."

I hung my head, more tears streaming down my face. Maybe I should want him to go to jail for what he did, but I didn't. I knew it wasn't *my* Bruce who had done it. *My* Bruce would never do something like this.

I realized that I no longer heard Bruce's voice coming from the living room, but I did hear my mom and dad's.

I walked around the police officer out into the living room where Mom and Dad stood talking with another police officer.

My dad's jaw set with anger when he saw me while Mom's face seemed to fall in heartbreak. I must have looked like hell to garner those reactions.

"Sarah," Mom began. Dad continued talking to the police officer, relaying everything they had heard, I'm sure.

I couldn't even bear to think about the ramifications of this night. If my parents had hated Bruce before, they would hate him tenfold now. I knew there would be no coming back from this.

Mom grabbed the dishtowel that was hanging from the stove and brought it over to me to hold up to my nose. I accepted it wordlessly and held it up to my nose, trying to stem the flow that didn't seem to want to stop.

Mom wrapped an arm around me and held me to her side, and I let her. I was no longer sobbing, but rather crying silently.

I heard one of the officers mention something about an ambulance, and that broke me out of my reverie. "No!"

I said adamantly. "I don't need an ambulance. I don't want to go to a hospital. I'm fine."

"Are you sure you don't want to get checked out?" one of the officers asked me.

I nodded my head emphatically.

"Well, do you have someplace safe to go tonight?"

"I'll be fine," I said. I didn't want to go anywhere. I just wanted to stay here and think about what I was going to do. Everything was such a mess. I hadn't even processed it all yet. Bruce was in jail. What was I going to do? I couldn't just leave him there, could I? I had to get him out. He didn't mean this. He would be sorry when he got out, and it would never happen again. It should have never happened.

"Sarah, you need to come stay with us," my dad said.

"You don't need to be alone tonight," Mom added.

"We'd feel better if you went with your parents too," one of the officers chimed in.

I didn't have the strength to argue with anyone. And the soothing way mom was running her hand up and down my back was comforting, and after the night I had just had, I found myself wanting the comfort of my mother.

I let her lead me into the bedroom where I mechanically gathered up some clothes. Actually, she packed most of the clothes in a small tote bag I had hanging up on the door. I didn't even question the fact that she was packing more clothes than I would need. She probably packed enough for a week, but I certainly didn't plan on staying with them that long. I didn't have the heart to tell her that at the time, though.

I just had to get through that night.

By the time Mom and I came out of the bedroom, the cops were gone. Dad came over and took my bag while Mom got my purse and phone for me.

My entire body was still shaking so badly, from the alcohol or from the shock of the night's events, I didn't know. Nevertheless, Mom must have noticed because she held onto my arm tightly and led me down the porch steps before helping me into the back seat of their SUV.

It was freezing outside, and I pulled my coat closer around me as Dad shut the door to the backseat. My strength left me then. I laid down on the back seat and curled into myself as much as I could, wondering how in the world things had gotten to this point.

My entire world had come crashing down around me in one night.

And I didn't have a clue how to begin picking up the pieces.

CHAPTER 19

I DON'T KNOW what time it was when we pulled up to Mom and Dad's house, but it was pitch black outside. It had been dark when we left my place, but the sky was lighter there anyway since we lived within city limits.

I felt a ball of dread settle in the pit of my stomach when I took in the pristine cottage-style home that I grew up in. Not that long ago I had sworn off any communication with my parents. I certainly never thought I would be back here—at my childhood home.

My head was foggy. I was walking around still dazed from the night's events. I couldn't think straight. I still couldn't believe what had happened. Bruce was in jail, and it was my fault. I might as well have put him there. When I'd called my parents, I had sealed his fate.

Then I remembered the anger in his voice, the blackness in his eyes, the rain of his palms down on my skin, striking me over and over again. I trembled at the memory. I had never seen him that angry before. The way he told me he would never let me leave him. The way he said he would kill me if I did. That had just been the alcohol talking, though, right?

When we got into the house, Dad went into the living room and collapsed down into his recliner. He could hardly look at me, and no wonder. He was probably ashamed of me. Whoever would have thought that me, the straight-A student with such a bright future ahead of her, would have been reduced to this—a battered woman?

Bruce was right. I was disgusting. I disgusted myself. I was filled with a rush of shame so deep that I almost collapsed.

I don't know if Mom sensed it or what, but she gently steered me toward their bedroom, closing the door behind her.

"Sarah," she began tentatively once we were behind the privacy of the closed bedroom door, "is this the first time this has happened?"

I looked into her eyes that were filled with a mixture of worry, concern, and a mother's righteous fury that her child had been attacked. I swallowed and looked away before answering, "Bruce would never purposefully hurt me. He loves me."

Mom made a strangled sound of disbelief before saying, "Sarah, this is not love. He beat you."

"He was angry," I said weakly. "We'd been drinking too much. It was the alcohol."

I looked at her, pleading with her with my eyes to understand, "He's not like that at all when we don't drink. I made him angry. It was my fault—"

She cut me off with a firm denial, "No, it was *not* your

fault." She emphasized her statement with, "Do you understand me?"

"Come here," Mom said gently but firmly. She led me over to the mirror and prompted me, "Look at yourself."

I lifted my head and dared a peek, but I quickly looked back down, distraught by what I saw. Blood crusted underneath my nose, and there were dark spots along my jawline, on my forehead, and under my eyes along my cheekbones.

"Does that look like love?" Mom asked me. "You're lucky he didn't break your nose. Or maybe he did. I don't know," I glanced back up, and my eyes met Mom's in the mirror.

The pained look in her eyes caused my own to fill with tears.

I swallowed again before saying, "It's not broken. Just sore. He didn't hit me with fists."

"You can't stay with him, Sarah," Mom said, shaking her head. "This is unacceptable. No man should ever raise a hand to a woman. I know you know that. We didn't raise you to accept this kind of behavior."

Her words stabbed at me because I knew they were true. I remembered watching Lifetime movies growing up, ones where men hit women, and I always swore that if a man ever barely laid a finger on me, I would leave. I could never understand how they would stay with them.

I was beginning to understand now. Things were not always as simple as they seemed.

Despite how my skin pulsed and throbbed where Bruce's hands had connected, I couldn't help thinking of the man I'd fallen in love with. I thought of all the fun Bruce and I had drinking before things went too far. I remembered those early days when I first moved in with him and was a virgin and how he patiently waited for me to be ready before he slept with me. If that didn't prove he loved me, what did?

I thought of everything we had gone through to be together. Why would he put up with all this stuff from my parents if he didn't really love me?

But then my thoughts swayed back to what my mom said. Bruce had hit me. It was more than just pushing me down and holding me down now. It was more than grabbing me too roughly and shaking me. He had pummeled me over and over again, screaming threats at me, calling me vile name as if he hated me. And I should hate him for that, shouldn't I? If I had any sense, I would never want to see him again. I would want him locked away for what he did to me. I would be terrified of him.

And I was—terrified, that is. Both of him and of the prospect of being without him. I had been with Bruce twenty-four-seven for so long now that I couldn't imagine life without him. Even the time we'd spent apart when he was still in Florida and I was up here with my family, we'd talked multiple times a day on the phone. I couldn't imagine a day going by without having some sort of communication with him.

What would I do? I had no money of my own anymore. I didn't have a driver's license to get a job around here. Sure, I had my writing gig, but it wasn't stable. Sometimes I could make great money, and other times, it was slow. Besides, I hadn't worked in so long. Bruce didn't like me working. He wanted to be with me all the time.

My heart broke all over again at that thought. He was

so possessive and jealous of me. Why would he be like that if he didn't really love me? He was the only man I had ever been with. My first kiss, my first boyfriend, the first one to hold my hand, my first everything. He was the only one I ever wanted. I never wanted to be with another man. I couldn't even fathom it.

How could I leave him? Move back in with my parents? Go back to letting them control every aspect of my life? Because that is for sure what they would do. Now that they saw what had happened when I had left, if I ever moved back in with them, the reigns would be tighter than ever.

But I knew that if I left Bruce, that was what I would have to do. I didn't have the means to support myself. I hadn't even cooked anything in years. I was completely dependent on Bruce, and my chest ached at the thought of not having his presence in my life. Sure, even when he was sober, he could bitch and moan. He could have a shitty attitude that totally got on my nerves. He was impatient and boorish at times, but I was still terrified at the thought of never seeing him again.

And then there was what he had said—that he would never let me go. Would he really let me just walk away? Somehow, I didn't think it would be that easy.

No, I had married him for better or for worse.

Mom walked over to her dresser, opened the top drawer, and pulled out her digital camera.

"What are you doing?" I asked her skeptically.

"Why don't you let me run you a bath? It'll help you feel better. And let me take pictures of all the bruises on you, just to show you what he did to you."

I instantly shook my head to protest, "No, I don't want to see."

"You need to see what he did to you, Sarah. I know this is hard, honey. I can't imagine how you're feeling, and I hate this for you. I really do. But you need to face the truth about this. Bruce does not love you the way he says he does, or he would never have hurt you this way."

I continued to shake my head, but I could tell that Mom was not going to be deterred, so my shoulders slumped in dejection. What did it matter anyway?

I allowed her to lead me into the bathroom where she began running water into the tub. I watched as she poured a generous amount of bubble bath into the water followed by a couple of cups of Epsom salts.

"It'll help with any swelling," she informed me.

A lump caught in my throat as I began taking off my clothes. I listened to the mechanical whirl and click of the digital camera as it flashed and captured every bruise on my body. Apparently, they were numerous if the amount of clicks I heard were any indication. She started with my front and then circled around the back, clicking and flashing all the way.

"Good Lord," she murmured, "you're covered in marks."

"I black out a lot when I drink," I told her honestly, "and I do fall down a lot and run into stuff."

"How do you know that if you're blacked out?" she asked me pointedly.

I didn't answer, knowing that if I said it was because Bruce told me so, she would doubt his word, and I guess I couldn't blame her now after seeing what he had done to me. I knew how it looked from the outside. But none of them understood. They didn't know Bruce the way I did. I knew he didn't mean to do this. I couldn't believe it. My heart wouldn't let me, regardless of what my mind and eyes told me.

When she was finally done making her photographs, I stepped over into the warm water and lowered myself down into it, drawing my knees up under my chin.

I couldn't stop shaking. I felt warm water dripping over my back where Mom had placed a washcloth and was squeezing it. She proceeded to wash my back before tilting my head back and using a cup to dump warm water over my hair. She lathered my hair and washed it for me too.

The whole time I sat there, not saying a word, too weak to move or talk or even think.

It was officially the worst night of my life, and I didn't have the energy for anything.

"I love you, Sarah," Mom told me as she was rinsing the suds from my hair. "And your dad loves you too." She paused before she went on, "We love you more than anything in this entire world, and we are here for you. You're going to get through this. Everything is going to be okay."

I still didn't speak. I didn't see how anything would ever be okay again.

Mom gave me a big T-shirt to sleep in after I got out of the bathtub. She offered to sleep with me that night, but I insisted on sleeping alone. I knew that I would have trouble sleeping anyway, as I was prone to do if I didn't drink until I passed out.

Mom and Dad both hugged me and told me that they loved me before I went to bed just like I was still a little girl. Mom even insisted on coming upstairs to my old bedroom to tuck me in and make sure I was okay and offer again to sleep with me if I needed her.

I assured her that I was fine and sent her downstairs to sleep with Dad where she belonged.

I tossed and turned all night, never really sleeping. Every time I woke up from a light doze, my reality came crashing back down on me with a swooping feeling of dread and depression.

I'd never felt so lost in my entire life.

I lay awake most of the night, my nerves in a bundle of uncertainty and tension until I finally heard Mom and Dad stirring downstairs.

I got dressed in a pair of stretchy pants and hoodie before making my way down the stairs.

Mom and Dad greeted me with a cup of coffee. The smell of bacon cooking in the microwave turned my stomach.

I glanced down at my phone and saw that it was Saturday. So, the night before when Bruce was arrested had been a Friday night.

Although food was the last thing on my mind, I tried to force down a few bites at Mom and Dad's prompting.

Talk was stilted at the table that morning. It was awkward, like no one knew what to say. We were all dancing around the elephant in the room, none of us willing to talk about why we were all once again in the same room.

I think maybe Mom and Dad were hesitant to bring anything up because they didn't want to upset me, but what they didn't understand was that I was perpetually upset. Nothing in my world was right anymore. It had all been turned upside down in one night.

Dad was the one to finally broach the subject. "I'm sorry about all this, Sarah," he said awkwardly. "You can stay here with us as long as you need to," he offered.

I nodded before saying, "Thanks, but can you please take me back to my place now?"

My parents shared a glance before Mom cautiously asked, "Are you sure that's a good idea, honey?"

"It might not be a good idea for you to be alone right now," Dad said.

"It looks like I'm going to have to get used to it," my voice broke with the words, "so I might as well start now."

"You could always move back in here," Dad said.

I shook my head. "I just need some time to figure things out. Please," I added.

Mom and Dad shared another look, communicating without words in that way they did. I could tell the idea didn't sit well with them. They probably never wanted to let me leave their house again, but they also knew that I was legally an adult, and they legally couldn't keep me here. They had tried that before and look how that had turned out.

I could tell they weren't happy about it, but they did take me home.

They gently reminded me not to drink anymore if I still had alcohol in the house.

"Trust me, that's the last thing on my mind," I told them honestly.

The truth was I couldn't imagine drinking without Bruce. We always drank together. I had never drunk without him.

I had told them the truth when I said drinking was the furtherest thing from my mind. No, I needed to be sober for Bruce's first appearance in court.

I started to pour the remaining alcohol out but then thought better of it and put it away in the cabinet instead.

I straightened up the house—not that it was particularly dirty anyway, more like disorganized. I cleaned the bloodstains out of the carpet in the room Bruce had wailed on me in, a lump in my throat and tears pricking my eyes the entire time.

My nose was sore and ached every time I touched it, but I knew it wasn't broken or anything. It looked normal, but there was dried blood inside of it that was bothering me. However, every time I blew my nose to get it out, that would restart the bleeding, so I had to go around with basically a stuffy nose.

The house was unnaturally quiet, so I turned on the TV to generate some background noise and try to take my mind off of everything. I couldn't focus on anything. Everything on TV reminded me of Bruce and the shows we watched together while we drank. Every corner of the house held memories—some good, some bad.

Bruce had been the one constant in my life for so long

now. My world felt strange without him. I felt alone—
more alone than I had ever felt in my entire life.

The day was tortuously long. Nothing could hold my
attention. I couldn't eat.

All I could do was sit in the chair that Bruce liked to
sit in and think, analyzing every aspect of the night Bruce
was arrested.

Part of me knew that my parents were right—that I
should leave Bruce and never look back. But there was
that other part of me that still believed I loved him and
that he loved me and that he hadn't meant anything that
he had done, that it had all been due to the alcohol and
the stress that my parents were constantly putting on our
relationship.

My parents called me to check on me and make sure I
was okay. I assured them that I was, though I think we all
knew that I wasn't.

My grandma called me. I think her phone call was the
worst of all. It was obvious Mom and Dad had told her
what had happened because there was no way to hide it.
Grandma never had been good at hiding her emotions. It
was obvious she had been crying, thinking about what
had happened to me. She didn't ask about the details,
and I was thankful for that because I wouldn't have told
her anyway. She just kept saying that she wished I would
come stay with her or Mom and Dad, but I refused,
telling her the same thing I had told Mom and Dad—that
I was fine.

She said what Mom and Dad didn't say, though.

"You're not fine, Sarah," her voice was sad and wobbly.

I didn't argue with her. I just told her goodnight and
got off the phone with her.

I had to do this. I had to be left alone with my thoughts. I had to figure out if there was a way I could live without Bruce.

And when I went to bed that night, it was torture. I missed the weight of my husband beside me, even the sound of his snoring. My mind went back to all those nights when we didn't drink, and I would lay with my head on his chest, and we would watch TV together until I fell asleep in his arms. I remembered the feel of him stroking my hair, my arms, my shoulders, my back. I remembered the gentle way he used to touch me and hold me.

And I cried. I cried until my chest ached and my throat hurt, until my eyes were so swollen no amount of makeup would be able to hide it.

I had never felt the type of pain I felt that night. It gripped my heart with harsh fingers and twisted, and the thought of being without Bruce again only made it worse.

I couldn't stop thinking about if he was angry with me. If he hated me now. Would he even want me anymore? Maybe he would decide that I was too much trouble.

But then I shuddered when I remembered him saying he would never let me leave him and that he would kill me if I tried.

I didn't want to leave him. It was the last thing I wanted. But I also didn't want to live in fear of him either. I just wanted things to go back to the way they used to be when things were good.

One thing was sure.

I didn't think I could live without Bruce.

And my parents were going to hate me for it.

CHAPTER 20

I ENDED up getting in touch with a bail bondsman to see if a bail had been set for Bruce yet—except the bail bondsman wasn't a man. She was a woman.

She was surprisingly compassionate. She told me that even though a bail had not been set yet, one should be set the next morning: Monday morning when Bruce had his first appearance before the judge.

Although I didn't understand why he didn't have a bail set yet, she told me that sometimes the judge waited to review any evidence pertaining to the case when it involved domestic violence cases. It was something about the laws in Tennessee concerning those types of cases.

She explained that since I was the alleged victim, if I was there to say that I didn't want to press charges, then the judge might just release him with no bail, so that was, of course, my game plan.

However, she assured me that even if he had a bail set, they would be able to get him out.

I asked her what time I needed to be at the courthouse so I would know what time to have a cab bring me.

But she was hearing none of that.

"I have to be at the courthouse in the morning anyway for other clients, so why don't I just swing by and pick you up?" she offered.

I was taken aback by her kindness. "Wow, are you sure?" I asked hesitantly. "I don't want to be a bother or put you out."

"It's no trouble at all," she assured me.

She told me what time she would be at my house the next morning, and that was it.

Then, I spent the rest of the day on pins and needles waiting for it to hurry up and pass so that the next morning would come.

The next morning, I was ready an hour before the bail bondswoman was set to come pick me up.

It was still in the dead of winter, and it was freezing outside — quite literally. It had to be in the twenties. Unfortunately, I knew it wouldn't be acceptable to show up in court wearing stretchy pants and a hoodie.

I managed to throw together an outfit that consisted of my thickest leggings, a turtleneck sweater dress, and my long black boots that came up over my calves nearly to my knees. I wished I had a pair of boots that didn't have heels on them, but I didn't, so I would have to make do with these. I hoped the way I had paired them with the leggings and the conservative sweater dress made for a classy outfit rather than a trashy one. I knew these were the kind of boots that could go either way. They could make an outfit look fashionable and pulled together, or they could make it look like you were a tramp.

I finished it all off with my thick winter coat, hoping that it was presentable enough while still keeping me warm.

I was careful with my makeup that morning, applying it so that it covered any redness or discoloration around my nose and along my jawline. I knew Bruce wasn't a fan of me wearing makeup, but he would have to understand in this instance when I was doing it to save his ass.

I felt a twinge of trepidation at the thought. Would Bruce be angry with me about everything, or would he just be glad to see me? Did he still love me?

I finished applying my mascara and then stood back to survey my handiwork. I fluffed my hair and decided I was as good as I was going to get. And I would find out how Bruce felt soon enough, I reasoned.

That still didn't stop my nerves from getting to me. The bail bondswoman called me to tell me she was waiting outside, I grabbed my ID and debit card and stuck them in my coat pocket. She had already told me there was no use taking a purse to court since this court wouldn't allow you to bring in cell phones or anything of that nature.

My legs shook with every step I took down our slippery porch steps that were frosted over with a light film of ice. I held onto the railing, praying that I didn't fall and bust my ass in my hooker boot heels. That's all I needed at this point.

"Good morning, sweetie," Susie, the bail bondswoman greeted me. "Oh my, look at you. You look like a little doll."

I thanked her for the compliment and greeted her good morning back. "Thanks again for doing this. You totally didn't have to, but I really appreciate it."

"Think nothing of it," she said with a smile. "I'm happy to help when I can."

I was super grateful to have her next to me when we entered the courthouse. Otherwise, I would have felt totally lost trying to navigate through everything on my own. She knew exactly where to go, so it was like I had my own personal guide. We stood in line to go through the metal detector that was stationed right outside the courtroom. The guard working it greeted her like an old friend. Apparently, she was there a lot, which made sense since she was always bailing people out.

The courtroom was already packed when we entered, but she secured us seats on a bench near where the prisoners sat.

"Which one is your husband?" She asked, her eyes flicking over all of the male prisoners who were sitting facing us.

As if drawn by the heat of his gaze, my eyes immediately found his. He caught me in his stare, and my heart began pumping harder in my chest. I was nervous, so nervous to see him again, wondering how he would feel. I hated seeing him in the green and white jail suit. It wasn't a jumpsuit but rather a shirt and pants set. His hands were handcuffed in front of him like all the prisoners. I don't know how I managed to notice all of that when his eyes held mine captive so I couldn't tear mine away.

"That's him," I whispered to her. Out of my peripheral vision, I saw her head turned to follow the direction of my gaze.

Bruce's lips were moving, and my heart stuttered within me when I made out the words that he was mouthing.

I love you. I love you.

And then he smiled at me, and I felt a rush of relief. Everything was going to be okay. It had to be. Bruce still loved me, and he wasn't angry at me. No doubt he had realized that that night was just a horrible instance caused by too much alcohol. When he got out and we were back together, things would be different. I just knew they would.

Susie squeezed my hand and smiled at me when she saw him mouthing *I love you*'s at me.

I just gave Bruce a tiny smile in return before one of the guards noticed him trying to communicate with me and shut it down.

"No talking to anyone." The guard's stern voice rang out over the heads of the prisoners. "Prisoners face forward."

Bruce turned his head obediently forward, but where the prisoners' benches were was perpendicular to the rest of the court, so even though he kept his head forward, I saw his eyes constantly flitting over to look at me.

"How do I get to talk to the judge?" I asked Susie. Sure, I had been through a bit of this song and dance before in Florida, but each state and each courtroom was different, and I wasn't sure how things worked here. Hell, I hadn't been sure how they'd worked in Florida, but I'd just floundered my way through.

"When they read off his charges, they'll usually ask if there's anyone concerning the case here. That's when you'll stand up and make your presence known. The judge will usually ask what you want to see happen, and she'll take whatever you have to say into account."

I nodded silently, my stomach twisted in knots at the thought of standing up in front of all these people. A quick glance around didn't show anyone that I knew, though I knew it was possible that there were people here who knew me through my parents or other relatives. That made it a whole different ballgame than the courts in Florida where no one knew me.

Susie squeezed my hand again and reassured me," It's okay. I'll let you know when and what to do."

I smiled at her gratefully and nodded again, once again so thankful that she was there to guide me through all of this.

I screwed up straighter when the judge finally called Bruce's name. I watched as he walked to stand in front of the podium and have his charges read off to him. I didn't fully understand what he was charged with, but it was more than just simple domestic violence. I heard terms like "assault" and "battery" and "aggravated."

Just like Susie had said, the judge asked if anyone concerning the case was there. I felt Susie nudge me and shakily stood to my feet.

The judge gave me permission to approach the bench. Nervous as hell with at least a hundred pairs of eyes on me, I walked up to the front of the courtroom.

The judge asked me to state my name, and I did so. She glanced over at who I assumed must be the DA, and he supplied for her, "The victim." I hated hearing myself termed as such. It made me sound weak and pathetic. It made Bruce sound like a monster. Neither of which was true.

"Well, Ms. MacKenzie, what would you like to say to the court?" The judge asked me.

In typical Judge Judy fashion, she sported a short haircut and had a thin frame. However, I couldn't say she was quite as stern as Judge Judy. Oh, she was stern, but she also seemed to have an element of humanity and fairness about her. She didn't strike terror in me, though I was nervous knowing that she held the fate of my husband in her hands.

"I, um," I tripped nervously over my words before I found my voice, "I don't want to press charges."

"Why not?" she asked me frankly.

"Because it was all just a big misunderstanding," I answered. "We just had a normal argument. We'd both been drinking a bit too much. That's all." I didn't know if I was saying the right things, but I prayed that I was and that I wasn't making things worse. I hated being put on the spot like that.

The judge glanced at the DA, and he stood and went to speak quietly with her. I waited with bated breath while they spoke, wondering what was going on.

When he returned to his seat, she addressed me with, "Unfortunately, that's not up to you. It's up to the DA, and judging by these photos in front of me—especially the one of your bloodied nose." She shook her head before going on, "These coupled with your parents' testimony," she continued rifling through the pictures in her hand, "I tend to agree with him."

I was struck speechless, not knowing what else to say. Photos? Testimony? How and when had my parents contacted the DA? My mind flicked back to the night I spent in my parents' house. How mom had insisted on taking pictures of me. She had claimed they were to show *me* the bruises on my body.

It suddenly clicked in my brain what she'd really been doing: gathering evidence. She'd tricked me so that she could turn all this in to the court.

Had Mom and Dad anticipated that I would try to get Bruce free? And they wanted to make sure that they could try to keep us apart as long as possible?

My heart sank within me. Bruce was completely right about everything. There were no lengths my parents wouldn't go to to get their way.

The judge dismissed me and told me to be seated once again. Feeling helpless and with my cheeks burning red, I did as she said.

The judge called Bruce back to stand before her and went on to set his bail, though she looked between him and me both when she read the conditions of that bail.

"You are not to consume any alcohol or partake of any illegal substances. You are not to have any contact with the alleged victim. You will report to all your court dates..." On and on she droned reading it all off, but my mind had shut off after the "you shall have no contact with the victim" part. I didn't even catch the amount that his bail was set at, but thankfully Susie had.

When court was over and all the prisoners started filing out, Bruce blew me a quick kiss and mouthed another *I love you* to me before he was escorted out back to the jail.

Susie led us from the courtroom, and then she turned to me with a reassuring smile, "See? I told you he'd get a bail. Don't worry. We'll get him out."

"But what about the no contact order? "I asked her.

"How do they expect that to work? Bruce and I live together."

She brushed it off with, "I'm not advising you to break the law or anything, but usually those things aren't enforced unless someone turns you in for being together or unless the cops come out to your residence on a call and find you together. The police force doesn't have the manpower to constantly scout out and see if no contact orders are being followed. In other words, they're not going to be actively looking to see if you've broken it."

I nodded, relieved at her reassurance. I hadn't seen my parents in the courtroom that morning, and why would I? They were both at work that morning, and I, of course, hadn't told them that I was coming to court that morning. As far as they knew, I was still at home, trying to cope with everything.

As far as they knew, Bruce was still in jail and was going to stay there. In fact, judging by how much "evidence" they had supplied the court, they were probably pretty confident that he wouldn't be getting out of jail anytime soon, so they wouldn't know if I bailed him out. As far as they knew, I was going to leave Bruce and move on with my life. I had purposefully let them believe that. It was for the best that they believed that, and this right here was exactly why.

"So, what do we do now?" I asked her, looking to her for her expert guidance.

"Well, we have to wait for the paperwork to be filed, and as soon as it is, I'll post his bail, and then we'll have to wait for the jail to release him."

I nodded.

"When's the last time you've eaten?" she asked me suddenly.

I paused, caught off guard by her question, "Um, I don't really remember." That was a lie, though. I did remember. It was the couple of bites of breakfast I'd forced myself to eat back at Mom and Dad's house, so I guess it had been more than forty-eight hours since I'd eaten.

I didn't want to tell Susie that, though.

"Why don't we go get lunch?" she offered. "My treat?"

"Oh, um, thanks, but I'm not hungry," I smiled at her apologetically. It was true. Food was the last thing on my mind.

"Are you sure? You need to eat, hon," she gently told me.

"I promise I'll make myself eat something when I get home," I told her.

"Okay, well I'm not going to try to pressure you. I understand," she said kindly.

"Thanks," I told her gratefully. "Not just for that, but for everything. You've been amazing. I don't know what I would've done without you."

"Oh, you're welcome, honey. I'm happy to help. And everything is going to be okay. We'll have your man home in no time," she assured me again.

I hoped she was right.

I waited impatiently for any word on Bruce and when he would be getting released. I paced the living room, chewing on my fingernails nervously—a bad habit I'd always had as a child. I'd successfully broken it as a teen, but my nerves were so frazzled I was reverting back to it now.

I didn't know what would happen after Bruce's bail was posted and he was released. I'd paid the ten percent of his bond with my credit card, but Bruce's wallet was still laying on our bedroom dresser where it had been sitting the night he got arrested, so he didn't have any money on him, so I didn't know how he would get home. Since I didn't have a license and my car was parked away at my parents' place, I wouldn't be able to be at the jail to pick him up.

I took a deep breath and tried to calm my worries. All of my pacing and worrying wasn't helping anything. Plus, I still hadn't eaten anything, a fact that wouldn't be comforting to Susie or any of my family members.

Despite my anger at Mom and Dad for tricking me with the photographs, I tried not to let on that anything was wrong when I talked to them on the phone earlier. They'd called to check up on me on their lunch break, and I tried to act as normal and heartbroken and depressed as possible. I didn't let on that I'd been in the courtroom that morning or that I knew anything more about the state of Bruce and his charges. Of course, Grandma had called as well, and all of them had reminded me to eat before getting off the phone with me.

I grabbed a package of peanut butter crackers from the pantry and mechanically bit into one. It tasted like cardboard on my tongue, but I pushed through and managed to eat three of the tiny squares before I wrapped up the remaining three in the pack and put them aside for later. There. Now I could in all honesty say I'd eaten something.

I contemplated calling Susie to get an update—any word—on what was going on, but I didn't want to bug her after how amazing she'd been. I trusted that she was doing the best she could to get everything settled as quickly as possible. Plus, I was sure my husband wasn't the only person she was bailing out that day. I just needed to be patient.

It was hard, though, as the hours ticked by.

When the evening wore on, I finally heard the crunch of gravel outside and peeked out of the window to see Susie's car crunching up the driveway.

My heart leapt into my throat when the passenger-side door opened up and Bruce stepped out. I hadn't expected Susie to pick him up from the jailhouse and drive him home, and my heart swelled with gratitude toward her again.

He was wearing exactly what he'd been arrested in— a white undershirt and jeans, and I knew he had to be freezing with no coat or anything to cover his arms.

It didn't seem to matter to him, though, if the way he stormed up the stairs toward where I already had the front door open and pulled me tightly into his arms was any indication. I melted into his embrace as he kissed the side of my head.

"I missed you so much, baby," he told me, while still hugging me tightly. "I'm so sorry for everything," he apologized, pulling back to look down into my eyes. "You know I love you?" he asked me with a desperate look in his eyes, like he needed me to believe him.

I nodded with my cheek pressed against his chest.

We pulled apart when Susie walked up the steps.

"Thanks so much for getting me out and giving me a ride here." Bruce told her. "And for helping Sarah through all of this," he added, glancing down at me and then wrapping his arm around my shoulders to pull me to his side.

"It was nothing," Susie shrugged off his gratitude. "Y'all just be happy and be careful and enjoy being together. Everything will be okay. Whenever you need a ride to the courthouse for any of your court dates, don't hesitate to call me. I have to be there anyway, so it's really no trouble to swing by here and pick you up," she spoke to both Bruce and me.

"Thank you," Bruce said, "we'll do that."

"Well, I'm going to leave you two lovebirds alone now," Susie winked at us before she turned and walked back to her car.

Bruce held up a hand as Susie began pulling out of the driveway, and then, still holding me tight to his side, he ushered us through the doorway and closed the door behind us.

"Bruce I —" I began, but he cut me off.

"I know, babygirl. I know you've been scared. Susie told me she's never seen anyone shake like you and how her heart immediately went out to you to help you."

I listened to him with wide eyes. That's what she'd said about me?

"It's okay," he assured me. "I'm back now, and I'm just glad your parents haven't turned you against me. That was my number one worry when I was locked up — that I would get out and you would no longer want to be with me."

I shook my head, "I missed you." My voice came out weak and wobbly—how I felt.

"About that night... That night was—" I began, ready to tell him how sorry I was for calling my parents.

Bruce interrupted me again, though. "A mistake," he supplied. "It was all just a huge mistake, baby. We both made mistakes that night. Ones that your parents were more than eager to capitalize on. What matters now is that we move on and that we stay together no matter what."

He took my face between his palms and looked directly into my eyes while he said vehemently, "We can't let them tear us apart. I won't let that happen. Do you trust me?"

I nodded. "So, the things you said," I stumbled over my words, "how it was all my fault..."

"Forget any of the things I said in anger. I wasn't myself that night. I never should have gone back to drinking hard liquor. It's just wine and beer from here on out, angel. I promise you."

He pulled me in for another hug. "I never want to hurt my sweet babygirl ever again. I'm just so glad to have you back in my arms. I'm so glad that you're okay."

My heart finally calmed as I melted against him.

This right here. This was all that mattered. Bruce and me together. Yes, we both made mistakes, but we loved each other.

I took comfort in his embrace, my world finally feeling right again with his presence back in it.

But I knew that there was something we would have to talk about sooner rather than later.

My parents.

CHAPTER 21

I TOLD Bruce everything that had happened since he got arrested. His jaw tightened throughout my delivery, especially whenever I got to the part about how Mom took photos of me.

"I'm sorry," I faltered at the look on his face. "I swear I didn't know what they planned on doing with the photos. And I was still coming down from all the alcohol, and I was in shock, and I just couldn't think straight. I didn't have the energy to argue with them that night, Bruce. I pleaded with him to understand.

"It's okay, babygirl," he assured me. "I'm not angry with you. They took advantage of you. They caught you when your defenses were down and used you to try to get at me. No doubt, in their witness testimony, they'll be telling that judge that every single bruise on your body was put there by me." He frowned.

He sighed and began to pace while smoking a cigarette and thinking. "You realize there's no going back from this, don't you? They're never going to stop now,

Sarah. They're trying to lock me up to keep me away from you." I heard the restrained fury in his voice.

I felt a chill run up my spine at that thought. I looked up at Bruce with fearful eyes before I admitted, "It's probably not safe for you to stay here. What if they send the cops over here and they find you here with me and you go back to jail?"

Bruce scoffed. "They can't send them over here without a valid reason, so we won't give them any. You'll keep checking in with them every day like you've been doing, that way they won't be able to justify a welfare check. And we'll stay on the down low. They won't find me here, baby. Don't worry."

"I don't know," I said chewing on my lip in worry. "Maybe you should stay at a hotel until after your case is settled."

"You want me to go to a hotel?" Bruce asked me disbelievingly.

"No," I admitted, "but I don't want you to go back to jail either. We have a no contact order between us, Bruce. If you're caught near me, they'll take you back to jail."

Bruce set his jaw, and his eyes hardened as he said, "I'm not going anywhere. This is my house. I pay the rent on it. You're my wife. I'm staying right here with you. I'm not leaving you all alone, babygirl."

I looked at him skeptically, my worry showing plainly on my face, I'm sure.

Bruce came over and hugged me again. "Don't worry, angel. You're never getting rid of me," he tried to joke. "Everything will be fine. You'll see."

I hugged him back and chose to believe him. What

else could I do? At least I wasn't alone anymore, and Bruce was back to his loving self.

Just like Bruce was breaking the no contact order, so was he breaking the no drinking order. After taking a bath and showing me in no uncertain terms just how much he still loved me and how much he had missed me, Bruce went into the kitchen and poured us some drinks. We had a couple of brand-new bottles of wine we had yet to open, so he popped the cork on those and poured us each a glass.

I didn't even bother trying to talk him out of it. I knew he wanted to relax, and after the stressful days we had both just had, we both needed to unwind.

He told me about his time in jail and some of the guys he had met in there.

"Man, babygirl, you should have seen their faces when I was telling all those other sorry pricks about you. They can't believe I had such a young, beautiful girl, but then they saw it with their own eyes in that courtroom," he looked at me with pride. I knew that Bruce loved boasting about how young and pretty I was to other guys. At least he was proud of being with me and wanted to show me off. Of course, I remembered how that only applied whenever he was in the mood for it. He certainly didn't like random guys checking me out. That had led to one too many arguments and was part of the reason why I rarely wore makeup anymore.

I didn't say much. I just listened to him and let him vent while I sat beside him with his arm around me. Oddly enough, despite the circumstances surrounding everything, our short time apart only seemed to knit us closer together. Bruce kept touching me more than usual and pulling me close to him as if he was afraid he'd never get to hold me again. He kept reiterating to me how much he loved me and how he'd never hurt me.

And I just basked in the warmth that was his love.

Everything went fine for a couple of days. I talked to Mom and Dad and Grandma every day and never said a word about Bruce, and they didn't either. So, I mistakenly believed that they bought the whole act, that I was really set on leaving him and that I hadn't heard anything else about him—that is until a knock sounded on the door one day around noon. Surely it wasn't my parents because I knew they were both at work, so that left only one other option: the police.

I shared a panicked look with Bruce who swore softly under his breath before whispering to me, "I'm going to go hide. Answer the door, but don't tell them that I'm here. Try not to let them search the house unless you absolutely have to."

I swallowed nervously and nodded, taking my time walking over to the door so as to give him time to go wherever he planned on going.

Just as I thought, I opened the door to a pair of police officers.

"Hello?" I looked confused to see them.

"We're here on a report that your husband might be here. He was released from jail a couple of days ago. Have you seen him?" they asked me.

I shook my head, "No, I don't know where he is." It

wasn't a total lie. I didn't know where Bruce had gone to hide.

"Mind if we come in and take a look around?" one of the police officers asked me.

I knew I couldn't refuse or question them without it looking suspicious, so I merely stepped back and let them in, inwardly praying that they wouldn't discover Bruce wherever he was.

Only one police officer came in. I stayed in the living room as he did a quick sweep of the house. I saw the other police officer walking along the outside of the house.

I had to stop myself from visibly sagging with relief when they both came back to me empty-handed.

They apologized for taking up my time and then took their leave. I waited until they were completely out of the driveway and driving down the road before I ventured to whisper Bruce's name.

When he didn't hear me wherever he was, I spoke more loudly, walking throughout the house, calling his name.

He finally emerged from the bedroom closet where he had hidden behind all of my clothes that were hanging up.

"Man, I'm one lucky son of a bitch. I thought that f— was going to find me when he opened this closet, but he didn't look deep enough. I guess it was too dark to see me." He released a relieved breath.

"We got away with it this time. We were lucky," I told him, "but we might not be so lucky again next time, Bruce."

"I know," Bruce frowned.

"I really think you should go to a motel," I told him. "Just to be safe," I added.

Bruce's lips thinned as he thought it over, and then he cursed my parents.

"We'll both go," he suddenly said.

"What?" I asked.

"We'll both go to a motel. They won't know you're with me. And they won't know what motel we're at or which room we're in. And motels are not allowed to give out that kind of information. It violates their guests' privacy, so if your parents want to call around to try to find us, they won't be able to."

It sounded risky, but one look at the stubborn set of his chin, and I knew this was happening. Bruce was not going to be separated from me again.

"Are you sure this will work?" I asked him. "Plus, this is quickly going to get expensive," I reminded him.

"We can get a discount by paying a weekly rate," he told me. "Most hotels will do that, so it won't be that bad. Besides, we'll just do it long enough for you to get the contact order lifted or for my case to be settled."

I nodded. According to what Susie had told us, there was still a chance that I could get the no contact order lifted if I talked with the DA and explained my side of things to him and told him that I wanted it lifted. In fact, she was supposed to drive me to the courthouse the next morning to do just that.

Bruce didn't wait for my acquiescence. "I'll call the cab. You start packing," he instructed me.

I moved to do as he said. I just hoped we were doing the right thing.

Bruce booked us a room in the motel he had stayed at back when we first met. Turns out he was right. The owner of the place ended up giving us a discount to pay by the week.

The good thing about the motel was that it was centrally located. Bruce could walk right across the street and get us a burger or something to eat, and there was also a liquor store next door where he could get wine and cigarettes.

The next morning, I left him to go to the courthouse with Susie where I spoke to the DA before court started. Although he was older than me, he was a younger guy, younger than my parents and certainly much younger than Bruce.

His stern gaze made me nervous, and I had barely gotten my request for him to lift the no contact order out of my mouth than he gave me a flat refusal, telling me that if he had his way, he would stick my husband underneath the jailhouse for what he had done to me.

"I've seen his record. This isn't the first time he was arrested for assaulting you, but this isn't Florida," he leaned in and leveled me with a stare, "we're going to give him the maximum we can here in Tennessee."

I hated the DA in that moment, and it struck me as ironic that he was trying to be such an intimidating hardass with the alleged victim. If I was the victim, wasn't he supposed to be on my side rather than talking to me as if I was a criminal too?

Of course, he'd probably say he was on the side of justice. If there's one thing I'd learned, it was that all those Lifetime movies were bullshit. They always made it look like charges were dropped if the victim didn't want to press them, but that was far from the truth.

When it came to any type of charge—especially domestic violence—it was up to the state. The DA was ultimately the one who held all the power and decided if the state was going to waste its time prosecuting someone even if the alleged victim didn't want them to.

Susie was sympathetic but unsurprised when I told her what had happened. From her experience, the DA was a hardass hellbent on winning as many cases as possible. If he thought he had enough evidence for a conviction, he went in for the kill every time. "I can't tell you how many couples I've met just like you and Bruce who had an argument and then were tore apart by the justice system because their families got involved," Susie told me.

I'd never admitted to Susie that Bruce really had hit me. I'd only told her we'd been in an alcohol-fueled argument, which was a half-truth, I knew, but still. Bruce was *my* husband. It was *my* life. If I didn't want to press charges and was willing to forgive him and move on because I knew that wasn't really him, then what business was it of anyone else's—much less the court's?

Susie told me that if Bruce was convicted of what he was charged with, it carried a maximum penalty of a year in jail.

I barely made it three days without Bruce. An entire year would kill me. And I hated to think of him being locked up in there. He'd told me the longest time he'd ever spent in jail was six months, and I wasn't even entirely sure what it was for.

I didn't want him ripped away from me for a whole year. I just wanted to be with him and for everyone to leave us alone. Bruce was right. All of our problems stemmed from outside sources. If it was just me and him, everything would be fine, and we would be happy. He only got so angry because he loved me so much and couldn't bear to let me go.

That's what he'd consistently been telling me ever since he'd been released from jail, and I believed him because I wanted to, because I had to, because it would destroy me to believe otherwise.

When Susie dropped me back off at the motel and I told Bruce what had happened, he scowled. "No," Bruce said, "what it really is is he's a little f— prick who's out to prove something. And he thinks he has an airtight case thanks to all the pictures your parents gave him and the testimony I'm sure they're just dying to give."

Once we found out the DA was determined to see this all the way through, we knew we would have to find a good lawyer to represent Bruce.

Thankfully, Susie was able to help with that too. Apparently, she had gone to college with a local lawyer, and she vouched for him, saying that he was the best criminal lawyer in the area and that he was fair with his fees. So, Bruce and I determined to set up an appointment with him. There was no rush, though, since his court date wasn't for a couple of weeks.

Mom and Dad called me that same day too.

I barely got the 'hello' out of my mouth before dad asked me pointedly, "Did you bail that asshole out of jail?"

"I don't know what you're talking about," I lied. Bruce was sitting at the table in our small hotel room, listening intently with furious eyes, though he was careful not to make a sound.

"Where are you?" they asked me.

"At home," I lied again.

I think they knew I was lying, but they didn't call me on my bluff perhaps because if they did, they would have to admit that they had swung by the house or something, which I totally did not put past them at this point. In fact, they had done it before, like the night they had had me committed to the hospital against my will.

"Sarah, if you're with him, please leave. Stay away from him. The police officer who arrested him told us how they had seen this time and time again. Women stay with the men who abuse them because they believe their lies when they tell them they're sorry and that'll it'll never happen again, but it always does," Mom said.

"If he hit you once, he'll do it again, and, frankly, we believe this has been going on for a long time," she went on.

I opened my mouth to deny it, but Dad jumped in before I had a chance to. "He told us this always ends one of two ways: either he'll kill you or you'll end up having to kill him in self-defense. Now, that's not us talking, Sarah. That's a man who's seen it firsthand."

"I hear you," I said, my voice clipped, "but, like I said, I'm at home. I haven't seen him."

Bruce nodded, approving of my lie, though his eyes were still blazing with indignation at Mom and Dad's words.

I could almost feel their frustration suffocating me over the phone. The tension was that palpable.

When I finally got off the phone with them, Bruce

wasted no time telling me how full of shit they were and cursing about how pissed he was that they and those cops were trying to scare me away from him.

He spent the rest of the night proving to me how much he loved me with massages and touches and caresses and kisses and doting on me in general.

He continued on in that way for days.

In many ways, it was just like back when we had first met. Bruce couldn't keep his hands off me and wanted to have sex multiple times a day. It's as if he was trying to prove to me just how much he cared about me, like he was trying to permanently erase the night he got arrested and everything my parents had said from my mind.

When we drank, he talked about my parents and how much he hated them for what they had done to us. He blamed every bit of our current situation on them. And I believed him, especially when he kept feeding me words of love in between his bad mouthing of them.

He told me they were trying to brainwash me against him, and I believed him.

It's like we were more in love because of rather than in spite of our circumstances, and that's how we carried on.

Until we were ripped apart again.

In retrospect, it shouldn't have come as such a surprise when it happened. Bruce and I had been drinking every day as we did when we were together. We'd been listening to music and talking, and we let our guard down in our drunkenness. Although I never left the motel room, Bruce did. He went out to get wine, cigarettes, and food, and he also started going outside to get fresh air while he smoked. He still smoked in the room too, of course, but sometimes he just wanted to step outside.

That, it turned out, would be his downfall.

One evening Bruce came in from smoking in a rush. He shut the door and then peeked out the window that we always kept closed for privacy.

"What's wrong?" I asked, instantly on alert, thanks to his paranoid behavior.

"I swear I think I saw your parents' SUV drive through the parking lot when I was out there." He was still peeking out the window.

"What?" I sat up straighter, alarmed. "Bruce, maybe I should leave and go back to the house for in case the cops show up here. As long as they don't find us together, they can't take you back to jail."

Actually, that wasn't true. If they found Bruce and smelled alcohol on his breath, they could throw him back in jail since he wasn't supposed to be drinking either.

"No," he barked sharply. "You're not leaving me! That's exactly what they want—to separate us, and we're not going to let them."

"But if you go back to jail, we *will* be separated," I tried to reason with him.

He finally dropped the curtain back down and stepped away from the window and door, turning to look at me stubbornly. "Even if it was them, they didn't see which room I came in, and they shouldn't be able to find out what room we're in. I explicitly told the owner of this place not to release our names to anymore. No one should be able to find out we're here, and the cops shouldn't be able to just go door to door knocking and disturbing all the guests on the chance that we might be here."

I nodded, taking another sip of my wine. "Okay," I said slowly, "but just to be on the safe side, please don't go outside any more than you have to. Just smoke in here. The more you're outside, the more risk you take of them seeing you in case they are cruising around looking to find us."

"Okay, baby," he agreed. "I can do that."

Bruce claimed he wasn't worried, but the way he touched me that night was more desperate than usual—like he was afraid he'd never get to again. He kept me up all night with sex and drinking. He didn't go outside anymore, though.

It didn't matter, though, because it seemed that somehow Mom and Dad had discovered what room we were in. Either that or they had pressured the police enough that they asked the hotel manager which room Bruce was in, and I imagine the manager couldn't *not* disclose the information to them.

It was midday the next day when the police showed up.

Bruce and I both knew it was them as soon as we heard their signature policeman knock on the door.

"F—!" Bruce cursed before heading to the bathroom. I don't know why he even tried it as if the police wouldn't find him there. We'd been lucky back at our house. There was no way we'd get that lucky again. There was no way they wouldn't find him in such a small motel room.

With dread settling in my stomach, I went to open the door.

I furrowed my brow and tried to look confused, asking the officers, "What's going on?"

I recognized one of them as one of the ones who had been at the house the night Bruce was arrested. He leveled me with a knowing look and said, "You know why we're here. Where is he?"

I shook my head and tried to play dumb, "I don't know what you're talking about."

He looked down at me firmly before issuing a warning, "If you try to keep us from enforcing a no contact order, we can arrest you too."

I pursed my lips together as that shut me up really quick. As much as I didn't want Bruce taken back to jail, there was no sense in both of us being thrown in jail. In fact, that would be horrible. If he was going to be locked up, he at least needed me out here to secure him a good lawyer.

I stepped back and allowed the police officers to enter the room. They scanned it with their eyes before going to the bathroom where Bruce had apparently heard everything if his completely dressed state was any indication. He must have grabbed some clothes before he went into the bathroom in anticipation of just this happening. I guess he wanted to make sure that he was better dressed when he was hauled off this time since the police didn't give a shit whether you were wearing clothes when they cuffed you or not.

"Damn, man, easy with those cuffs. I'm cooperating, aren't I?"

The cop who was cuffing him had absolutely no sympathy. "This is your own fault, dude. You were told to stay away from her."

If Bruce's eyes could shoot fire, the police officer who'd said that would be dead.

"I love you, baby. Don't forget that," Bruce told me, his eyes boring into me as they pulled him past me.

I couldn't speak past the lump in my throat and the tears I were trying to keep from falling. I didn't want to be seen crying in front of yet more police officers. Besides, my tears wouldn't stop anything. They wouldn't change anything. They would just make me look like the weak, little victim that the entire police force already thought I was.

The police officer leading my handcuffed husband out of the motel room had a look on his face that clearly said he didn't believe Bruce's pronouncement of love for me. I frankly didn't care what they thought. They didn't know us or anything about us. All they knew was what my parents and the DA had told them.

While I might have made a valiant effort to not sob my heart out while the police officers were in the process of removing my husband from the premises, as soon as the door closed shut and I was left all alone in that dark motel room, I broke down—once again.

CHAPTER 22

ONCE I HAD GATHERED myself together enough to where I wasn't constantly crying anymore, I went into the bathroom and washed my face. Then, I called a cab and went about gathering up all of our things from the motel room. Now that Bruce had been taken back to jail, there was no need for me to keep staying in this motel and paying them money. I could go home.

I called the lawyer Susie had recommended as soon as I got back home and set up a time for me to meet with him. I might as well start getting everything underway.

I was painfully alone once again without the man who had come to be my everything despite his some-times-volatile temperament and all.

I was in agony, and I was pissed. I was done playing dumb with my family.

When they called me that night, I answered with a huge chip on my shoulder.

"How are you doing?" they asked, sounding more chipper than they had in the past few days. I'd been keeping up communication with them even while Bruce and I were at the motel with him just sitting totally silent to the background. I did it to keep up the ruse that I was just at home and wasn't with Bruce, though I knew that they weren't really buying it.

Well, playtime was over. I was tired of playing their stupid little games. I was done. I was out.

"You ought to know," I retorted back before I hung up on them.

They called back several times before they finally gave up when they figured out I wasn't going to answer. I was done talking to them. When Grandma called me later that night, I didn't answer her phone call either. As much as I loved my grandma, I knew she was in cahoots with my parents. She would just report anything that I said back to them, and at that point, I didn't even care about talking to them so that they would know that I was okay. They were the enemy. They were on the prosecution's side, and I had to be careful to make sure I didn't say anything else that they could use against Bruce in court.

Let them send their little welfare checks if they wanted to. The cops would eventually get tired of coming over to my house every two days to check on me, and besides, I didn't care if they came over anymore or not. Bruce wasn't here, and I wasn't doing anything illegal, so there was nothing for them to find.

Although Susie had offered to drive me over to the lawyer's office for my appointment, I took a cab instead since it was later in the evening when I was meeting with him. I knew Susie had her own family to attend to, and I didn't want to pull her away from them.

The lawyer Susie had recommended, who went by

Andy, was exactly as she said he was. He was down to earth and nonjudgmental, and he seemed fair enough about his fee. He was only going to charge us a flat fee to handle the entire case.

During the consultation, he asked me a few basic questions about what had happened the night Bruce was first arrested. He was upfront and honest with me about what could happen with the case. He assured me that he would defend Bruce to the best of his ability, but he couldn't assure me that he could get him completely off. However, he did say that if the case went to trial, it could go either way. He could end up getting the maximum sentence allotted by law, but more likely he would be able to at least secure him a plea bargain where he wouldn't have to serve as long in jail if it came down to that. He assured me that he would be able to let me know more about what his strategy would be once he received all the documents from the court, such as the arrest record, the evidence that the prosecution had, etc.

Either way, it was clear that we needed his services, so I promptly put him on retainer and then went back home, feeling more hopeful that maybe everything would all be resolved favorably.

Andy had told me that he would go to the jail to talk to Bruce since technically Bruce is the one who would be his client. He would have Bruce sign paperwork saying that he was allowed to talk to me about his case, and then he would end up interviewing me and talking to me more about anything that he needed to know once he looked all over all of the paperwork from the discovery.

I expected that process to take a lot longer than it did. I was surprised when barely two days had passed, and Andy called me and asked me to come down to his office for a meeting.

"I want to show you something," Andy said as soon as I walked into his office.

"Okay," I said cautiously as he motioned for me to have a seat across the desk from him.

He sat back down behind his desk and slid a piece of paper toward me. I glanced down at it and then looked back up at him questioningly.

"You know what that is?" He pointed down at the piece of paper with a half-smile, his eyes shining with barely suppressed victory.

I looked down the paper again and shook my head slowly. "It looks like the arrest report?" I guessed.

He grinned and nodded. "Correct," he praised me, "but look more closely. What's missing?"

I looked down at the piece of paper, wondering what he was getting at.

And then I saw it.

"There's a blank at the bottom that hasn't been filled in," I answered.

Andy was full on grinning then as he nodded his head up and down. "Exactly," he pointed back down at the piece of paper again. "This document was not properly signed before it was filed. You see there?" He pointed at all of the blanks along the bottom of the paper. "It was never signed by the arresting officer before it was filed. The only signature on there is the clerk's stamp."

"Okay," I shook my head and looked back up at him in confusion, "but what does this mean?" My heart was starting to feel lighter already because even though I didn't know the significance of this, I figured it must be pretty darn significant to elicit such a reaction from the lawyer.

"What this means," Andy sat forward against his desk eagerly," is that the entire case is going to be thrown out."

I gasped in shock before stammering," Really?" I had already begun mentally preparing myself for the likelihood that Bruce would have to do some sort of time with the way the DA was after him. I had been hopeful that at most the lawyer would be able to get a plea bargain where he would only have to do a few months in jail and then spend the rest of the time on probation and attending anger management classes. I hadn't even allowed myself to entertain the hope that maybe he would get off completely scot-free.

"Yep," Andy leaned back in his chair again, looking smug. "It's a small technicality, but it's going to have a huge impact. See, there are procedures that must be followed during arrests and when filing paperwork. When something like this is off, then none of the evidence that they have gathered matters. Because none of it is legal. Because the arrest was never legal to begin with."

"Wow," I shook my head in disbelief, still not believing our good fortune. "So, what now?" I asked. Would Bruce simply be released from jail? How would all of this work?

Andy knew what I was asking without me actually voicing all the questions.

"Well, we still have to go through the motions," Andy

said. "We don't want anyone to find out about this because we don't want them to have time to see their mistake and try to fix it. So, make sure you don't tell anyone,"He warned me. "Especially anyone who might want to help the prosecution," he added.

I shook my head firmly before telling him, "Oh, that won't be a problem. I won't tell anyone. I'm not even in communication with any of my family at this point."

Andy nodded, "That's probably for the best."

He sat up straighter in his chair and placed his forearms on his desk before telling me, "Now, what we're going to have to do is go to trial. Since you were the alleged victim, you're going to be the first person that the prosecution calls to the stand."

My heart began beating faster in my chest as my anxiety ticked up. "I'm going to have to testify?" I asked nervously.

"The way it works at trial is that the prosecution gets to go first. I just need you to hold the stand until it's my turn to take the floor, and then I'm going to ask to approach the bench, where I'll point out to the judge this little technicality, and then this will all be thrown out, and none of it will matter."

"But what do I say?" I asked him worriedly. "What kinds of questions is he going to ask me while I'm up there?"

"Well," Andy began, "you admitted yourself that you had both been drinking all day before the incident. That's even written in the police report. Most of the time when people drink for that long their memory tends to get fuzzy. Maybe you don't remember everything that happened that night."

I nodded in comprehension. "So, everything that he asks me, I can just say I don't remember?"

"Well, I would never tell you to perjure yourself," Andy said, "but if you don't remember exactly everything from that night because you had been drinking heavily, then you don't remember."

"Okay," I nodded at him slowly, taking it all in.

"It's up to you what you say," he went on, "though it would be best if you tried not to say anything too incriminating, but of course you need to tell the truth to the best of your ability. Like I said, it doesn't really matter either way because the case will be dropped on a technicality..."

I nodded again.

"Oh, but make sure you answer the simple questions, of course. He'll start off asking what your name is, what your birthday is, stuff like that. Obviously, don't say you don't know as the answer to questions like that," he gave a chuckle, and I smiled, grateful that he had lightened the mood somewhat.

He then went on to inform me of when the trial date was set for. Andy was really worth all of the money that we paid him in that he was able to get the date set just a few days away. Then he told me that he was going to go by the jail that afternoon and tell Bruce everything that he had just told me.

I thanked him for everything he had done for us and then stood to go.

"Oh, Sarah, your husband asked me to give you a message the next time I saw you."

I turned back from where I was standing with my hand on the door handle.

"He said to tell you he loves you," the lawyer told me with a small smile.

I spent the next few days anxiously awaiting the trial. I was nervous about having to get on the stand. Obviously, I had never had to testify in anything, and the prospect was overwhelming, even if I did already know everything that I was going to say.

I just wanted everything to hurry up and be over with.

I thought so much in those days I was surprised my brain didn't explode. I thought about the people who had stepped in to help us, Susie and Andy, and how great they had been to us. But then I was pricked by a moment of guilt when I realized that I hadn't told them the whole truth. I hadn't told either Susie or Andy that Bruce really had done what he was accused of.

But I hadn't actually voiced to anyone that Bruce really had hit me because I didn't want anyone to think he was a monster. I didn't know if anyone would understand the circumstances surrounding that night. All of the stress of my family coupled with the alcohol had just made for a ticking time bomb that had finally exploded. Yes, I knew that Bruce really had hit me, but I believed that he didn't mean it and that he would never purposefully hurt me.

I found myself wondering if I was a fool for staying with him. Shouldn't I leave him for actually hitting me? I had always excused the way he would push me down and grab me and shake me as *well, he's not hitting me, though, so it's not abuse*, but now he had crossed that line.

Memories of the victim awareness class I had been ordered to take in Florida came crashing back to me. Bruce had checked a few of those boxes then, but he checked even more of them now.

I worried my thumbnail between my teeth as I sat on the couch with my knees pulled up to my chin, deep in thought.

It wasn't as simple as a simple formula, though. I knew that Bruce and my circumstances were different, not only because of our age difference but because of the dynamics of my family.

Bruce loved me. He had to. He loved me so much he couldn't fathom letting me go. He said he would never let me go.

My mind flicked back to all of the memories I had of Bruce and me laughing, of how sweet and caring and attentive he could be, of how I used to talk to him online and tell him more than I had ever told anyone in my entire life, of how he knew me better than anyone else.

But then I thought of all the drinking, of how it didn't seem like just being with me was enough. Yes, he had given up drinking for me before, but now we were back at it. I thought about how he had accused me of wanting to be with other guys even though he was the only man I had ever been with in any form or fashion. He could be insanely jealous—not just of other guys looking at me but of me spending time with my parents.

He was inpatient and outright brutish at times. But then again, no one was perfect, right? There were things about my dad that my mom couldn't stand and vice versa. That was true in every marriage, right?

I had married him, so it wouldn't be right for me to

give up on us, would it? I had told him I would love him forever, and he had told me the same thing. How could I leave him no matter what he had done? It's not like he had cheated on me. It's not like there was another woman. Quite the contrary, he was obsessed with me. He wanted to be with me all the time. He never wanted me out of sight. His desire for me was never-ending, so much so that he didn't want to share me with school, family, or a job. Some women would kill to have a man love them like that. At least I would never have to doubt his faithfulness.

I shook my head and forced myself to my feet. I was over analyzing everything too much. We were so close to getting Bruce free so that we could be together again. Now was no time for me to start doubting and having second thoughts.

I walked over to the cabinet and pulled down the liquor left over from the night that Bruce had been arrested.

I hadn't tried to drink without Bruce. I'd never drunk alone before, but maybe it would help relax me and take my mind off of everything.

I poured myself a shot and quickly downed it. I went over to the computer and turned on some of Bruce and my favorite music videos.

I continued drinking while watching music videos and funny clips, the things that Bruce and I did when we drank together, but it wasn't the same without him. I couldn't enjoy the music. I couldn't enjoy any of the little clips. Everything reminded me of him and things that we had done together.

All the alcohol did was make my emotions even more raw. I missed him so much it hurt.

And then I thought about my parents and Addison and that saddened me too. My relationship with my family was probably irreparably damaged. Nothing would ever be the same. And if I had to choose between them and my husband, I knew I would choose my husband every time. It was only right. Because he didn't have anyone. He wasn't close to his family. His mother had died. And I remember how he had once told me he would kill himself if I ever left him. Whether he was serious or not, if he ever did that, I would never be able to live with myself. Of course, now he had gone to telling me he wouldn't let me leave. Had he become this desperate because of all the stress my parents had put on us? Didn't he realize he didn't have to make those kinds of threats? I never wanted to leave him to begin with.

I had to believe that things would be different now after this scare. When we had been in that motel room together for those days before the cops found us, Bruce hadn't seemed to be able to get enough me. He had been my completely loving and devoted husband once again, the husband who would never hurt me and who always wanted to be with me even if that devotion was tinged with a touch of madness and desperation.

When it became clear the alcohol was only going to send me spiraling into a deeper depression without him, I put the cap back on the bottle and put it back in the cabinet. Then, I went and laid down and cried myself to sleep.

Somehow, I got through the next few days, and then it was the date of the trial.

Susie drove me to the courthouse bright and early that morning like she had when Bruce had his first appearance before the judge.

Andy had already told me that the trial would be after all of the other court cases were settled, so I was in for a long wait.

But Bruce was as well. The jail only transported the prisoners over once, so he was there at the buttcrack of dawn too.

He grinned when he saw me, and he mouthed *I love you* to me. I simply gave him a small smile back before looking straight ahead. I didn't want him to get in trouble for trying to communicate with me. The way the DA had it out for him, I wouldn't put it past him to try to bring some more bogus charges against him if he thought it would help secure him a conviction.

The hours ticked on until finally we were some of the only ones left in the courtroom. It was after one o'clock before the trial officially began and I was called to take the stand.

My body betrayed me in that typical way that it always did as I shook with each step I took up to the stand. I hated the way it made me feel so weak and timid, but I couldn't control my nervousness anymore then I could keep the sun from rising.

There weren't that many people left in the courtroom, but as my eyes quickly scanned over the crowd, I saw my mom and dad sitting on a bench together, staring at me.

I don't know why it was such a shock for me to see them there. Of course, they would be there. They were the prosecution's star witnesses. They were probably itching for the chance to sit on the stand and tell the world how horrible they thought my husband was.

I quickly looked away from them and studiously didn't meet their gaze again. Instead, I glanced over at Bruce who gave me an almost imperceptible nod of encouragement.

Then the court officer was standing in front of me, prompting me to raise my hand so that he could swear me in.

It was surreal, that moment of me sitting on the stand being sworn in to testify against my husband.

Do you promise to tell the truth, the whole truth and nothing but the truth so help you God?

I heard my voice say "I do" as if from a great distance.

The DA sauntered over in front of me, his eyes gleaming down at me like a predator stalking its prey.

Just like Andy had said he would, he started off easing me into the questions with the basics.

And then he went in for the kill.

"Did your husband strike you on the night of..." He called off the date that Bruce was arrested.

The courtroom was so silent you could hear a pin drop as I sat there on the stand, my hands clenched together tightly in my lap. I heard the ticking of the secondhand of the clock that was staring down above the heads of everyone else in the courtroom from right in front of me.

This was it. The moment I had to decide whether to tell the truth or perjure myself.

When I finally spoke, I lied.

"I don't remember."

A wave of annoyance passed over the DA's face, but he moved on to the next question.

"I don't remember," I answered.

He asked another question.

"I don't remember," I answered again.

On and on we went with this dance of him asking questions and me shutting them down, claiming that I didn't remember what had happened. His face got redder and redder with each answer, until I thought he was going to lose his cool and scream at me.

By the time he flung his hand up in the air, snarling that he had no more questions and glaring at me like he wanted to murder me himself, I was ready to collapse from the intense pressure.

It was obvious to everyone in the courtroom that he hadn't bought a word of my *I don't remember* lines.

It didn't matter, though, because Andy was as good as his word. I didn't have to say another word because he approached the bench, and I heard the entire conversation from where I was still sitting on the witness stand.

If it was possible for the DA to look any more furious, he did when the judge called him up and showed him the error on the arrest form.

She shook her head and then promptly dismissed the case. If the look on the DA's face was anything to go by, someone on the police force would be having their ass handed to them later.

I didn't care. The police force's incompetence ended up being our gain.

I chanced a glance at Mom and Dad's faces, which were just as disgusted and angry looking as the DA's.

Then, I looked at Bruce, who was shaking hands with our lawyer and grinning triumphantly.

Bruce mouthed another *I love you* to me before he was escorted out of the courtroom and back to the jail where he would be released.

I was relieved that this nightmare was finally all over with, but oddly enough, I felt a twinge of guilt hanging over my head too.

I had just lied on the witness stand.

I had committed perjury.

I had committed yet another crime.

But I had done it all for love.

I just hoped I didn't live to regret it.

AUTHOR'S NOTE

Dear reader,

It is my sincere hope that you enjoyed this book as much as I did writing it. Don't worry! This is only the fifth in the series. The story will continue onward, so all your unanswered questions will be addressed in due time.

I thank you in advance for your patience between book releases. I assure you I'm working to get them to you as fast as I can.

I always love to hear from readers, so if you liked this book, please leave a review and let me know what you thought. Your thoughts truly do matter. After all, this book was written for you!

Subscribe to my newsletter to be the first to know when new releases are available and for sample content.

Blessings to you always,

Kayla

COMING SOON

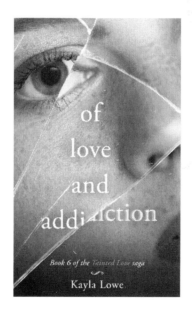

Of Love and Addiction (The Tainted Love Saga Book 6)

The lines have been drawn. Sarah made her choice between her family and Bruce again in a dramatic way on the witness stand where she lied to protect her husband. Will her decision finally prove to him just how much she loves him, or will her forgiveness be something she comes to regret?

ABOUT THE AUTHOR

Kayla Lowe is a Christian romance author who dabbles in poetry and loves reading. She's an editor by day and writer by night. She enjoys novels about the Phantom of the Opera as well as an eclectic mix of fiction and non-fiction. Kayla has been writing professionally since 2007, and in 2011, she was one of the "Top 100 Writers on Yahoo! Voices." She's been an editor since 2017. When she's not writing or editing, she's curled up with her Yorkiepoo or Pomeranian daydreaming up future stories.

Kayla loves hearing from her readers. Go to her website at www.kaylalowe.com to connect with her and find out how to follow her on social media.

OTHER BOOKS BY KAYLA LOWE

Maiden's Blush

The lovely and graceful Katrina Weems is on the brink of the successful life she'd always been waiting for. Yet, far from her home in Tennessee and betrayed by a man she thought her friend, she finds herself seeking the shelter of a stranger in Massachusetts. Trapped by fear, she gratefully accepts the protection of two kind men, but when matters of the heart intervene and she must choose between them, her world is thrown into even more chaos. This young maiden must endure much more than she had ever anticipated before finding the One who can truly save her.

Phantom Poetry

From author Kayla Lowe comes a collection of poems inspired by the classic tale of The Phantom of the Opera. Originally published by Gaston Leroux in 1909 and then later transformed into the Broadway award-winning musical by Andrew Lloyd Webber, the tragic story of the disfigured musical genius who lived in the bowels of the Palais Garnier has captivated audiences for more than a century.

Never before has anyone published a book of poetry pertaining exclusively to the love triangle that existed between the Phantom, his ingenue (Christine Daae), and her vicomte (Raoul de Chagny). This poetry collection consists of three chapbooks that explore these characters from a poetic standpoint. Divided into three parts, this collection features more than 100 poems that take readers on a dramatic journey to the past and into the infamous Phantom's lair where passion, obsession, music, love, and artifice reign.

Of Love and Deception

Sarah MacKenzie is a college student with her whole life ahead of her. Her family has high hopes for her, and she does too – until she begins chatting with a mysterious stranger online. As her priorities begin to shift, she'll make choices that will affect her life and the lives of those around her for years to come. Is her online suitor all that he seems, or has she been deceived? How high a price will she have to pay for the love she thinks she's found?

Love...deception...violence...abuse...crime...sin...addiction... betrayal...Explore the complex dynamics of online romances, family relationships, and self-perception in the Tainted Love Saga, a powerful story of one woman's journey through abuse and much more.

Of Love and Family

Sarah MacKenzie made a life-altering decision when she chose the supposed love of her life over her family. Did she make the right choice? Can she still hang onto her family while following her heart? More importantly, is her boyfriend all he seems? Moving out just may have made her life more complicated than ever before.

Love...deception...violence...abuse...crime...sin...addiction... betrayal...Explore the complex dynamics of online romances, family relationships, and self-perception in the Tainted Love Saga, a powerful story of one woman's journey through abuse and much more.

Of Love and Violence

Sarah MacKenzie is ready to begin her exciting new life in Florida with Bruce Stone, the man she met online, but will it be all she expects it to be? What will their new life together far from her family really be like? Far from home, will Bruce start to show more of his true colors, or will they indeed live happily ever after?

Love...deception...violence...abuse...crime...sin...addiction... betrayal...Explore the complex dynamics of online romances, family relationships, and self-perception in the Tainted Love Saga, a powerful story of one woman's journey through abuse and much more.

Of Love and Abuse

Sarah married Bruce in a spur-of-the-moment decision brought on by financial circumstances. Sure, they were engaged, but she's not sure she was ready for marriage yet, especially when Bruce starts acting even more obsessive after she becomes his wife. Did she really marry the man of her dreams, or is she married to a violent stranger?

Love...deception...violence...abuse...crime...sin...addiction...betrayal...Explore the complex dynamics of online romances, family relationships, and self-perception in the Tainted Love Saga, a powerful story of one woman's journey through abuse and much more.

OTHER WORKS

Poetry by K. L. Lowe

Ever wanted to know where Kayla got her knack for writing? It came from her father...

K. L. Lowe is a secondary school teacher in the state of Tennessee where he teaches Agriculture and Life Sciences to high school students. He's also an adjunct professor for the University of Tennessee at Martin where he teaches Plant Science. He obtained his Master of Science in Education at Trevecca Nazarene University and his Educational Specialist professional degree at Union University.

1989 is his first published work: a chapbook with impressions of the entitled year. Lowe's poetry illuminates life, memories, family, and faith in a profound and sometimes even humorous style.

1989. The cusp of a decade. A time of endings and new beginnings. In this chapbook, you'll find impressions from the year. From life and memories to family and faith, Lowe's poetry illuminates the journey we all face in a profound and sometimes even humorous style that's distinctive as much as it is down-to-earth.